Links to Infinity

Book 6 in The Dimensional Alliance Series

By Bonnie K.T. Dillabough

Cover art by Rick McKenzie

Also by Bonnie K.T. Dillabough

The Dimensional Alliance Series
The House on Infinity Loop
Infinity on Fire
Mirrors of Infinity
Ripples of Infinity
Chords of Infinity

Watch for more at dimensionalallianceheadquarters.com.

Acknowledgements:

With so many amazing people who have supported this work over the last 4 years, I could potentially take up several pages to thank each and every one. But for now, let me say how grateful I am for the steadfast support and encouragement of my fans. You know who you are and to name names would potentially invade someone's privacy or even worse, unintentionally leave someone out.

Instead, let me say this. I couldn't do this without you. At any point, on a day when I wonder if all of this work is worth it, and I get a text or message from one of my fans saying, "I couldn't put it down," or "When does the next one come out?", I find what I need to dig deep down and get back to work.

Thank you. Thank you. THANK YOU!

Dedicated to all those who came before me, who lived and loved and lost and persisted, so that I could have the life I have and do the things I do. Because of your stories, I have stories to tell of my own.

Table of Contents

Prologue

Jenny stumbled slightly, stepping off of the treadmill in the Alliance infirmary. She had misjudged the roll of the deck of the treadmill, but she quickly righted herself before the healer could reach out a hand to steady her.

Ulla smiled and shook her head. *"You are doing well, much better than before, but I'm afraid we still don't want you to cut your recuperation time any shorter. Please continue the regimen we have set up for you. We still do not know the long-term effects of 'the shout' ability and are concerned about your getting back into active duty before you are fully recovered."*

Jenny had been sure that would be the prognosis, regardless of how well she performed in the stress tests and other results of the healers' exams today. She felt they were definitely erring on the side of caution, but part of her was actually glad. One more week at light duty would give her the time to finish what might be the most important of Lizzie Japhet's journals.

The third journal in the box inside her MDP contained the experiences of Lizzie during her time as a gate guardian. Jenny somehow felt this would give her the vicarious training she had lacked in her journey so far.

"Thank you, Ulla," she sent with an answering smile. *"I definitely feel much better, but I will go by your judgment in the matter. I had no idea it would take so long to come back from it. Can you tell me, or do you have any information about whether doing 'the shout' again would cause more damage?"*

"Please don't try it, Gatekeeper. Be content that it didn't kill you or permanently injure you this time. Leave the battles to your generals. Your duties don't generally require you to be at the head of an army, nor should the issue come up again. Remember that the council has access to innumerable hosts of well-trained troops. You will be fighting this war on a completely different plane. We're depending on you to do your proper part, and we thank you for it."

Jenny nodded in acquiescence, knowing that she really didn't even want to argue the point. She didn't think of herself as some kind of warrior maiden out of ancient tales, after all.

Burt entered the room at that moment, grinning. *"One more week?"* he queried the healer with one eyebrow raised at Jenny and his usual cocky grin on his face.

"Yes, Agent Scout, she is improving greatly and can increase her daily exercise to alternated jogging and walking, every hundred steps. She is to continue to eat well and get plenty of sleep, only doing light duty in her role as communications liaison. She can return in one week for what we hope is a final evaluation."

"Thank you, Ulla," Burt acknowledged with a smile and a nod. *"And with that, I will escort my wife, the Gatekeeper, to her nice cozy house and her nice cozy chair, where I know a certain weighty journal awaits her."*

Ulla nodded and left. Burt put his arm around Jenny. "Well, Mrs. Scout, shall we go?" Jenny loved to hear him call her that. Jenny Scout didn't have the same alliteration as Jenny Japhet, but it was glorious, just the same.

They took the elevator down to the basement, and on the way down Burt took that moment in the roomy elevator to kiss her fervently, breaking apart only when the large doors began to slide open.

The transition from the gateroom at Alliance headquarters to the gate office in the house on Infinity Loop only took a moment. Even though she had only been away an hour, Jenny had to admit she was glad to exit from the door in the hallway to be almost formally escorted by her attentive husband to her chair in their sunny living room. Tidbit and Chidwi, side by side on the window seat, were both watching the birds out in the front yard perching and singing from the bougainvillea arch that led out onto the driveway, and they looked up when she and Burt entered from the hallway.

"Jenny is well? Jenny is good?" Chidwi asked, hopping down and running to leap into her lap as Jenny sat in her reading chair.

"I am well, Chidwi. One more week and we can get back to work."

"This is good. Lizziebot says lunch will be ready soon. Burt will stay?"

"Sorry, Chidwi. I have to get back to the lab. Bob and Cornelium think they are on the verge of a breakthrough, and I want to be there. Then I have a couple of assignments regarding the latest intel on the growing list of the dimensions

compromised by the Inseni. I'll grab a bite at the lab. Besides, I think Jenny is anxious to get into that next journal."

He bent and kissed the top of Jenny's head. "Have fun, my wife. I'll expect a full report at the pool tonight."

The pool he was referring to was the little pool by the Merced River, the imagined setting where they met every night in Jenny's mental wanderings. Her ability to contact anyone she knew well or had been mentally introduced to, even across dimensions, gave them the chance to be together, even when their schedules didn't allow them to spend time together in person.

This had been very useful, since their current schedules as newlyweds didn't intersect much, Burt being away from home more often than not.

"I will see you there," she agreed. "Be careful and give Bob and Cornelium hugs from me." This had been an ongoing joke, Burt objecting fervently that he wasn't comfortable with hugging either of them, but that he would pass on the message. Jenny chuckled as Burt disappeared into the gate office door in the hallway.

She sighed and reached into her MDP for the box containing Lizzie's journals, papers, and photo albums. Lying on top of the two previous journals she had read in her light duty assignment at home was the third and final of Lizzie's memoirs. She lifted it out and carefully sat it on the table next to her chair, then placed the box safely back into her MDP.

When Burt had turned to leave, Chidwi had scrambled up onto her favorite perch on the back of the chair and was crooning softly to herself. Jenny knew that due to the linkling's ability to read minds Chidwi had been experiencing Lizzie's adventures right along with her. She thought perhaps part of Chidwi's fascination with the journals was that her ancestor Ynni was also spoken of in Lizzie's story and had been linked to Lizzie.

Ynni had been the founder of Chidwi's tribe and was honored by the others of her clan. Now, as Jenny read, Chidwi had the opportunity to be a part of this story. Jenny felt it made their own bond even more significant, as Lizzie continued to learn more about how beneficial the link between her and Ynni could become as Lizzie expanded her own mental abilities.

"Are you ready?" Jenny sent to Chidwi.

"Ready! Yes, I am!" Chidwi replied, continuing to croon gently.

Chapter 1: And So, It Begins

Lizzie entered the gate office with Gaston at her side and Ynni perched on her shoulder, stepping in a single moment from the basement of the Alliance headquarters building into the house that would now become her own.

"There are arrangements that will have to be made," he was telling her. "For one, we will have to legalize the sale of the house from my name to yours. The Alliance has created a corporation through which they do all their transactions of this sort. With the passing of the key from one guardian to the next, the title of the property it resides on passes to the new guardian legally, according to the laws of that particular country.

"Also, this week you and I will be working on your cover story, the explanation we will give all who know us regarding these changes. Accounts are being set up, and a dummy company that will masquerade as your employer will be depositing any necessary funds into your current account.

"In addition, a special 'passport' is being arranged that is embedded with a unique technology that allows it to change to suit the situation, satisfying all international travel circumstances, with the exception of countries at war.

"You will be receiving instruction from Miriha, the current Gatekeeper, regarding your specific duties, as well as from me. I will be staying on here, bunking with Arvid for a few weeks, to make sure all arrangements are properly made.

"Nita's son will be coming by this week to pick up her things from the garage apartment. In the meantime, you will notice the house looks a little sparse at the moment. I left the basic furniture here, so you don't have to start from scratch, but I have removed most of my personal items from the house to give you the opportunity to truly make it your own."

Lizzie didn't speak for a moment. It was so much to take in. As her dad would have said, the Alliance didn't "let the grass grow under their feet." Once the transfer of the key had been made, they immediately turned her over to Gaston, telling her he had his instructions and that she was in good hands.

"I hate to take your bed," she began, but he rushed in with, "Not at all. It's a new bed, just for you. The linens and blankets are also new, but you can replace any of it that isn't to your taste. Arvid doesn't snore, so I'll be fine."

Lizzie chuckled at that. "Okay, professor. I think it's back to how we began. I'm your student. I'm ready to learn."

They both laughed at that. "I guess we really have come full circle, in a manner of speaking, haven't we? Speaking of which, I have arranged for the university to give you that degree you were pursuing, related to 'credits' earned in your internship with the corporation we were just discussing." And with that, he pulled a document out of his MDP with a flourish, like a magician pulling a rabbit out of a hat.

He solemnly handed it to her. "Once you submit your doctoral thesis, this will be upgraded from the Master's degree in your hand to a PhD in the sciences. You should be able to do that in the next several months between your training and your initial gate guardian duties. I am registered as your sponsoring faculty member."

Then, into his open hand from his MDP expanded a graduation gown on a hanger, complete with mortarboard hat and tassel. "We'll get a photo of you in this with your diploma to send to your family," he said, "and let them know that the graduation ceremony took place in a top-secret lab, so unfortunately you were not able to give them an invitation. If I judge correctly from what I know of your parents, they will be happy to have bragging rights that you have been included in such a 'hush-hush' program."

Lizzie nodded, dumbfounded. She took the hanger in the hand not holding the diploma and just stood there for a moment. Then, careless of what she had in her hands or the linkling on her shoulder who leaped onto the floor with a squeak, she threw her arms around the professor who had stood there with his head typically cocked to one side like a sparrow on a branch.

"Thank you so much!" she exclaimed, then straightened, still holding the diploma and the gown. "I knew they would have been very disappointed if I had not gotten my degree, not that it changes anything for me, but they will be so glad."

"You earned every bit of it," he said sincerely. "Go put the gown into your closet. It's emptied out, as well as the dresser. Speaking of which," he said following her down the hallway to the bedroom, "we need to do something about your wardrobe."

"My wardrobe?" Lizzie wasn't sure she understood what that had to do with anything.

"If we're going to put it about that you have a high-income position at a muckety-muck high-security research firm, you need to be able to be seen dressing the part whenever you go out in public, especially when traveling, as you will be doing a lot of that over the next several years.

"Do you think your mother would be interested in helping you pick out some business suits? Maybe let her know that because your job requires you to be very active, you need some dress slacks as well as some nice but serviceable blouses and nice shoes that will allow you to spend long hours on your feet."

Lizzie shook her head but answered, "Yes, she would love that." However, her eyes clearly asked, "Do I have to?"

"Most of the time you can wear your usual Lizzie style, but because people often believe more of what they see than what we say, you need the wardrobe to carry off the cover story. Over the next several weeks, we will be building the foundation for what people will believe of you for all the years going forward. Trust me. It will be worth the effort," Gaston said, putting a comforting hand on her shoulder and looking into her eyes with some sympathy, although she could tell he was also somewhat amused by her attitude, as if he had expected her objections.

Sure enough, as she hung the graduation gown in the empty, nondescript bedroom closet, she saw that nothing in the house, other than the basic furniture, gave any hint that anyone had lived there before. The double bed was perfect, neither the cot she had gotten used to during agent training nor the more luxurious options she had been given as an intern or agent. But there were no longer any photos or paintings on the walls in any of the rooms of the house.

"In all the time I've known you," Gaston remarked, "I've yet to see you leave any clue behind that you had thought of putting down any roots. This assignment is for life. Make this place your own, Lizzie. Give it a personality. For now, it's a blank canvas, an empty sheet of music, if you will. Over the course of your adventures as a gate guardian, you will acquire many interesting things that you may decide to display or to put in the gate office (things that may bring up uncomfortable questions from future visitors).

"In the meantime, you and I have a lot of work to do. Go ahead and call your parents and arrange for a shopping trip and a short visit. By the way, you can call as often as you'd like. The 'corporation' pays the phone bills."

Lizzie almost felt like her whole body was buzzing as she dialed her parents' phone number. She had wanted adventure and new experiences, and she had gotten them. She had wanted to learn new things, and once again she found herself in training mode. Her dad had always said to be careful what you wish for. She smiled and shook her head, as her mother answered the phone.

"Hey, mom, it's Lizzie! I'm back for a bit with some good news. I have a new position with the firm I was interning for and I could use your help. Any chance I could come for a visit this coming week? I need you to help me with some wardrobe issues and to fill you and dad in on my new status. When would be good?"

She hadn't even given her mom a chance to say more than hello, but she jumped in as soon as Lizzie paused.

"Lizzie! So good to hear from you. Your letters said things were going well, but we still feel clueless. What about your schooling? How long can you stay for your visit? I have so many questions."

"I'll have plenty of time to fill you in when I come out. Gaston will be bringing me, and he needs to know what day would be good so he can schedule. He has news too. I don't want to run up his phone bill. When would be good?"

Even though she knew the phone bill was not an issue, she knew her mom could keep her on the phone for hours if she let her and she didn't want to give out much more information until she had her cover story well in place.

Her mom consulted with her dad, and they agreed she could come out that coming Saturday, if that would work for Gaston. Lizzie agreed and told her she had to get back to work, which was true. When they hung up, she slumped for a moment in the loveseat that sat next to the little telephone table.

"Well, that's arranged. Now we need to take care of some details," Gaston jumped in, not giving her much of a chance to get introspective. "I know it's going to require a bit to take all of this in, but you'll have to do it on your breaks. I expect to fill up your schedule as much as you ever did at agent training." And he grinned a deliberately wicked grin, rubbing his hands together and arching his eyebrows.

Lizzie couldn't help but chuckle. "Thanks, Gaston. I'm ready. What's next?" If she was honest with herself, she didn't really feel ready, but it wasn't in her to hesitate when the chance to learn something new presented itself. Ynni patted her cheek, the linkling version of a hug, and Lizzie knew her little companion could feel her roiling stomach through the bond between them.

Gaston beckoned her out into the backyard. Arvid had been keeping it presentable, but other than that, it was as she had remembered it, with the exception of the clotheslines, which had been removed. Gaston noticed her look and said, "I went ahead and got that electric dryer. I couldn't see putting it off any longer."

Lizzie didn't comment. She understood it might be a little painful to think about clothes on a clothesline, considering Nita's death. Like the house, the yard was pretty much a blank slate. There were some bushes along the eight-foot fence that circled the yard and a marginal flowerbed, mostly marigolds, which Lizzie knew required nearly no tending to thrive.

"I've never really done anything with this yard," Gaston told her almost sheepishly. "It's nearly exactly the same as when I first came to the Gate Guardian position years ago. My wife would have done more with it, but she was so engaged in community projects, that we neither one did much more than come out here to eat. The patio is new, but other than the concrete slab and the picnic table with the umbrella, I haven't figured out what more to do with it.

"I only tell you this because I want to emphasize once again, this is your place now, including the outside areas. Give it some thought. I think the space deserves a lot more attention. You'll be busy, no doubt, but there will be times when you may find yourself here on your own with nothing more to do than to fiddle with the details that make the place more enjoyable for you and your visitors."

Lizzie only nodded. Her recent time in Linaria had made her appreciate plant life in a brand-new way. This would do for now, but she did have some ideas. Unexpectedly, Ynni spoke up, sending, *"This place needs a tree,"* almost wistfully.

"Then you can help me choose the perfect tree and we will make this a garden like Amenia's, shall we?" Lizzie felt more than heard Ynni's assent, and the linkling began to croon expectantly.

Gaston turned and they went back into the house. Arvid was just coming in through the front door, several shopping bags hanging from his hand. "Welcome home, Jenny," he said with a welcoming smile. His English was only slightly accented, which surprised Jenny, as she had previously only ever spoken to him in mindspeech.

"He's been to the Farmer's Market, picking up some goodies," Gaston said by way of explanation, as Arvid strode directly into the kitchen. "Since Nita passed, he's been doing the cooking and I can hardly get him out of the kitchen. He prefers the Farmer's Market to any grocery store. I guess it's much more like how they buy food where he comes from. He's figured out the concept of a taxi, and he can't begin to understand why anyone would want to own a car if you can just make a phone call and have someone chauffer you to your destination. Of course, the Alliance is footing the bills, otherwise, he might think differently."

Lizzie laughed. There was no accounting for the unique attitudes of those from a different dimension. She tried to think of Geln or Gi on her home world and smiled as she imagined their reactions to how things were done here.

Once inside, Gaston sat her down at the dining room table, removing a packet from his MDP and setting it between them.

"This is all the legal stuff," he said, pulling the first sheaf of papers out of a folder. "First, we need you to sign the bill of sale and the check for the mortgage to the house. Appropriate deposits have been made."

Sure enough, a check from her bank inscribed with her name as the account holder was paperclipped to the pile of documents representing the mortgage and the home insurance agreements. The amount on the check stunned her for a moment, but then she shrugged, recognizing the Alliance was ultimately responsible for the amount, and she dutifully signed all three documents.

"I have already put the utilities in your name. I put up a 'For Sale' sign in the yard for a couple of days and then added the 'Sold' sticker to it last week. As far as anyone in the neighborhood knows, you bought it.

"Moving vans will pull up and remove everything from the garage and any furniture you want to replace. Another moving van will deliver the furniture you are going to buy to replace it. This will keep anyone from wondering how you came with nothing and from out of nowhere to take over the house. This means that one of our tasks before you go clothes shopping will be to go furniture shopping. As I said, I intend to keep you very busy. Any questions so far?"

For a fleeting moment Lizzie's thoughts went back to the time she had spent with Reloi, planning their little cottage in Grild. The flash of pain was replaced by his final words to her, sent across the dimensions on that dark day of destruction, *"My Lizzie, my wife. I will meet you again in a new dimension at a future time. Do not despair. The most destructive force in the multiverse cannot destroy our love."*

She shook her head and then amended, "Actually, I don't really know where to start on that task. I'll be glad for your help with that."

"That's our plan for tomorrow. I have some catalogs you can look at today if that will help. But for now, a little more business...Here's your packet for your PhD thesis. I recommend you work on it on slow days. You have a full year to complete it, so, if you pace yourself and set regular research and writing goals, you should have no problem."

He handed her a manila envelope with her name on it and then held out a peculiar-looking booklet. "This will be embedded with your information later today when we visit Miriha with Tarafau. This is her bailiwick, but from now on, you will keep it at the ready in your MDP. It's a peculiar bit of tech that doesn't look like tech—in my opinion, the best kind. I'll let her explain it to you."

Lizzie compliantly put the PhD envelope and the little booklet into her MDP, another peculiar bit of tech that didn't look like tech, for which she was deeply grateful.

Through all of this, Tidbit had been hanging out on the brightly sunlit window seat, Ynni seated next to him, looking on with interest. Lizzie found herself wondering how he fit into all of this. Once again, she was on unfamiliar ground with more questions than answers, but this time she realized it didn't make her stomach clench thinking about it. After all her training and experiences so far with the Alliance, she had finally begun to realize there would always be more questions than answers and, to her surprise, she recognized she was okay with that.

"By the way," Gaston remarked, as he noticed Lizzie's glance in Tidbit's direction. "Arrangements have been made for your linkling to be able to have access to the backyard with her reflection turned on. A special filter has been created extending twenty feet above the fence that will show Ynni as a squirrel scampering around the yard if others happen to peek over the top. The same filter will also block any sound or conversation from being overheard, so Ynni can croon as she desires."

"How wonderful!" Lizzie exclaimed, distracted from her questions. *"Ynni, did you hear that?"*

Lizzie knew that if she heard something and understood it that Ynni could immediately translate the thoughts in her head to her own language, but she habitually used mindspeech to communicate with her.

"This is good!" Ynni chortled, clapping her tiny hands.

Suddenly, Lizzie realized something was missing. "Where's Thumble? I expected to see him the minute we popped out of the gate office."

"Thumble is currently residing at Sanglarka, getting things ready for my stay there. He loves the freedom of the place, as he is allowed to roam the surrounding countryside alone or in company, and he is fascinated by the concept of snow, something he never experienced here in L.A.," Gaston answered with a grin. "I'm sure he will be sad he missed the three of you, but we'll be visiting Sanglarka as part of your orientation after your trip to San Diego next week, so you'll get to see him then."

So much to do! And she hadn't even gotten started yet. She was glad she had Gaston to walk her through all of this. She remembered when he was her professor in college that she had always been impressed with his down-to-business approach to his classes. He knew how to make even the subjects that seemed most boring interesting because of the energy with which he tackled everything he did.

"Is everything in your MDP? Yes? Good. Then, let's go to the gate office. There are some things we must do there to get you set up."

They went down the hallway between the dining room and the bedrooms and bathroom and there was the door that led to the gate office and the gateroom. She felt her key warm as they approached. "As you know, this door will be invisible to anyone without the proper documentation." And he touched the infinity symbol at his own neck and nodded to her, noticing that she had subconsciously touched the key as it warmed.

"After you," he said, gesturing to the door handle. She turned it and entered with him, Tidbit on her heels and Ynni on her shoulder.

It was a generous office space, with room for not only a large old-fashioned desk and a wooden swivel desk chair with a red corduroy seat cushion, but it was also lined with shelves, mostly empty and a white wicker cat bed with a red cushion roomy enough for Tidbit to stretch out in. Two other chairs faced the desk, and a little side table near the desk chair looked as if it had been used for holding a snack or lunch.

The office space was more than ample for the furniture and shelves, with room to spare. On the door opposite the hall door was a second door. Lizzie knew this led to the impossibly long carpeted hallway lined with door after door, like an endless hotel corridor.

"You will note that I have removed much of my own detritus from the shelves, leaving you free to fill them with anything you wish. I did leave a few interesting volumes for research purposes to start your own library. I have no doubt it will fill up quickly, knowing your insatiable curiosity. The desk is empty, with the exception of a few office supplies. That being said, there are a few important, umm, 'accessories' that you need to be aware of and that we need to personalize for you."

He tapped a button on the desktop and a screen appeared, transparent and apparently unsupported, hovering over the desk. Lizzie had seen something similar in offices in the Alliance and at Sanglarka.

"Please get out your tablet, Lizzie," he said, motioning her to sit in the chair behind the desk.

Obediently, she sat and invoked her tablet from her MDP. "Now slide the tablet under the screen and wait for a moment."

She did so, and in a few seconds a message appeared on the screen. "Welcome, Lizzie Japhet. Please acknowledge your identity by speaking your name and sliding your hand palm up between your tablet and the base of the screen."

She did so, and a new message appeared. "Identity, handprint, voiceprint, and DNA confirmed. In the future, simply say your name and this unit will tie to your tablet and all information contained therein."

"Now you will find instructions in your tablet to access the floor safe under the desk as well," Gaston said with a satisfied smile. "This is an extra layer of security for anything you wish to keep hidden. The likelihood anyone will ever be able to break into this room without proper access is next to impossible, but it never hurts to have a few unexpected secrets."

Gaston appeared to be relieved to have that done with. "Now the office knows who you are and has synced your key and your tablet to all the tech as the official Gate Guardian. I understand Arvid has put together some sandwiches and some pink lemonade for us to have for lunch. He's planning something for supper when we get back from Miriha's, but for now I think we can take a lunch break before we head for her office."

"Sounds good," Lizzie replied with a smile. Gaston knew from experience that a sandwich and pink lemonade was her standard for lunch. This almost felt like back in the day when she was an unknowing college intern, and they would have lunch together during the time she was working in his "lab." That now seemed like ancient history to her. So much had happened since he first invited her to his so-called "special project."

They ate out on the patio, Ynni munching on a bowl of raw veggies and Tidbit daintily enjoying his bowl of "cat food." He had confided in her at one point when she had made a face about it that the so-called "cat food" was actually privately canned with a special label with his favorite stew from home, and that one of the "special flavors" was actually roasted bud crawlers. Anyone visiting would think it normal cat food.

Lizzie also knew that Tarafau generally ate with his wife, Amenia, on his apparent nightly wanderings as a cat, travelling dimensionally in his special way directly from the back porch on Infinity Loop to his home planet where Amenia would have a nice meal ready, anticipating his return.

They finished with some brownies that Arvid had baked the night before, and Lizzie helped Gaston clear the table and wash and dry their plates and cups—in her kitchen, she realized. Her kitchen! This was now all officially hers, or at least as long as she continued as a gate guardian. She almost wanted to pinch herself to see if she was dreaming all of this.

They reentered the gate office and proceeded directly through the door on the opposite wall. The first door on the right was the door that led to Miriha's dimension. The gem-eyes, like giant dragonflies, were there to greet them, scanning them up and down before they stepped down from the porch that appeared to be attached to a small, thatched roof beach hut.

Ynni began to get excited as they walked down the long beach to the path between the trees that led to Miriha's village. They could hear the sweet crooning of the linklings that lived in those trees long before they got close.

"Ynni can visit with the tribe today?" she asked. *"Lizzie doesn't mind?"*

"Of course, you can visit your family," Lizzie sent. *"And we will see that you get to visit your family at Tarafau's grove often also. It is now an easy trip for us."*

Tarafau, no longer in his cat form, now strode along beside them. For such a kind and gentle person, he did look formidable. He was dressed in his native costume of a brightly colored tunic and breeches, and as they walked, the sun sparkled on his shiny bald head.

The contrast of his nearly blue-black skin and the bright colors accented his broad chest and muscular shoulders and his height, easily a head taller than Gaston. Lizzie remembered that the first time she saw him she didn't even notice how his ears at the bottom were pointed, much like the tops of so-called elvish ears.

Even now that she knew him well, she could never discount the sheer presence of the man. No one in their right mind would ever challenge him in anger. She also knew that this was no show. He was a deadly fighter even with just his hands. Put a quarterstaff in those hands and beware. He had been their instructor for a time at the Alliance agent training center, and only Lall even came close to his skill in close combat.

As they entered under the canopy of trees over the path to Miriha's village, the crooning intensified and a troop of linklings swarmed down the trees. Ynni hopped down, and there was much cheek patting and excited chirruping as they greeted one another.

"Lizzie has returned Ynni to us!" one of them exclaimed excitedly in mindspeech. *"We missed her. She can stay?"*

"I'm sorry, but she can only stay for a little while. I will need her back, but we will come and visit again more often, I promise." Lizzie sent back, apologetically.

"We will love her while she can be with us, then," the same linkling said without rancor.

They left them behind, hooting and chirruping and crooning all at once. As she looked back, Lizzie noted there was some serious dancing going on as well. She couldn't repress a grin of delight.

They entered the little town square during what appeared to be the busiest time of day in the open-air market. As usual in this little alien village, since it was normal for the townspeople to communicate in mindspeech, there wasn't the noise you might expect from an active market, but throughout the various booths, customers appeared to be haggling with the merchants or asking questions about their goods, as indicated by their gestures and body language.

Among the crowd, children ran and played, some hanging on their mother's skirts, others apparently having animated conversations with one another. As usual, no one seemed to pay any mind to the strangers going about their business, nodding to them in passing with welcoming smiles.

Lizzie loved this place and found herself wishing she could have spent some time here as an agent intern. They seemed like such a peaceful and happy people, and she couldn't imagine anything bad ever happening here.

They strode past shops and what might have been an inn or restaurant until they got to the large green building at the apex of the square. The two uniformed guards at the door greeted them with broad smiles and opened the doors. They shed their shoes by the entrance, left them on the shelves provided, and proceeded up the long curving staircase that led up to the rounded room beyond the balcony on the second floor.

The moment they drew close to the door, a chime sounded, and the door swung open into an amazing egg-shaped room that was full of light, with rainbow-like glints reflecting off of many surfaces. Miriha stood before them in the center of the room holding both hands out, first to Gaston and then to Lizzie in turn and finally to Tarafau.

Each took her hands, and then she gestured for all of them to sit in the chairs that faced her own.

Miriha had always seemed to Lizzie to be the essence of calmness and peaceful self-assurance. *"Welcome, new Gate Guardian! I knew when I first met you that you had the heart and mind to do this. Gaston chose well. Before you can begin, we have a few things to do. First, please remove the booklet from your MDP."*

Lizzie complied and put it into Miriha's outstretched hand. She laid the booklet down on the small table beside her and sent, *"Now give me your hand."*

Lizzie did so and suddenly a needle appeared in Miriha's hand, evidently pulled from her own MDP. Before Lizzie could react, she jabbed Lizzie's middle finger and then reached for the little booklet. She tapped the booklet to the tiny drop of blood on Lizzie's finger. Lizzie put the finger into her mouth without thinking then rubbed it on her pant leg.

"What was that all about?" she asked a bit sulkily. *"You could have warned me."*

Miriha's mischievous grin and Gaston's lack of surprise told her that this reaction was expected. *"Just watch,"* was all Miriha sent in response.

To Lizzie's shock, she noticed the little booklet was transforming before her eyes into an exact replica of a U.S. passport. The cover of the little blue booklet now bore the official seal of the United States government. As Miriha flipped open the light blue pages with their official watermark, Lizzie noticed it bore a photo of herself from her college yearbook, and her fingerprints.

"How did you do that?" she sent in wonder. *"There is no such thing as magic... no... such... thing."* Then she remembered a common saying among her scientist friends, "Magic is only science we don't understand yet."

"*This is very advanced technology. This particular booklet is made of paper that is actually a very high grade, flexible computer screen. It can replicate pretty much anything we can send to it. This is now attuned to both your DNA and your tablet. It feels exactly like paper but cannot be torn or damaged except by fire. The information on the paper is updated based on need. When we need it to be a U.S. passport it will be; if we need it to be a different document, for instance from another country, you simply go into the application on your tablet to change it.*"

Lizzie thought she had seen everything, but once again was struck with how little she actually knew about what was possible.

"*Now that this is out of the way, you may put it back into your MDP and we will move forward. It is time for a new lesson on gate guardianship. As a guardian for your planet and dimension, you have a number of responsibilities, probably the most important of which is to shield your unaware neighbors and the citizens of Earth from the knowledge of the gateway network.*

"*It is vital that, until they are ready, they be guarded from that knowledge. As you might guess, incursions from gateways in other dimensions, fallen into the wrong hands, could spell disaster not only for your home planet but for any dimensions they might encounter, either by intention or by accident.*

"*Your neighbors must see you as that slightly eccentric person who travels a lot and works for a private corporation on sensitive scientific research. You must give the impression of normality and friendliness at all costs. The gate you guard is of ancient date, and the Alliance intervened by creating a domicile on that property when it was discovered by one of our agents, back in the days of the California gold rush.*

"*There had been rumors of some strange incidents of unusual creatures seen roaming the area, and mysterious disappearances of explorers. Once our agent located the gateway, measures were taken to legally purchase the entire area that surrounds this neighborhood and to connect it to the Alliance gate network.*

"*For many years it was simply a ranchero, the Gate Guardian raising cattle and investing in orange groves and the like. Over time, when the area became more of a suburb of Los Angeles, a new plan was made and this neighborhood was constructed around the house that currently houses the gateroom and gate office.*

"They were careful to make it appear that this house was simply purchased by a new homeowner moving into the neighborhood, like all the rest. Gaston is only the third guardian to live in the little house on Infinity Loop. This is the only gate on Earth that exists in a neighborhood environment, making it rather unique.

"Like any other new person moving into such a community, you will be expected to meet your neighbors and get to know them. By the time you are ready to do that, your cover story and all its details will be firmly in place.

"No one entering your house who does not have the appropriate Alliance identification will even be able to see the door in the hallway, although it will always be obvious to you. With the Gate Guardian key around your neck, you will also be able to sense any other gateways you encounter in your visits to the other Gate Guardians' gates or in any other dimension you travel to.

"Soon, you will revisit Sanglarka, the training headquarters for the Earth Gate Guardians and initial training facility for potential Alliance agents, and you will begin a round of visitations to the other gates throughout your planet. Each guardian will have something interesting to share with you, and it is important for you to know each other well.

"In addition, from time to time you will visit other dimensions to meet with guardians there. Also, I understand that you have taken an interest in the refugees from Grild, as is appropriate. I suggest you make regular visits to each of the different locations of these refugees. You should know the Alliance is currently working on finding them an appropriate planet to resettle them all in one place, so they can begin again to rebuild their culture in a secure environment on a planet they can call home.

"Also, as you are considered an ambassador to Tarafau's planet, you have been given a dispensation to visit there as time permits, especially since your linkling, Ynni, has a vested interest in the grove behind Tarafau's home.

"You will be reporting directly to me for the first year of your initial training. The training you have already received as an agent is usually considered the fledgling aspect of training for a guardian. Now you will study gate theory much more intensely and expand your understanding of the various dimensions we deal with on a regular basis.

"You may also visit other dimensions from time to time in relation to special assignments by the Alliance as indicated by your unique skillsets and talents.

"One other duty you should keep in mind is that eventually all gate guardians either die or retire from service and as a result, you need to be on the watch for an appropriate successor when that time comes for you. You will receive training on best practices and how to do that. Gaston's method is only one of many to choose from.

"Regardless of all of this, your primary duty is to keep up appearances of normality in your neighborhood to protect the secrecy and security of the network. I know enough about you to understand that this could be a bit of a challenge on any given day. However, I also know you have a lot more to you than meets the eye and that you have grown in some significant ways since beginning your agent training."

Miriha once again reached both hands out to Lizzie and Lizzie grasped them in return, the possibilities of what Miriha had just told her buzzing insistently in her head.

"Lizzie Japhet, do you take on these responsibilities, as explained to you, with full understanding that this is a lifetime commitment and that you still have much to learn? Do you promise to be faithful to your commitment as an agent and gate guardian of the Dimensional Alliance? And do you promise to guard the network to the best of your ability, as long as life shall last?"

Lizzie looked long into Miriha's eyes, not even glancing in Gaston or Tarafau's direction. "I do, Miriha. I will."

Miriha first touched her own key and then Miriha's key warmed once again, but this time Lizzie also felt a warm glow spread throughout her, not physically, but more like the warmth of a hug from a dear friend or loved one. In that moment her heart reached out into the vastness of the dimensions and to Reloi, to what she thought of as her true home... the home of her heart.

And strangely, there was no sadness there, only joy and hope. It was like awakening from a longtime illness and being fully healed.

Miriha looked steadily back into her eyes, and Lizzie felt that somehow Miriha understood what had just happened. "There are many benefits of doing what you know in your heart is right," she sent privately to Lizzie. "You will do much good and make a difference in the multiverse in ways you cannot yet imagine. I see this in you. You need to see it in yourself."

Lizzie nodded somberly, considering the implications of not only the commitment she had just made, but also Miriha's statement, directed to her in private. *"Thank you, Miriha,"* she sent back, knowing that one of the benefits of mindspeech was that it sent not only the meaning but the intent of what was being said on a deeper level.

Miriha smiled and Gaston stood. He reached out and hugged her and she hugged him back with a full heart.

"Now the real fun begins," he sent with a chuckle. *"We will be back in a few days to do a day or two at Sanglarka, but tomorrow we get to go shopping!"*

Gaston could always make her smile. She knew he understood the significance of the last few moments for her and was so glad he had chosen her out of all the potential prospects to enter on this path.

Chapter 2: Hijinks and High Jumps

*(R*emembering her own beginnings with the Alliance and how much it *had begun to mean to her, Jenny blinked back tears. There was so much she hadn't understood until she herself had been through so many things she had never expected. She was excited to get to this part of the journals which would hopefully reveal the more complete training for the Gate Guardian position Lizzie would have experienced.*

She also wondered a lot about how that would affect how she would deal with what was coming up in her own journey as the Gatekeeper. With the war against the tyranny of the Insenium and their search for solutions to prevent future issues of a similar sort, in addition to her responsibilities that included the security of the entire Dimensional Alliance gate system, she knew her life was about to become much more complicated.

She reflected on the fact that she hadn't received the full training for any of her positions, either as a gate guardian or as the Gatekeeper. For now, these journals were turning out to be the lifeline to understanding more fully what she had gotten herself into.

Her time was short. She was determined to complete this final journal before her recuperation was finished.)

The promised shopping trip had been more fun than Lizzie had expected, and after the movers finished taking away the old furnishings and the new furniture had arrived, Lizzie found herself looking forward to her days at Sanglarka.

She was sure it wouldn't be all welcome home parties and hanging out with the other gate guardians. Sanglarka's whole purpose was training and keeping the gate guardians organized and unified; and they were serious about that purpose.

In Miriha's office once again, Lizzie was somewhat glad Miriha rushed them through to the gateroom right away after a smile and a hug. *"You have much to do, and it is already late in the day in Sanglarka,"* she said cheerfully.

Grenheim met them as they came through the rose covered arch that represented the Sanglarka gate. *"Oak and the rest are all assembled in the dining room,"* he sent as he escorted them down the path that led to the big lodge in the valley surrounded by frosted mountaintops.

In the wintertime the path would have been surrounded by tall snowdrifts, but for now the valley was green and lovely as a picture postcard. This time of the year the days were long, and the Sanglarka residents and visitors seemed to take advantage of every moment. She determined she would get some photos to take to her mom when she went home for her clothing shopping expedition.

Livia was waiting in the large lobby of the lodge, just outside the double doors that led into the expansive dining room furnished with a long table roomy enough for a dozen people. At the moment, all of the staff of Sanglarka were in attendance, along with the other eleven Earth gate guardians.

They looked up as Lizzie with Ynni perched crooning softly on her shoulder, Gaston, Tarafau, Grenheim, and Livia entered, and there was a smile of welcome on every face. Even Meta was there, something that surprised Lizzie, as the last she had heard Meta had resumed her instructor position at the agent training center.

The table had been extended to include the additional guests. Lizzie took the indicated seat at one end of the table, with Grenheim on her left, facing Gaston with his wide grin. She didn't quite know where to look. All eyes were on her, not a position she normally would have taken voluntarily.

Grenheim stood and intoned in his deep bass mental voice. *"Welcome, one and all. We are here to celebrate the retirement of our good friend Gaston and the addition of a new gate guardian to our number. Lizzie Japhet has exceeded expectations during her training, internship, and first assignments as a certified agent of the Alliance. As Gaston had proposed when he first found her, Lizzie will be taking his place as the Los Angeles Gate Guardian.*

"We are also pleased to announce that Gaston will be spending his retirement with us. I should say, 'semi-retirement,' as he will be continuing as

a consultant and will also be participating in the future training of new agents here in Sanglarka.

"We also welcome Lizzie's official Guide, Tarafau Bane. We are happy to see him continue to offer his wisdom in the cause of the gate guardians of Earth. Lizzie will be with us for a few days as we conduct her initial orientation and allow her to catch her breath before plunging into her official duties.

"Let us give thanks for the blessings of these associations and the wonderful banquet that has been prepared, shall we?"

He bowed his head and all followed suit, each giving thanks in their own way in the quiet that followed. Finally, Grenheim raised his head and with an expansive gesture sent, *"Let's eat!"*

The staff of Sanglarka all stood and headed through the swinging double doors that led into the kitchen and returned wheeling several serving tables laden with an amazing array of foods from salads to home-baked bread and large tureens of soup, as well as several interesting looking casseroles. The aromas that rose into the room were enticing.

As each of them served themselves while the food carts were wheeled around the table, mindspeech conversations bloomed happily around her. There were questions about her training experiences. It was obvious from those questions that the Sanglarka team and the other Earth guardians had kept up to date about what was happening with her.

Their common bond of having all gone through the training and internships early in their own experience as agents before being promoted to gate guardians made it easy for Lizzie to share, and she began to feel very much at home with the other guardians.

Lizzie remembered how, whenever her dad had encountered another army veteran, even when they had never met before, there had been a common bond between them because of the similarities of their experiences. This felt a lot like that.

The food was excellent and the company was pleasant. Once they were done, everyone rose to help clear the table while the staff put away the few leftovers and took care of the dirty dishes.

As soon as the table was cleared, Grenheim stood again. *"Lizzie, we all remember how intense it was for each of us to begin the journey you are about to undertake. It is important for you to realize that the gate guardians, even though our gates are spread over vast distances throughout the Earth, are all part of something more than just a team. We are a family.*

"Political borders, distance, differences in culture and belief systems mean little here. As a group we are focused on protecting all beings on the planet Earth. For this reason, we meet on a regular basis as a group via a telecommunications network provided for us by the Alliance. This technology is very advanced compared to anything we have on this planet and is accessible only via deeply encrypted coding and special shielding applications programmed into your tablet.

"This means we don't have to be in proximity to stay close to one another, and no outside scanning equipment can interrupt or interfere with our signals.

"Via this same network, we can communicate one on one. Much of your training will happen in this manner."

He scanned the faces before him. *"But for this stage of her training, each of you will make arrangements for Lizzie to come and visit your gate to give her a feeling for the different ways each of you fulfills your responsibilities and to give her a perspective of her own duties. This should be a comfort, as right now, we all know how overwhelmed she is probably feeling. We've all been where she is now.*

"Lizzie also has a rather unique addition to her situation, as she is bonded to Ynni, an admirable linkling from Miriha's planet. Some of you, including Yaw, may be able to advise her on how to make this companionship work in her favor.

"Let us adjourn to the lobby and spend some time catching up and taking turns with Lizzie. We have a few hours before we must go to our beds and prepare for a long and interesting day tomorrow."

With an immediate scraping of chairs, they all proceeded into the lobby. Lizzie was seated in the apex of a circle of comfortable chairs near the huge stone fireplace. From where she sat, she could see the long row of windowed French doors that led out onto the balcony, which overlooked the breathtaking Sanglarka Valley. The sun was just beginning to set over the mountains, their snowy slopes sparkling and taking on the colors of the impending sunset.

Lizzie knew from her last visit that once the sun set there would be an awe-inspiring view of the northern lights to replace the sun. She found herself wishing she could spend a few weeks here instead of the few days on her current schedule.

As they gathered around in the big circle of chairs, it appeared that they had already organized this portion of the program. They took turns, each re-introducing themselves with their gate designation. All had taken out their tablets and were using the amazing connection and scheduling application that would make all of this so much easier than writing it all down on a calendar or in a daily journal.

Not only would they be able to continue communications throughout the process, even when they were at their home gates, but they could update information or change arrangements in a moment, without phone calls or letters going through the mail. Because the connection was secure from any form of current Earth technology that might allow snooping, they could be free with their conversations.

In a world where every phone was connected to a wire and most international mail took weeks to arrive at a given destination, this practically took Lizzie's breath away when she considered how far her planet yet had to go to even begin to approach this kind of convenience.

As she began to make these appointments and arrangements, she was equally interested in the fact that the Alliance had taken her world's cultures into account, and the mechanisms necessary to do business were always circumspect. Nothing they were doing would stand out because no new tech was ever adopted until it could be done without attracting attention; and all tech they used was disguised as something earthlings would consider ordinary and unworthy of notice, such as the MDP bracelets.

For instance, the China and the Sanglarka gates were inaccessible via normal transportation methods, so, in those cases Lizzie would travel first to Miriha's gate and then directly to those gates. It was one of the peculiarities of the gate network that although one could travel across entire dimensions directly from a gateroom, one could not travel from gate to gate on the same planet.

Other than China and Sanglarka, however, the Alliance had a direct relationship with a private travel agency that would allow her to book flights when necessary, via her tablet. The Alliance had created an entity that produced all the necessary paperwork and payments to give their agents and gate guardians full access to travel by air, ship, or train, as well as accommodations at major hotels and resorts.

Most of the time, when Lizzie visited a gate area, she would be accommodated by the gate guardian. Nearly every gate had at least a guest room that worked for most visitors.

Lizzie thought of the little guest room in the house on Infinity Loop and realized that, in some cases, there must be other options she didn't yet know about.

Fortunately, she wouldn't be going into this blind. The other guardians were happy to walk her through the process. Each of them related stories of their own early days as guardians, some of which were very funny and others perhaps more in the nature of cautionary tales. In either case, she was quickly beginning to realize that, like with her podmates, these people would soon become close companions and friends.

This was a comfort in what might have been an uncomfortable situation. She was glad she had become acquainted with them briefly before her agent training.

By the time they had all made some arrangements with Lizzie, she could see her schedule would be remarkably full, even in the beginning of her time as a guardian. She had initially pictured her time in this new position more like being a receptionist sitting around in the little gate office, her travels and adventures in the past.

However, if she learned anything from the tales told by her fellow guardians, it was that, if anything, her life had become more complicated, and the potential for new adventures had just increased by a significant margin.

At one point, with a shock, Lizzie realized that many of her companions were yawning and stretching. For most of them, the time difference probably meant they should have been in their beds hours ago.

"I'm guessing we have an early start tomorrow?" she sent to the group. *"Thank you so much for all your help. I'm looking forward to spending time with each of you, but I think we probably need to find our beds for now."*

They all nodded in agreement and Livia, who had been sitting just outside of the circle with her crocheting, gestured to Lizzie to follow her. They proceeded up the stairs to the balcony lined with several doors that overlooked the lobby. There was a similar balcony on the other side of the lobby that meant that at least a dozen rooms were reserved for guests here in the lodge. At the second door, Livia paused, opened the door, and nodded for Lizzie to precede her into the room.

To Lizzie, it almost felt like home. In her early training she had spent weeks here at the lodge, and the accommodations were impressive. Her room was more like a suite, with a door that led from a sitting room to a bedroom and bathroom. At one end of the room was a large picture window that overlooked the valley below. Just below the window was a desk. On the desk was a large journal, much like a ledger, along with fountain pens and an ink jar.

"This will be your permanent room here at Sanglarka, Lizzie. Every gate guardian has their own space here. The journal is a gift from the staff here at Sanglarka. We know there will be many new and interesting episodes in your journey. Gaston tells me you have a habit of journaling, and we thought it appropriate to give you a fresh start for this leg of your journey.

"Feel free to take it with you. As you may remember, all meals are taken in the dining room. Breakfast is a gathering meal and the evening meal as well. Lunch is usually a buffet with sandwich and salad ingredients laid out for you to assemble your preferred lunch meal, and there is no schedule for that. At any time during the day, if you need a snack, the kitchen is available for your use.

"Bathing necessities are all arranged in the bathroom for you. Morning routine is still a breathing and stretching session followed by the group's working the forms of quarterstaff. We generally do breakfast immediately following that.

"Grenheim has created a training schedule for you for the next two days. After that, the remainder of your training will take place partially as visits to the various Earth gates; and in addition, some lessons will be sent to you on your tablet from various experts in the Alliance, including the Alliance Council and training staff from the agent training center.

"I know this is a lot to take in, but you'll do just fine. My advice is to take it one step at a time and just do your best. We know you have what it takes to become a great guardian and want you to always feel welcome here at Sanglarka or at any gate on Earth.

"Is there anything special we need to prepare for your linkling?"

It was the longest speech Lizzie had ever heard from Livia, and she could feel the motherly tone of it. She found that oddly comforting, although previous efforts of someone to mother her had felt slightly insulting, as if she wasn't adult enough to manage on her own. In this case, due to the benefits of mindspeech, she could sense the honest care and kindness intended.

"Ynni usually can eat most of the things I eat, although she prefers raw fruit and vegetables. Other than that, she shouldn't need anything special. She can sleep on the pillow next to me on my bed, and we use the same bathing facilities."

Livia nodded with a smile and left them to it.

The next morning, she woke before the alarm bell sounded and was quickly up and dressed, with Ynni perched happily on her shoulder, looking forward to the day like a little kid at Christmas. She knew the first part of the day would feel pretty routine, slipping back into the habits of her previous time in Sanglarka before she had gone to the Alliance agent training center.

The morning exercises and defense forms were actually fun, as she got to do them with the entire staff and all of the attending gate guardians, including Tarafau. Ynni had cheered with delight as she managed to do the forms as perfectly as anyone could have wanted. She felt so much more confident than she had when she had last been to Sanglarka. All the hard work and agent training through the Alliance had paid off.

Breakfast was also enjoyable, mental conversations weaving in and out between the guardians and Lizzie and the various Sanglarka staff. Ynni enjoyed the happy interaction as well. This group treated her much as Lizzie's podmates had, as one of the team, not a bit out of the ordinary. Thumble had shown up with Gaston that morning, and Ynni and Thumble acted as if they had been pals for years, evidently chuckling over some private conversation.

When it was obvious that everyone was finished with their breakfast of the traditional crisp rye crackers, homemade lingonberry jam, cheese, fruit, and eggs prepared in a variety of ways, Grenheim stood.

"Today and tomorrow is all about exchanging experiences and doing some basic training on the practical side of gate technology. We will now adjourn to the Sanglarka gateroom. Today, Ernst, the Switzerland Gate Guardian, will be our lead in this part of the training. However, Lizzie, feel free to ask questions of anyone in the group. Let us go. The staff will clear up after breakfast. I want to get as much work into this day as we can."

Ernst nodded to Grenheim, who led the way from the dining room to the room between the library and the workout room. Lizzie realized with a start that she had never noticed the door there in her previous visits to the lodge. Obviously, it was true that she had been given new authorizations she didn't have before.

They entered into a generous office space similar to Miriha's and her own house, easily fitting the fourteen of them without crowding. The now familiar door across the space led into a hallway so long that the end disappeared around a gentle curve. When all had filed into the wide corridor, Grenheim stopped and gestured to Ernst.

Ernst nodded. Lizzie found herself front and center of the disparate group of gate guardians and felt herself to be the focus of Ernst's piercing gaze.

"Lizzie, the first thing you need to understand is that every one of us is going to see this place slightly differently. The gaterooms are based on perception and don't exist in any real form. As I'm sure you were taught in your classes in agent training, every gate exists like a minuscule particle that is not seeable by our physical eyes. Somehow, the technology that created the gaterooms allows us to visualize these particles in a way that makes sense to us personally. There is no actual mass or size to any given gateway. To a dragon a gateway will look one way, and to a dwarfish race or the denizen of a water planet it will appear to be something very different.

"We know this from the descriptions we have been given as we researched the gates and how they work. Unfortunately, the notes or documentation of the originators of the gate system are lost in the eons of time since it was originally created.

"One of the conveniences of the system is that, although this gateroom appears to most of us as an unending hallway, you don't have to wander for miles down the hallway to find the gate you need. You simply need to picture in your mind where you are going, and the gate will appear within your current view.

"Generally, only the guardian of a particular gate can arrange the gates to suit themselves. For example, as I picture it, the first gate is Miriha's gate; and it is marked, to my eyes at least, as a green door with a flourished swash imprinted in blue over a silver doorknob.

"If you have been through that door from another gateroom, you may see it differently."

Sure enough, just in front of her, the plain green door from her own point of view did not have the blue swash over what appeared to her to be a brass doorknob.

"Do any of the rest of you see it differently?" she sent to the group.

"For me it is a Paifang," sent Wang Xiu, the China Gate Guardian. *"The trim is silver, and the doorway is shielded as by a gentle waterfall."*

"I see a door that I must stoop to pass through, as are the doors in our traditional villages. The curved edges of the door frame are painted in white, red, and black," sent Yaw from Ghana. *"Traditionally, our homes are made from clay, brick, and straw, so our doorframes are rounded, molded by hand."*

"To me the door looks of weathered wood, with a brown frame and a wood handle," Lela sent with a gentle smile. *"The winds and storms from the sea beyond my home dinna leave much untouched, ya know."*

And so it went, each guardian describing the gateway before them, none of them exactly the same as what Lizzie saw plainly before her.

"You see?" Ernst continued. *"Each of us sees our gaterooms in a very personal way. And it also follows that we organize what we see differently. Each of us has easy access to the gates we intend to enter, by simply picturing that gate in our minds, and we organize the order of the gates based on the ones we use most frequently.*

"The gateroom also appears differently depending on whether you are entering from the gate office or from a different gate. Any questions so far?"

Lizzie almost laughed. Questions? Her mind was buzzing with them, but she asked the first one that came to her mind.

"What about if you wanted to explore a random gate? How would you do that?"

Ernst's eyebrows rose in apparent disbelief. *"Explore an unknown gate? Do you have any idea how many there are? I suppose this is a good time to talk about gate safety,"* he sent in a musing tone. He looked around him at the other guardians as if looking for confirmation. Several of them nodded somberly.

"It hasn't happened in a long time, but there have been, er... umm, shall we say, incidents? Not every gate leads to an atmosphere or environment that

is safe for human use. Some go to water planets where all life is aquatic, for instance. Some lead to gates that are on non-member planets where the native life is not particularly friendly and would not appreciate unannounced visitors. And some... well, let's just say, as united as the Alliance appears on the surface, not all members are in agreement about how much interaction they wish to have with other Alliance member dimensions.

"Just as you would not walk into the house of a stranger without an invitation, you should never just go visit a dimension you have not visited before without making advance arrangements.

"That being said, there are ways to get invitations and to make those arrangements. One of the courses Meta will lead you in today will be about how to use your tablet to do just that.

"We do encourage you to learn more about the dimensions and their various cultures. Even on the planets that are inimical to human life, there are often safety measures that can be taken to allow you to experience those dimensions. For now, I would recommend you start with the meetings you have already arranged with your fellow Earth guardians. They will be happy to introduce you to some of their favorite dimensions."

Lizzie only nodded, admitting to herself that she was a bit disappointed in the answer, even though she saw the need for caution. She was a bit embarrassed, as she knew she should have reasoned this out by herself. It made logical sense.

Yaw put in, "When we are finished with you here in Sanglarka, you will be making another trip to Alliance headquarters, where you will be outfitted with an extensive kit of tools and supplies to support you in varied environments and situations.

"Your MDP will soon hold every item you might possibly need to survive pretty much anything nature in any dimension might subject you to. I have to say, some of these things have even come in handy here on Earth in several instances."

Ernst spoke up again. "One of the safety measures you carry with you is your tablet. Even ensconced in your MDP, your tablet makes a notation every time you change locations via a gateway. The tablet is connected to the actual portal in the MDP via your key, and it senses when that portal has moved. This means that wherever you go in the gate network, Alliance security is aware of your travel.

"From time to time, this has made a life-and-death difference for an agent or guardian traveling outside their own dimension."

Lizzie nodded her understanding. She realized why she hadn't been told this in agent training, as an agent might not need to know any of this, considering they could only go through a gateway with the assistance of a gate guardian.

"So, will I have people going in and out of these gateways in the gateroom without knowing it is happening? Kind of like Grand Central Station behind the gateroom door?"

"No," Ernst replied with a grin, "that would be a very disorganized way to run the network. There are no layovers or transfers between gateways. With few exceptions, a person or persons travel directly from their origin gate to their destination gate. When they come to visit your gate, they won't even see the gateroom at all, but will enter directly into your gate office through the scanner there. That's one more reason we don't travel to another gate without making arrangements ahead of time, with the exception of the gate on Miriha's beach and the one at Alliance headquarters, but even the Alliance gate is minded by Alliance troops."

"So, what is my job again?" Lizzie asked, feeling a bit sheepish, like she just wasn't seeing what must have been obvious to the rest of them.

To her surprise, they all seemed to be grinning at her.

"Right to the point," Ernst sent with a note of pride in his mental voice. "Your job is not to monitor the comings and goings of people in the network. You are there to receive visitors from time to time, but more importantly to keep anyone from suspecting there is anything any different about your house than any other house around you.

"You need to get to know your neighbors, give them a reason to think of you as just another householder, just another person going about their normal business.

"You are also expected to reach out to gate guardians in other dimensions for reasons that will become evident to you as you move forward. You are now a part of the council of Earth guardians, and you will also meet from time to time with the main body of the Alliance Council and even once in a while with the Chief Councilor in the private council chamber.

"One of the reasons Gaston singled you out as a potential candidate as an Alliance agent was because of your incessant thirst for knowledge, as your time as a representative of the Alliance will be a constant learning curve. We have every confidence that you will acquit yourself well."

Lizzie was once again grateful for her training in keeping her face passive, as she only barely withheld a blush at these words of praise. She simply sent, "Thank you for your confidence."

"Okay. Let's take a quick break, and you can spend some time with Meta before lunch. I told you we were going to work you hard in the couple of days we have you here. Take a deep breath, get a glass of water, and meet Meta in the library," Grenheim sent, a clear dismissal to them all.

And so it went, meeting with one group or individual after another over the next two days, soaking up every detail she could in order to prepare herself for what was coming. By the end of the third day Lizzie felt wrung out, even looking forward to something so frivolous as a shopping trip with her mom.

Chapter 3: Plantings

(*Jenny sighed happily. She wondered if there was something transforming about the very idea of owning your first home. Remembering her own joy and awe when she inherited the little house on Infinity Loop with all its wonders and getting to make it her own, she empathized with her aunt as she settled into her new home.*

She also felt again the trepidation and concern she had felt when she began to realize the responsibility she had taken on as a guardian and now as a newly minted gatekeeper.)

Lizzie turned once again, looking at herself in the dressing room mirror. She shook her head in disbelief. Was this really her in this sleek taupe business suit with its crisp white blouse and the smooth lapels of the matching jacket? The dress pants that went with it were, to quote the shopkeeper, "just the thing for the modern businesswoman." Her mom looked on in approval.

"You look very professional, Lizzie. Are you sure you don't want to try on the skirt instead of the pants?"

Lizzie sighed. "Mom, I don't sit at a desk much. Most of the time, I wear a lab coat or even blue jeans, as I am very active in my research. I wish I could tell you more than that, but this will do very well for most of my more formal meetings."

"Well, we need to get you a black cocktail dress. I'm glad you don't drink, but there will be parties. There always are. A fashionable but modest dress and a pair of matching heels, not really high, and that rope of pearls we gave you on your sixteenth birthday should work very well. I'm impressed at the clothing allowance they gave you, you being just out of your internship and all. Yes, a black cocktail dress is next."

Lizzie barely restrained herself from rolling her eyes, but replied, "Of course, I hadn't remembered that. Thank you, Mom."

She knew she would probably never wear it, but it wouldn't hurt, and money wasn't an issue. This trip was a lot more about bonding with her mom, bolstering her cover story, and giving her a chance to settle her head as she moved forward into the Gate Guardian position.

So far, they had settled on three suits—one navy blue, one black, and now the taupe. They each had white blouses that could be interchanged between outfits. Of course, there had been shoes and hosiery and a serviceable coat to go with it all. She felt like she had been trying on clothes for hours, definitely not her favorite activity.

"Well, I told the shopkeeper to look for some options for you. Let's see what she has," her mom said with a twinkle in her eye. Obviously, this was as satisfying for her mother as playing the mbira was for Lizzie.

Ultimately, they were able to agree on a dress and some not-too-high-heeled shoes.

Lizzie took her mom to a late lunch at a nice restaurant with an ocean view just off one of her favorite beaches. When they got home, her dad and Gaston met them at the door. They were both grinning, and Lizzie guessed they had been discussing some sporting event or another... men stuff. They helped them in with their packages.

"Gaston was telling me about some of your college hijinks," her dad said with a wink. "Evidently you weren't his average student. Did you really argue with him about the grade on your science project?"

"I wouldn't exactly call it an argument, Dad," Lizzie objected. "It was more of a negotiation. He did raise my grade. He saw the logic of it in the end."

Gaston grinned and her dad laughed outright at Lizzie's defense. Lizzie allowed herself a blush. It was her dad, after all, not some alien Alliance official that she needed to impress.

They spent the evening just chatting, and it felt good to hang out with her parents and Gaston. All too soon, she and Gaston headed back up the coast after Lizzie promised her parents that she would invite them up to her house as soon as she was completely settled in.

They had been so proud to receive the photo of Lizzie in her cap and gown, holding her diploma. As they drove home, Gaston assured Lizzie that she had done well and that her parents didn't suspect anything out of the ordinary.

Although Lizzie hadn't slipped up at all in her cover story, she had been glad to be able to answer their questions truthfully without stumbling or giving anything away. She had been very thoroughly drilled by her fellow guardians during her time in Sanglarka. Gaston had informed her parents that, because of the security requirements of her job, she would never be allowed to tell them anything more, and they accepted it without question.

She felt this had been a very successful dry run and that if she could do this well with them, she could manage with anyone else she met in her neighborhood.

Now that she had jumped this particular hurdle, she still had a lot to do.

The next morning, she and Arvid and Gaston had an early breakfast out on the patio and chatted about what was next on her schedule.

As Ynni happily munched on the cantaloupe they were having for breakfast, Lizzie explained to them what she thought she wanted to accomplish in the back and front yards. Both areas were extremely plain, mostly lawn with the exception of the bougainvillea arch in the front yard, but when Lizzie looked at the hacienda style homes in her neighborhood, she knew she wanted something that fit the Hispanic theme.

"I think I'd like to create a little pool with fish and a fountain, like something I saw on Fanilia. I'd like a tree and some helpful herbs. I've seen a lot of good things done with herbs, and I want to study them in my spare time," Lizzie confided to her two companions.

"You should meet Lacey Longtree, next door on the left. She loves gardening and can be one of your first neighbor contacts. She grows roses, and she also works for the university as an assistant professor at the college. I doubt you've taken one of her courses, though. She teaches botany and ethics and spends most of her time in the college greenhouses. If you'd like, I'll be happy to introduce you."

"That would be wonderful," Lizzie agreed. "Once I've talked to her, I'd like to take Ynni with me to a greenhouse to help me pick out the tree. She can keep her reflection turned off."

Going into the house after breakfast, she surveyed her little house. She was beginning to feel very much at home there, especially with one of her mom's crocheted Afghans draped homily across the back of the loveseat.

With a contented sigh, she sank into the comfy overstuffed chair next to the bookcase. Gaston and Arvid sat on the love seat, and Tidbit and Ynni scampered up to the window seat. She would be hanging some new draperies when they arrived from a mail catalogue, but other than that, the room felt nearly complete.

She had considered hanging Geln's painting, featuring her podmates under their tree during one of their spontaneous concerts, over the mantlepiece; but she decided to hang it in the gate office instead, as the features of the participants would be considered a curiosity to any Earthling visiting in her home. So, the mantle really needed some kind of painting, but that would have to wait.

"Okay," Lizzie said to Gaston and Arvid as they sat there, catching their breath and considering the new look of the room. "Now what?"

"Let's go to the farmer's market," Arvid replied with a grin. "It's time to stock up your cupboards and fridge with some goodies you like. We can also stop at the supermarket down the road and pick up some canned goods and the like. You need to get out for a bit, I think."

"Ynni, would you like to come?" Lizzie sent.

"Yes, please," Ynni enthused. *"Ynni will keep her reflection off."*

Lizzie was surprised by how much was required to set up a household from scratch. Everything from wastebaskets to kitchen and bathroom supplies, not to mention little thises and thats that she already had in her MDP but decided that for convenience' sake she would buy separately for the house.

She felt she would be able to move and travel quickly, without having to pack and unpack every time she needed to go to another gate or dimension, by simply having duplicates of necessary supplies and clothing in both places.

Gaston did indeed introduce her to several of her neighbors, including Elias and Melinda Mensch and Professor Lacey Longtree.

She invited Lacey over to a picnic out on the patio in the backyard to discuss her ideas about the fountain and koi pond with the surrounding herb garden. She found they had a lot in common, as they were both fascinated by science and were voracious learners and readers. Lizzie could tell this was someone she could connect with.

Elias and Melinda were newlyweds, smart and excited about their new life together. Elias was a city planner and engineer, and Melinda was a librarian. They had been looking forward to getting to meet their neighbors, as they had moved in only a month before Lizzie.

All things considered, it seemed that this might not be so hard after all. Lizzie still felt a bit awkward at the whole making-friends thing, but by the time Arvid and Gaston said their goodbyes a week later, she began to be hopeful this would all work out.

The day she went to the local greenhouse with Lacey, she actually felt excited. She and Lacey (with discreet mental input from Ynni) had designed a landscape plan using herbs and flowers that would turn the entire left-hand part of the yard into a scent-and-flower experience instead of a standard flower bed.

Lizzie had been a bit apprehensive about going into the greenhouse, wondering if she would be bombarded by the thoughts and comments of the plants around her, but the greenhouse was surprisingly silent. She recognized a low murmur, as if hearing a conversation through a closed door. It took her a moment to realize that no one had ever tried to truly communicate with any of the seedlings here, and that the murmur was probably only the plants speaking among themselves.

She tuned it out as Reloi had taught her, so she could focus on her purchases. The gardener salesman who waited on her raised his eyebrows at her long list.

"Of course, we can fill this order, ma'am, but it may not be ready right away. Would you like to have it delivered?"

"Yes, please, and may I look at your tree seedlings? I want to buy a tree as well."

He nodded and led her and Lacey to a second large greenhouse, featuring row upon row of seedling trees from fruit trees to evergreens to shade trees. Lizzie could feel Ynni stirring on her shoulder with delight. She was glad she had brought her along, as ultimately the tree would be as much for her as for Lizzie.

Lacey was oblivious to the linkling as she pointed out various potential choices to Lizzie, expounding happily on their various histories and origins.

At one point, as they strolled between the rows of seedlings, Ynni sent, *"Stop, Lizzie and look!"*

They were in the evergreen section and most of the trees looked very similar to Lizzie, but she obediently stopped in front of a seedling with flat pointy leaves that were somewhat larger than pine needles. The label on the root ball said, "Yew tree, female," then listed the Latin genus of the tree.

"Female?" Lizzie said, arching an eyebrow to Lacey.

"Indeed. In many tree and plant species there are female and male genders. In the case of the yew, it's important to know which gender you are planting. If you have allergies or are planting in a populated area, the female is preferred, as the male yew tree has a very high allergic rating. During pollen season it can cause very uncomfortable allergic reactions like headaches, asthma attacks, and other symptoms such as itching eyes and a runny nose."

"Hmm. I can see why it would be important to know this before you planted."

To Ynni she sent, *"You like this tree?"*

"Yes, can't you hear it singing?"

Lizzie made a show of examining the seedling while she focused her mind on listening for the tree's voice. At first she heard nothing but the generalized ongoing murmuring throughout the greenhouse, until she finally sent to the tree, feeling a bit foolish, *"Little tree, can you hear me?"*

She was grateful for her agent training in controlling her expression when she got an immediate response.

"You speak to me? How is this so?"

"I have learned to hear and speak with your kind. If you will, what are you called?"

"I am Windsong. And you are?"

"I am Lizzie, and can you also hear my friend, Ynni?"

"Yes. She is somehow wonderful and strange to me."

"Would you like to come to my home? I would tend you and care for you always. Ynni heard your song, and we would sing with you, as you wish."

"This sounds like a good thing to me. I agree."

Lizzie turned to Lacey. "I think I like this one. Are they difficult to care for?"

"No, yews are hardy and thrive, as long as you don't water them too much. You needn't do much to them besides trim them from time to time to shape them. They have an ancient and honored history. You need to be careful that no one eats their leaves or the seed from the berry-like cones they produce, as the seeds and leaves are toxic to humans and some animals. Birds eat the berries and spread the seeds without harm, so you needn't worry about dead birds on your property."

Lizzie nodded. "Then, I think I want this one," she said, pointing to Windsong. She called to the salesman, and he tagged it as sold.

"We'll take it with us, I think. You can send the rest of it whenever the order is ready," she said to the salesman.

"This is a beginning," she sent to Ynni. *"This will be your tree... our tree, and we will sing together, shall we?"*

"Yes, Lizzie. This is the right tree for our home."

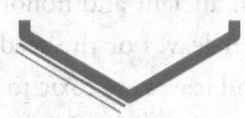

Chapter 4: Moving Forward

(J)enny laid down the journal and walked out of the French doors to the patio behind her house. She scanned the garden snuggled into the left-hand corner of the large backyard with its koi pond, the yew tree, whose branches extended over the pond, and the flowers, the herbs, and strawberry plants that surrounded the pond that was about the size of a large hot tub.

She had always had Chidwi turn off her reflection when in the backyard, but now she knew that this was unnecessary. Chidwi had become excited when Jenny had gotten to that passage in the journal and joyfully preceded Jenny into the yard, immediately scampering up the trunk of the yew tree.

She hadn't realized that Lizzie had been the one to plant the garden; she'd assumed it came with the house. She had always thought of her aunt as an adventurer, almost never home, somewhat mysterious to the rest of the family.

However, after beginning this part of the final journal, she saw the pleasant garden with new eyes. This was Lizzie's connection to her home, especially considering her talent of communicating with plant life. She wondered if this was something she could pursue with Amenia the next time she got a chance to train with her, remembering Amenia's own amazing garden area.

Amenia had never brought up this particular mental ability with Jenny, but at the time of their training, they had been focused on her talent for inter-dimensional communication, which continued to be a vital resource for the Alliance.

Now she found herself wondering what additional abilities might be available to her if she decided to work on them. Reloi's kinetic abilities and Lizzie's talent with mental music were opening her eyes to new possibilities.

She returned to the sunny living room and retrieved the journal from the table next to her reading chair. It was another beautiful Southern California day. Perhaps it would be appropriate to read the next few chapters out in the garden as she experienced the vicarious joy of how it came to be, and why it was significant to her own journey.

She settled onto the chaise on the patio, listening to the delighted crooning of her linkling, and turned a page.)

Lizzie surveyed the debris of the excavation of the pond area in the yard. She had decided to create a kind of oasis in one corner of the yard, leaving in place the bushes with their marigold borders that lined the back fence. She would use the dirt pulled from the pond area to form a small hill beside the place where she would plant the yew tree, creating the backdrop for the little waterfall that would circulate the water in the pond to prevent stagnation.

She had potted the yew tree temporarily into a large roomy pot with compost, and it stood near the patio, happily soaking up the California sun. She couldn't help but smile looking at Windsong.

As soon as she and Lacey had returned from the greenhouse with the little seedling, Lizzie had thanked her friend and bid her farewell so she could get back to grading essays. She immediately took the seedling to the gateroom, trailed by Ynni and Tidbit. She had promised to return to visit Bonwen when she had left Fanilia to take up her duties as a gate guardian.

She had some questions for Bonwen and wanted to introduce Windsong to the great tree.

Lizzie, Tarafau, and Ynni arrived at the gate near the main city. Gar, the Gate Guardian, was there to greet her, as she had sent him a quick note before coming via her tablet, per the usual protocol for cross-dimensional visits.

"To what do we owe the pleasure of your visit, Lizzie Japhet? We didn't expect your return so soon," he said with a smile and what might have been a shallow respectful bow.

"I wish to bring my little friend to visit Bonwen," Lizzie sent, pointing to Windsong, whose pot was held gently in Tarafau's large hands. *"I wish to nurture this tree friend and want to do it properly. I know I will receive wise counsel from Bonwen."*

"Indeed," agreed Gar. *"I can arrange transport, if you don't mind staying overnight? The day is well on, and we would be glad to greet you properly, as such a one as yourself well deserves. You have become somewhat of a legend to the Fanilian people, you know."*

Lizzie blushed, in spite of herself. She had only been doing her duty after all, hadn't she? Saving Bonwen from the "crawlies" had been a vast team effort. All she had done was to organize them and think through what she considered a logical solution. She had no idea how to reply to this, so she simply nodded.

Gar gestured for her and Tarafau to follow him down the forest path to the little town nearby. He then escorted them to what might have been considered a town hall at home. People in the streets around the public square waved and pointed at them as they went.

When they arrived in the meeting room, Lizzie was astounded at how many of the Fanilians had assembled there, since she had given them only short notice of her arrival. The news of her visit had obviously spread more quickly than she had anticipated or hoped for.

Gar led them up to the dais, where she was greeted by several of the notables of the surrounding villages. They touched hands to heart with every welcome; and Lizzie, Ynni, and Tarafau responded in kind.

After a short welcoming speech by Galauph, the speaker for the "over-tribe", the Fanilian term for their form of government, he invited Lizzie to stand.

"We remember you always, Lizzie Japhet, for what you did for our people. Please be welcome and know that anything you wish of us, that is within our power, we will do for you."

He quirked a mischievous smile. *"We noticed that last time you were here, you took a great interest in our beach sand, collecting many bags of what to us has little to no worth. Our children have taken to gathering sand in bags whenever they go to the beach to play. They call them 'Lizzie bags.'"* He chuckled, a deep rich sound, and the gathering also chuckled in appreciation of what was evidently a known joke.

"These have been collecting behind the inn on the square ever since you left. Please take them with you when you go."

Lizzie almost gaped in surprise. When she had taken samples out of the bags of sand she had initially gathered in her assignment on Fanilia, they had assayed as pure 24 carat gold. She had told the assayer that she had gotten the small handful of gold panning in a river while on vacation in Alaska at some well-known tourist spot.

She already had bags and bags of the stuff. And now they were offering her what would be considered a fortune on her planet, something the Fanilians would gladly just throw away or use to line the edges of a path as decoration. They had never considered melting it down and using it for anything, as they had said the resulting metal was soft and mostly useless.

She laughed with them, but not for the same reason. This was the kind of joke that she decided to keep to herself.

"We hear you wish to visit Bonwen, and we will be happy to take you there. A transport will be arranged for tomorrow after you break your fast. In the meantime, we would love to greet you. Assembled in this hall are all of those who worked with you to save our magic and release Bonwen from her pain. They would celebrate your return before we take you to your suite in the inn."

At his nod, the group swarmed forward, and Lizzie greeted those she recognized. Some had worked directly with her and her team to return the crawlies to their world, and some had worked in the background, providing technical help, meals for the workers, and other necessary services.

It was a joyful time for her, Tarafau, and even Ynni. The linkling had played an important role in the project, warning them of the impending danger of the crawlies and reading their minds to determine what kind of threat they were. If not for her, Lizzie would have probably perished before she had a chance to do anything at all for the Fanilians.

Lizzie had never been comfortable with large crowds, and even less with high praise. Nevertheless, she found herself laughing with various individuals over some of the funny parts of their adventure and crying with the relatives of the few who had perished in the attempt to save Bonwen and their planet from destruction from the crawly invasion.

By the time the chat had begun to wind down, Gar dismissed the crowd and escorted an overwhelmed Lizzie and her companions to the inn on the square.

It didn't have a name. They simply called it "the inn," as there were seldom travelers that needed its facilities. Gar, the current Gatekeeper, had a suite there, the one Lizzie had used while initially working with the Fanilians. There was a homey dining facility on the first floor, and the lift took them to the second floor to the guest suites.

After a good night's sleep and a traditional Fanilian breakfast of fruit and a sweet spicy cake made of some kind of fine flour, they followed Gar to the launch pad of one of their air transports.

The nearly silent engines of the plane made it feel like they were simply floating to their destination over the massive forests interspersed with small villages. But it was evident that, floating or not, they were moving quickly. In under an hour, they had traversed the jungle-like countryside and had arrived at the port near the village by the compound which had sprung up around the clearing where Bonwen stood, huge and regal.

As had become popular with the Fanilian people since the crawlies had been eradicated from Bonwen's branches, there was a reverent crowd of pilgrims gathered around the perimeter of the clearing surrounding Bonwen. Many had begun bringing newborn infants to the shade beneath the gigantic tree, hoping to infuse the child with the "magic" that Bonwen supposedly radiated.

Lizzie, with Ynni on her shoulder, and Tarafau, carrying Windsong, approached deep into the shade near the massive trunk of the great tree. As they approached, Lizzie could sense the great peace and joy of the tree, like music heard from a distance.

"Bonwen?" Lizzie sent tentatively. "I wish to ask a favor of you. Do you sense my friend, Windsong?"

"Ah yes, such a sweet seedling. She is not of our world, but of an ancient race. Greetings, Windsong."

Lizzie sensed that Windsong's answer was almost shy. "Greetings, Great One. This one is in awe of your strength and power. I am honored to be in your shade."

"As am I to see your potential, friend of Lizzie. How may I serve you both this day?"

"I shall plant this yew in my garden, Bonwen. I wanted her to know how she may be a comfort and joy to all those who come within and how she can protect and encourage the plant life around her. You are wise in this way, and I want my garden to be a place of peace and inspiration to all who are near it."

"Lizzie, you are wise and of a good and generous spirit. Leave Windsong beneath my canopy for a time and return."

Lizzie bowed her head in assent and gestured for Tarafau to place the pot at the base of the trunk. She realized that Ynni was crooning softly as if singing to the vast tree. It was a gentle and joyful sound, and Lizzie also noticed tears trickling down her own cheeks... tears of joy and peace.

Wiping her face on her sleeve, the three of them left the little yew tree in Bonwen's tender care.

As they exited from under Bonwen's branches into the sunshine, Lizzie felt a surge of warmth that wasn't from the sun but from gratitude emanating from the two trees who were already interacting with one another.

They spent the rest of the day enjoying meeting with the Fanilians who had come in pilgrimage to the great tree. The food vendors' booths that edged the compound refused to take any compensation for their goods from Lizzie, but gladly gave them meals. Lizzie suspected this was probably for bragging rights to say that Lizzie had eaten at their establishment, although she had noticed that the Fanilian people were a lot less focused on profit than most of the merchants of Earth, having a generous nature.

Just before dusk descended, Lizzie and Tarafau returned to retrieve Windsong.

"*Thank you,*" Lizzie sent. "*I'm not really sure why this was so important to me, but I really appreciate your help.*"

"*Windsong understands her duty to the land and to your garden. She will be a comfort and a joy to all who venture near to her. She is of a true spirit, and she is glad for her future and yours,*" Bonwen sent in return, tendering approval and warmth to them all.

"*Go in peace, Lizzie, and return whenever you feel a need for counsel and encouragement.*"

Lizzie thanked her again and she, Ynni, Tarafau, and Windsong departed, each of them filled with joy and peace.

Chapter 5: Growing Things... Glowing Hearts

(J enny looked out over the garden with a new understanding of the significance of the little oasis of green and growing things.

Jenny had spent as much time as she was able to out on the patio that looked out onto the garden since she had lived in her little house, never realizing why it felt so good to be there.

She was comfortable on the chaise, shaded from the direct sun but warmed by it. The only place she could think of that felt this good was the little pond by the Merced River where she and Burt spent time together in her dreams at night.

Chidwi and Tarafau were busy watching the koi swimming lazily in the pool, as they both perched on yew branches to give them the best view. Jenny now wondered if they were also having conversations with Windsong. She turned the page.)

Lizzie stood up from kneeling next to the rock lattice she had created at the edge of what would soon be a pond that would eventually be shaded by Windsong and that Lizie would stock with a pair of koi. The water of the pond would come to near the top of the rock lattice. Her strawberry plants would be supported by the lattice as their roots extended into the enriched water of the pond instead of garden soil.

Elias Mensch had helped Lizzie to dig out the depth and width of the pond, and they had poured the concrete shell after tamping down the earth around the perimeter. They had left a trough about a foot deep around the edge to contain the rock lattice. Lizzie had decided to add the rock lattice while the concrete was curing. The curing process would take nearly a month.

In the meantime, Lizzie was also establishing the various planting beds around the area that would be outside the shade of Windsong's branches. She had already laid down a layer of compost over the entire area, with special attention to the hole next to the little waterfall where she would be planting Windsong.

It was a lot of work, but she had company. Since Gaston and Arvid had left for Sanglarka, Lizzie had worried that she would have to do this by herself, but one of the last things Gaston had reminded her about was that she was supposed to be interacting with her neighbors and establishing relationships with them that would give the proper appearance of normality.

She heard the doorbell and, brushing off her knees, went to answer it to find Lacey. She had obviously just gotten off work, as she was wearing what she laughingly called her "professor suit." In her hands were Lizzie's mail and newspaper and a bag from which was emanating some delicious aromas.

"I knew you'd be puttering today and, knowing you, would probably not have even thought about preparing food. I didn't feel like cooking myself, so I picked us up some takeout. Chinese? I have eggrolls..." she trailed off with raised eyebrows.

"Oh yes!" Lizzie enthused. "I completely forgot about lunch. What time is it?"

Lacey laughed. "It's supper time, silly girl. Honestly, and I thought I was a gardening enthusiast. You have me beat by a mile. Shall we eat outside and admire your handiwork?"

Lizzie laughed with her, realizing that she might even like her role as a neighbor, something she had never imagined about herself. It wasn't really surprising that her former college classmates and even most of her relatives had thought her to be aloof and somewhat untouchable.

Looking back as she and Lacey ate and chatted about Lizzie's plans for the garden, she realized that this was one of those weird loops people created in their lives. She had always been thoughtful and introspective, and people had interpreted that to mean she was snobby or "stuck up." She in turn had construed their reaction to mean she was unlikable and that no one wanted to be her friend, so she had closed off that side of her to avoid being hurt.

Now she realized that both assumptions had been inaccurate, and Lizzie was just now beginning to appreciate that common experiences were important to creating relationships. It was what made her fond of the guardians at Sanglarka. It was what made her podmates so dear to her. It was what had bonded her to Reloi and his people. It was what made Lizzie want to return to Fanilia and Bonwen. And it was what would now return her to her family and help her become an intrinsic part of her new neighborhood.

As she and Lacey chatted about both the garden and Lacey's experiences as a fledgling assistant professor, Lizzie once again blessed Gaston for his interest in her and his willingness to offer her the opportunity to become an agent and eventually a gate guardian of the Alliance.

She and Lacey laughed together about the eccentricities of students and even the faculty of the college. They laughed about Lizzie's sore knees from kneeling on the ground all day.

"You know, you really need to get moving more," Lacey mentioned. "I've been thinking about taking up jogging around the loop after all day doing scholarly work. What do you think? We could become jogging buddies. Maybe we could even get the Mensches to join us? Safety in numbers and all of that."

"That sounds like a great idea, or at least whenever I'm not out on assignment," Lizzie agreed. She realized she hadn't been working out much at all since she took over her guardian duties. She didn't need to go soft, after all that time working out in her agent training. Who knew when it might be important to be in top shape?

"I guess I'd better get back home," Lacey said with a sigh. "I've got papers to grade, and I need to feed my fish."

A huge aquarium divided Lacey's living room from her dining room, and it contained many exotic tropical fish. She had been the one to recommend the shop where Lizzie had bought her fish that also happened to stock koi. Lizzie looked forward to the time when the pond would be ready for its denizens. In the meantime the fish she had chosen lived in a separate aquarium in the shop until the pond was ready for them

They cleaned up their mess, and Lizzie saw her out the front door with a cheerful wave and a thank you for a wonderful meal she hadn't had to cook.

Lacey's suggestion reminded her that she hadn't worked the forms for quarterstaff or hand-to-hand in several weeks. She had done so pretty consistently during her time as an agent. She noticed Tidbit curled up in his happy spot on the window seat next to Ynni, who was looking blissfully out the front window at the birds looking for worms on the front lawn.

"Hey you lazy cat," she sent, *"where can we go to work out? I'm gonna get fat and lazy as a tabby cat if I don't get in some workout time."*

"Hmm. Didn't Gaston show you the gym?" he sent back with a lazy amused tone and a twitch of his tail. *"Come on, I'll show you."*

"Ynni come too? Fun to watch, fun to play."

Lizzie nodded, somewhat confused. A gym? She beckoned, and Ynni leapt joyfully from the window seat to her usual perch on Lizzie's shoulder. The linkling was so feather light that Lizzie barely felt her land, wrapping one tiny arm and her fuzzy tail around Lizzie's neck.

Tidbit led the way to the gate office door, which Lizzie obediently opened for him, his tail up in the air with a crook at the end like a battle banner. Lizzie hoped she hadn't offended him. Like all cats, you could never tell with Tidbit.

He stalked across the office to the second door that led to the gateroom which opened for him. Two doors down, he paused expectantly. The door was painted yellow. She opened the door and stepped through. Suddenly she wasn't with Tidbit anymore.

Beside her, dressed in his gi, was Tarafau. He was over a foot taller than Lizzie and heavily muscled, his bald head glistening blue black in what appeared to be sunlight coming from windows arrayed down one side of the large room.

It was fully equipped with workout mats, full length mirrors down the wall opposite to the windows, and various kinds of workout equipment. Through an inner window at the far end of the room, Lizzie could see a small indoor workout pool and the door to a sauna. It was nearly an exact replica of the workout room in Sanglarka.

However, Lizzie knew it couldn't be that space, as you couldn't get to another gate on the planet from here. Lizzie had quizzed her instructors about the reasons for this, but at this point, none of them had an answer about why this was so.

"Let's start with a mental workout and go from there," Tarafau suggested.

Lizzie nodded and seated herself cross-legged across from Tarafau on the workout mat. It had been a while since she had done any of this; weeks, as a matter of fact. Fortunately, Lizzie had no trouble easing herself into the deep REM trance that allowed her to drift into her personal mental space.

She entered the space, as usual, through the well-appointed library she had created as her safe and happy place, and out the library doors into a sunny day. She and Tarafau trod down the stone steps between the statues of two lions that guarded the entrance to the library and out onto the sidewalk that circled the park and city square beyond.

They strode out toward the pond in silence down the path lined with spring flowers. Lizzie could see in the distance the little shops that surrounded the square. As they walked, Lizzie's heart swelled within her. This had been hers and Reloi's special place. Every little detail of the little town square with its lovely park reminded her of the countless hours they had spent here, exploring Lizzie's mental abilities and helping her to connect more effectively with Ynni, as well as discovering her ability to communicate with the plants around her.

Most of the sadness had faded into an ache like a healing bruise, obscured instead by the joy of her memories with him. As painful as the disaster had been that had separated them, nothing could ever erase the joy of his final words to her and the memories they shared. If she had any regrets, it was only that she wished she had connected with him sooner.

They paused at the park bench where she and Reloi had spent so many happy hours, talking and planning. Every moment with him had been instructive and yet so sweet. She determined that she would revisit the refugees of Grild, now that the foundation for her garden had been put into place. She knew she couldn't do much more until the concrete had set and cured. At that point she would begin the rest of the ongoing process of creating her garden.

It was Reloi who had started her on this path. He had been the one to expose her talent for hearing and communicating with the plants around her. He had been the one who had taught her how to filter those mental sounds so that walking through a garden or forest wasn't overwhelming to her. He had been the one who had given her the skills to rescue Bonwen from the crawlies and had saved another world, even when he couldn't save his own.

Tarafau was silent as they sat there, allowing her to rest in her thoughts for the moment. She wondered what he remembered most about all they had gone through together, since he had been her guide through her internship and her first official assignment as a certified agent. Now once again he was her guide in her new position as Gate Guardian.

She often wondered what had happened to start him on the path of an Alliance agent, since his dimension had no gateways that anyone had been able to discover. She still didn't feel comfortable asking him about it, however. It occurred to her that their relationship, as close as it had become during the last several months, still didn't allow her to ask something so personal.

"So what would you like to study here today?" he asked her, startling her out of her reverie.

"I'm not sure," she replied, turning to face him. His deep amber eyes were not catlike, the pupils round as her own, but she still always felt like she was looking into Tidbit's face. "Is there a list somewhere of the kinds of abilities one can learn? It all feels so random to me sometimes. For instance, when I started to learn with Reloi, I had no idea I would learn how to use my music to calm and heal or how to listen to plants. I did start to work on kinetics, but never got to be very adept at it, although Reloi could do amazing things manipulating physical objects with his mind."

"I'm not aware of a 'list,' but I imagine there might be some books in that library of yours, or you might want to do a search on your tablet when we get back. Perhaps for now, just getting here and allowing yourself some peace before doing our physical forms is enough for today. Usually, I like to start my mental jaunts with a purpose, either a question I have for myself or a goal of learning a skill. Let's retire for now and get to work," he concluded with his catlike grin.

So they faded back into the workout room. Ynni was waiting expectantly near her on the mat.

"You play now?" she sent, bouncing in expectation of the coming entertainment. Ynni loved to watch them do the forms and spar, often cheering them on with chirruping squeals and squeaks.

Lizzie strode over to the basket full of training quarterstaffs that sat near the window side of the room. She generally didn't use her "ceremonial" staff for practice exercises, although she could whip it out of her MDP in a motion that made it seem like it appeared out of thin air. As she lifted an appropriate sized staff out of the basket, she hefted it and paused looking out over a large valley featuring double suns in the cloudless sky.

"Where are we?" she asked as she took a few lazy swings of the staff, warming up and stretching her shoulder muscles.

"We really don't know. Evidently there are some gates on uninhabited worlds where the ancient members of the Alliance had created various facilities to be used by all Alliance members for a variety of purposes. You may even meet some of your fellow gate guardians here from time to time, although time differences, both across your Earth and within the dimensions, are so different that this would be a rare occurrence."

They stepped into the first stance of the quarterstaff forms, and Lizzie was calmed and energized at the same time as they stepped in perfect rhythm to the graceful, almost dancelike, movements of strike and thrust and parry, swiveling, turning, and stretching. They finished out face to face like a pair of ballroom dancers preparing for the final choreography of defense and attack.

Lizzie's entire focus was on doing each movement with precision, grace, and attention to detail. They finished with an acknowledging bow in the proper form and deposited their staves in the basket. Ynni hooted at their performance and Lizzie barely restrained herself from bowing to her appreciative audience with a grin.

Lizzie groaned softly. Only now that they had stopped did she realize how much her muscles ached. After hours of kneeling in the garden, absorbed in her work and now starting up this workout after weeks of relative inactivity in that direction, she could see that she would need to go slowly to recondition herself.

"Can we skip the hand to hand for now?" she sent, regretting the querulous tone of it.

Tarafau laughed softly. *"I suppose, but I don't intend to go easy on you in the future. You need to get back into your usual routines. Shall we say every morning before breakfast?"*

Lizzie sighed and nodded. Now she was committed to both a morning and evening workout.

She decided to take Tarafau's suggestion to research mental abilities on her Alliance tablet. Tarafau had transformed back into Tidbit and he meowed plaintively at the French doors leading outside. Ynni didn't follow him. They both knew that he was heading out to visit his family for the night. He would return in the morning to be let back into the house.

Lizzie considered this to be an excellent arrangement. He got to be with his family every day, so little Elizabeth and his sweet wife Amenia didn't have to do without him much more than any man who worked outside his home to make a living. From time to time, Ynni went with him to visit her own family, her tribe, which appeared to be growing and prospering.

Lizzie had learned while an intern agent on his planet that he was reimbursed for his time working for the Alliance with hours credits as if he was working any vocation on his planet. She liked their system. It was all about the time spent doing something useful. On his planet even homemakers and family caregivers earned credits for the hours they spent caring for others.

She had noticed that greed wasn't a problem on his planet, although Amenia had told her it hadn't always been so. In the years before they had changed their governmental system, it hadn't been much different than some of the worst years on Earth. It had interested her that the one who had instigated the movement that had changed everything had been a humble woman of no particular fame or influence.

Could she somehow, someday, be that woman for her own planet, without compromising her commitment as a guardian to the laws of the Alliance?

She sighed and sat down with her tablet, running through the messages from her podmates and Alliance news updates. It seemed that, like herself, many of them had already been through some harrowing experiences, but so far none of them had been drastically injured or killed. All of them were still active agents in their respective assignments.

Then, as she buckled down to her study, she was amazed once again at the technology that not only let her search the massive library of the Alliance but would instantly translate any document into her own language. It boggled her mind when she considered the millions of active Alliance agents and gate guardians of the gate network.

Delving into the history of mental abilities, as far back as she could go, she realized that she had only scratched the scratch of a scratch of the surface of what beings could do with their minds. She did learn more about the abilities, however, which encouraged her.

The amount of time it would take to study this one topic alone would extend beyond the average human lifespan. She found herself somewhat jealous of so many of the beings she had associated with in her time as an agent trainee and then as an agent. Some of them lived not just for centuries, but for millennia.

Sighing and feeling a bit defeated, she finally put her tablet away after she realized that Ynni was patting her cheeks to wake her up.

"Bedtime," she sent sternly.

"Bedtime," Lizzie agreed with a sigh.

Chapter 6: The Pieces of Her Heart

(J)enny looked up once again out into the beautiful garden Lizzie had planted with such love and care. Like Lizzie, she knew she had a long way to go to refine her mental talents.

Her own ability to communicate beyond dimensional boundaries had created quite a stir and had been a timely discovery. She knew using it was vital in the current conflict, because the ultimate goal of the Alliance was to defeat the formidable foe that challenged the safety and security of the entire multiverse. They needed her to stay focused on using her talents to that end.

Therefore, although she wished she could explore her abilities, the Alliance needed her to focus on continuing to act as the only secure way to communicate between all the active forces in play. This meant that even during her recuperation, much of her sleep time was dedicated to meeting with the various forces moving on what seemed to be a vast cubes board.

So far, the Alliance had made a dent in the Inseni threat, but they had uncovered something that was so much more than they had first believed. First, it had seemed to be the Groga under Sam's father's rule, but then they discovered the Inseni. They had thought Peril to be the ruler of the Groga forces, only to discover that he was only a puppet of Gall, the devious and evil ruler of a vast network of terrorists.

Gall had killed Sam's father and mother, Peril had been defeated, and Sam had killed Gall in retribution. The Groga, for the most part, had joined in the defense of the Alliance and their cause. The Alliance knew that there were still multiple dimensions under the thumb of the Inseni invaders even though, between the Alliance's attacks and Sam's destruction of Gall, they had effectively shattered the known government of the Inseni. Thereafter, the ethical stance of *the Alliance had been to seek out every conquered dimension and seek to free them from the tyranny that had been imposed on them.*

This, of course, was a task beyond Jenny's imagining. But, as the Gatekeeper of the Alliance and due to her mental ability to securely communicate across dimensions, she had become an intrinsic part of their strategy. Fortunately, she thought, she wasn't part of the team that created the battle strategies or who would fight in the upcoming struggle.

However, Burt, Bob, Elizabeth, and many of her friends and associates in the Alliance, including the amazing Mookookie, were actively engaged in planning and in the missions that would be shortly traversing the gate network to do battle and relieve the suffering of the conquered dimensions.

Much of what Lizzie had written about her earlier training filled in some of the gaps that Jenny had felt so keenly in her own preparation for her position, due to the series of unanticipated events that had led her to this point and had interrupted her formal training.

She couldn't feel grateful for being out of the action in the Alliance for three weeks, but if nothing else, she was learning so much more about her aunt and was beginning to feel such a kinship that it was almost worth it to be treated like an invalid.

She sighed and opened the journal again.)

Tears streamed down Lizzie's face. Seeing the plight of the Grildite people she had grown to love, brought back so many memories. Reloi had given his life to rescue them from destruction, but there was so much more yet to do.

The Alliance had set them up in individual refugee camps on four different planets in the Alliance network. The native people on each of these planets had given generously of food, temporary housing, and necessary supplies.

This was the third planet she had visited this week. She had gotten Elias to collect her mail, not that this was ever much more than bank statements and an occasional letter from her parents or siblings. She had let Lacey know that she would be on a traveling assignment and had someone taking care of Tidbit.

In every camp, Lizzie had been welcomed with delight. She found people she knew and had loved in each camp. At this particular camp she had been greeted by Reloi's family, or at least his mother and his siblings. Evidently his father had been assisting Reloi right up until the end, sending his family ahead through the gateway, promising them that they would follow when they could.

Lizzie was now surrounded by them, all of them touching her and hugging her in turn. Every face was wet with both reunion and mourning. *"You are my daughter now,"* his mother had sent privately to her. *"Reloi confided to us about your marriage, and we acknowledge you as his widow. You are a part of our family now, and that will never change."*

Lizzie had no words but simply held her mother-in-law tightly to her and they wept together.

There were over a thousand refugees at this particular camp. Lizzie could only remember that dreadful day like a movie played at triple speed. She had helped group after group of refugees over a period of several days through the Alliance headquarters gate, spaced ten minutes apart. She had slept very little, but the entire experience had passed in a blur.

Once again, reality hit her like it was yesterday. In the past few months, she had stayed as busy as she could, absorbed in new duties and learning new things during her various visits with the other gate guardians. But these faces, these very familiar faces, brought those devastating days all back in astounding and heartbreaking clarity.

Finally, when the tears had dried up, she once again asked the question she had asked at the first two camps.

"What can I do that will help you? What do you need? I'll be reporting to the Alliance. I know they're working hard to find you a place to make a permanent settlement, but until then, what can I do for you?"

Surprisingly their reply had been the same in all three places she had visited thus far. *"Play for us, Lizzie. We need to hear your music."*

After all they had been through, music seemed to be the one thing that still connected them all.

Obediently, Lizzie pulled out her mbira and began to play. The one thing she now knew about her musical gift was that it was strongly connected to her mental abilities. It was just another way of communication that allowed Lizzie to express things she couldn't find words for.

As the music began, Ynni, who had accompanied her to every camp, began to croon in harmony. What surprised Lizzie most was that many of the younger Grildites had brought their mbiras with them in the backpacks and bags that had accompanied every refugee through the gateways. They had brought so little with them, but these instruments had been their companions.

Many of them ran to fetch their mbiras to join in with her impromptu composition. Lizzie's talent linked to them and, like her concerts under the tree by her pod in the Alliance agent training compound, they anticipated the flow and direction of her music, harmonizing and syncing with her. Anyone else would have thought of this as a kind of magic, but Lizzie knew that this was just another expression of mindspeech, and it filled her with awe.

At some point she realized that beyond the music emanating from the small mbira orchestra, voices were joining in. There were no words, but the music had infused the entire assembly of refugees in a spontaneous composition, making the very air around them vibrate.

Once again tears streamed down every cheek, but they were no longer tears of sorrow. Instead, they were tears of hope for a future that before may have not seemed possible.

In her mind, Lizzie pictured a new home for these people—her people, as much as any of her family on Earth. She pictured them going forth to recreate the pastoral society they had known inside Grild. She pictured libraries and universities, craft halls and concert halls. She pictured a new generation of children, learning, growing, and creating.

All of this she poured into the music until, exhausted, she finally created a crescendo that faded to a gentle heartwarming climax, the music fading into silence.

For a long moment, no one spoke; and then a nearly deafening cheer went up from the onlookers. There was new joy and determination on every face.

"Thank you, Lizzie," was sent in almost a chorus, from the minds around her. *"Thank you. We see now, and we will go forth with hope and trust in our future."*

Years later, Lizzie would revisit this moment, and it would still bring tears of joy and healing. They surrounded her, each wanting to take a moment to touch her, to hold her hand or hug her. She didn't rush them or withdraw; she greeted each one with a gentle comment when it was someone she knew from before. By the time they had all had their moment with her, she realized they would expect her to say something. What could she possibly say that hadn't already been said by the glorious music they had created together?

"I will return when I can. I have one more camp to visit. I've been collecting messages to send back and forth between the camps and have been given permission to give you a gift. We know there is much planning that needs to be done for your impending migration to a new land that will be your own. This planning will be difficult with you separated in four different dimensions.

"I've been given this to give to you." And she withdrew a tablet from her MDP. She handed it to her mother-in-law. *"This will connect you to the Alliance network, specifically to the other tablets I am distributing through the four camps.*

"The leaders of each camp will be able to consult with one another and begin to organize everything that is necessary for a successful relocation. You will also be able to receive personal messages from those you love who are in other camps, as well as to receive instructions and updates from Alliance headquarters.

"I know this is technology you're already familiar with. In the near future, more of these will be distributed throughout your community for more widespread access. But for now, this represents the commitment the Alliance has to its newest official member. Although you are currently scattered and are living through hard times, you can be assured that you have not been forgotten, nor are you abandoned."

Once again, an exultant cheer ascended from the multitude around her. Lizzie was more than a little overwhelmed by the reaction to her speech. She had received the same response in each of her other visits. She was somewhat embarrassed, not feeling that anything she had done merited such a reaction, but she smiled.

Her goodbyes were poignant, especially her leave-taking with Reloi's family, but she had one more stop to make before returning to Infinity Loop.

When she finally got home, it was nighttime the next day, and she was glad for it. She curled up with Ynni and was instantly asleep.

The next morning, she awoke late, the sun already well up, peeking from beneath the curtains in her bedroom.

Yawning and stretching, she realized that Ynni was already up, but had not awakened her as was usually her custom. She knew that Ynni realized that she was exhausted and worn out by the last couple of days visiting the refugee camps.

She didn't feel like having an extensive breakfast, so she quickly made herself a peanut butter and jelly sandwich, poured herself a glass of milk, and sat down at the dining room table with her tablet next to her. The number of messages on her alerts was a little astounding. Not surprisingly, some were from the Alliance, congratulating her on her successful mission to the refugee camps.

There were also some from her podmates, updating her on their own adventures. But the majority of them were from many of her friends in the refugee camps, once again thanking her for her visit and the hope they now felt. The most surprising of all was a message from the newly reformed council of the Grildites:

"We would like to extend an invitation to you to be a part of our council. We know you are no longer an official agent of the Alliance, but we also know you can be a vital link to the Alliance council on our behalf. You need not attend every meeting, but we value any input you might have when you read the after-reports of the meetings of our council. Please respond as soon as you can."

Once again Lizzie found herself in awe of the futuristic technology that allowed this kind of communication. Other than telephones, most communication on Earth still relied on mail or telegraph, delivered across continents by air and sea. Often even letters from her parents that came from San Diego to Los Angeles took as much as a week to two weeks to get to her mailbox.

Here she was, receiving almost instantaneously a message from dimensions in the multiverse that she couldn't have even plotted on a star chart. Far beyond the edges of the universe as far as Earth scientists understood it, Lizzie had friends, acquaintances, and, yes, even family. This wasn't just light years away, but a distance that no one on Earth could measure. And yet, here were messages that had taken nearly no time to get to her, as she sat eating a peanut butter and jelly sandwich at her dining room table.

She hurriedly sent a reply accepting the proffered invitation to be actively involved in helping the Grildites in any way she was able. She owed Reloi and her new family that much, at the very least.

Catching up and answering her messages took her most of the morning. It appeared that while Lizzie was sleeping, Ynni had let Tidbit in, as both were lazily hanging out on the window seat. She realized that Ynni had probably told Tidbit not to wake her, even though she had promised to do her morning workouts.

"I know it's a bit late," she sent to Tidbit, *"but do you want to work out this morning? I think I have something I want to explore in my mental workout today. Something occurred to me during the impromptu concerts that happened on my visits to the refugee camps, and I want to work on it."*

In answer, Tidbit and Ynni simply sprang down from their comfy perch and followed Lizzie into the gate office and from there to the yellow door that led to their workout space.

Once inside, Lizzie immediately sank down onto one of the mats, Tarafau across from her and Ynni standing behind her, her tiny hands warm on each shoulder. Lizzie knew this physical connection would strengthen and support her mental abilities, something they had learned while being trained by Reloi and Tanata.

Inside her mind, they moved directly to the park from the library. Lizzie strode determinedly down the path to the little park bench that sat next to a large tree overlooking the placid little pond that reflected the sunlight in multitudes of sparkling diamond-like glints.

As they sat, Tarafau looked at her quizzically, his amber eyes almost glowing with curiosity.

"So what is this about?" he finally asked when Lizzie didn't speak for several minutes.

"I think I learned something interesting," she began and told him in detail about her several experiences with the Grildites.

She told him about their response to the music, their continued enthusiasm about the mbiras she had taught them to use during her time on Grild, and the fact that of the few treasured possessions they chose to bring from Grild during their flight from the destruction of their planet, the mbira was chosen by a majority of those who had been her students.

She told him about the connection she had made with her spontaneous compositions and the response of not only those with mbiras, but also the vocalizations that had harmonized so beautifully. She knew this was not "normal" by any definition she could think of, and she knew she needed to explore this.

One of the things she had noticed as she said goodbye at each of the camps was the complete shift that had happened in the faces and attitudes of the people around her between the time she arrived and her departure. She had often heard the quote from William Congreve: "Music has charms to soothe the savage breast."

She had been told by the teacher of that single music appreciation course she had taken in college that music was one of the most powerful forces for change that existed, but she had pooh-poohed the idea at the time.

However, the evidence of her own experience belied that initial conclusion. Those people had experienced a powerful shift in their attitude and emotions. She had felt from them a determined commitment to moving forward with hope as she left them, although they had initially sent out feelings of despair and hopelessness when she had first greeted each group.

Tarafau listened intently as she spoke. Finally, as she wound down, she asked, "What do you think about this? Am I rushing to unsupported conclusions here?"

Tarafau shook his head and, at first, Lizzie thought with irritation that he was going to shut it all down. But instead, he reached out both hands to take hers. This gesture was typical of his wife, Amenia, as well as Miriha, but she had never had him reach out to her this way before. She was shocked when she noticed tears glistening in his eyes, another first.

"I wish Amenia could be here right now. She is so much more skilled than I am in encouraging burgeoning mental abilities. But Lizzie... do you have any idea how amazing you are?

"I admit that when Gaston first singled you out as his potential successor, I was doubtful. But I can now see his wisdom confirmed. This gift—or talent, some would call it—may be unique to you. I have never seen it before, but I agree that you have only begun to scratch the surface of what you can accomplish with it.

"Combine that with your strong connection to the plant life around you, and I begin to believe that your adventures and accomplishments have only begun to approach your final potential. So I ask you, where do you think you would like to take this?

"Perhaps a visit to Amenia would be in order soon or maybe Liliath, if she can spare the time from her administrative duties at the training center."

Lizzie thought about this for a minute. She could feel the warmth of Ynni's hands on her shoulders, even though, according to her eyes in this place, Ynni was perched on a limb of the tree that shaded the park bench. She wondered how this tallied with her ongoing responsibilities as a gate guardian and what that really meant in the long run.

"I think I want to find out how this helps me to help the people around me without having to pull out my mbira or give a concert. Somehow, I have the feeling that there is more to it than that. The mbira definitely got me started, and I don't expect to start picking up other instruments besides the one your council gave me. I don't see myself getting a piano or learning to play the harp like Gi, for instance.

"But I can't help thinking I'm missing something important here. Liliath once told me that we are each given distinct and different gifts in the realm of mindspeech and mental abilities. She seemed to think that the Creator intended it that way for some specific reasons.

"My parents raised me to believe that God, our word for the Creator, gave what they called 'spiritual gifts' to each person to allow us to fulfill our potential and help the people around us.

"This feels like the same thing to me. So, regardless of what we may believe, don't I have a responsibility to continue to enhance what I've been given?"

Tarafau didn't speak at once. Again, he considered her soberly, searching her face as if there were answers there that she couldn't imagine.

At last, he said, "I think we all underestimated you, Lizzie. So, I would like to suggest that you probably already know, somewhere in your subconscious, what you need to do next. Are you ready to act now? Or do you want to give this some more thought before we continue?"

Lizzie thought about this. Now that she had laid out her concerns to Tarafau, she realized that he was truly a guide to her. It was not just a title. He really cared about her and was doing his best to help her reach her potential.

"I think I need a physical workout to get some oxygen flowing to my brain. I'll think on it while I work in the garden today and will tell you my conclusions in our workout tomorrow."

Chapter 7: Connecting Some of the Dots

(Jenny shook herself, coming out of the journal as if she had gone from one dimension to another; but instead of distance, it was the dimension of being in another time.

She found herself contemplating Lizzie's experience so much more personally than she would have when reading a biography of some famous person she wasn't connected to.

Lizzie's experiences, although unique to her, also seemed to parallel Jenny's own journey in many ways. The link she felt to her aunt was growing stronger as she realized that she too had far to go in honing her mental gifts. She also realized that Lizzie's trials, like her own, had a significant impact on Lizzie's progress, not only in her mental gifts but also in her changing perspectives.

She knew she should probably pause to eat the lunch she could smell Lizziebot preparing in the kitchen, but it would have to wait. She couldn't take a break now.)

Lizzie woke early the next morning without Ynni's prodding. Her dreams had been filled with the memories of the many concerts she and her podmates had shared under the tree between the pods—the tree that she later learned had been listening to and singing along with them the entire time.

Her first thoughts this morning had been that she would mentally serenade her garden as she planted it and, even once the plants were established, she would make a point to communicate with them and encourage them to grow and flourish.

She dressed and practically sprang into her workout clothes, pausing only to brush her teeth and run a brush through her tousled hair.

Ynni peered sleepily into the bathroom, chirruped softly, and headed into the dining room to let Tidbit in, who had been waiting patiently.

"Let's go, you two," she sent, striding purposefully to the gate office door.

"My, we're feeling enthusiastic this morning," Tidbit sent, amusement emanating from his mental tone.

Ynni chirruped in apparent agreement, and they followed her.

In the workout room she gracefully sat on the mat in her usual relaxing posture to prepare to enter the place her mind had created for her as a safe and peaceful place.

Without hesitation, Lizzie led them down the street in her mental village to the little music shop, but it wasn't so small anymore. In fact, it seemed to dominate the other little shops arranged around the square.

As they opened the door to enter, a little bell tinkled, and the shopkeeper emerged from a door in the back of the shop.

"Lizzie! Welcome back. How is your mbira performing these days? Staying in tune, I hope?"

"Oh, yes. Since you taught me how to keep it tuned, I have cared for it regularly. I have gotten much use out of it. As a matter of fact, I was hoping you could give me some direction moving forward."

Lizzie had been taught by Reloi that the answers she received within this place were really answers that already existed in her mind but were more available to her here. He had told her, after she had thought carefully about something, she could go to one of the shopkeepers and ask questions and receive insights that might be harder to come by in the conscious world.

This was what she was hoping for now. So, she asked, "How is my mind like the mbira? How can I create the same music and effect when I don't have the mbira in my hand?"

The shopkeeper laughed. "You have certainly come a long way. I don't think many music students ever work that out. Your music is more than just in your mind. It comes from something deep inside you. But it can also be influenced by the minds and hearts around you; and you, in turn, can influence them. Few learn to connect with the subtle personal music that surrounds them.

"Once you make that connection, it is very similar to mindspeech. Like any musical talent, it requires practice and intent to master. I think I have some sheet music that will help you."

"But I don't read music," Lizzie protested, shaking her head.

"Ah, I don't think you understand. You'll find this to be very different than any sheet music you have encountered in the physical world."

She went through the door in the back of her shop and came back out with a sheaf of papers in her hands. On them were imprinted the familiar tablatures Lizzie had expected, but when she reluctantly reached out her hands to take the papers, the shopkeeper drew them back.

"Stand still," she commanded, and Lizzie obeyed.

The shopkeeper approached closer and laid the sheaf of papers on top of Lizzie's head where, to Lizzie's surprise and continued confusion, they seemed to melt into her head. A warm feeling of contentment and a strange, calm confidence wafted from her scalp into every fiber of her being.

Lizzie had been taught that everything she saw in her mental wanderings in this place was intensely symbolic, but this verged on magic.

"What did you just do?" she asked in awe of the continued warm feelings spreading throughout her conscious mind and into her physical body still seated on the mat in the workout room.

"I just opened a conduit to something that has been waiting for you to accept it for a long time. It will take some time to manifest completely, but you'll begin to notice some differences in how your music expresses itself. It will be up to you to expand it and make it your own."

Lizzie looked up at Tarafau, who was grinning his delighted catlike grin, his amber eyes warm with pride. Pride? In me?

She thanked the woman and left, the little bell tinkling in their wake.

"What just happened there?" she asked Tarafau in wonder as they walked across the street to the park.

"I think you just answered your question," he remarked. Was that a tinge of wonder in his voice?

"So, how does that work, really?" she asked almost plaintively.

Tarafau laughed. "Lizzie, there are never enough answers for you, but I will answer as I can. If I understand it correctly, once you set your mind to a question that is important to you, your subconscious mind goes to work on it immediately. Then, as you do your own research and allow your mind to work on the issue in the background, your subconscious tugs and pulls and yanks and pushes on the question until it comes up with possible answers.

"Here, in this place, we have direct access to your subconscious mind in a very symbolic way. The shopkeepers in the various shops around the square represent the unique answers your mind requires.

"You've already found that the shops on the square change and some are replaced from time to time by others. These respond to your needs. What are you considering, thinking about, questioning or researching?

"One of the benefits of these mental exercises is to allow you to more fully connect with your mind to allow you to progress more quickly and efficiently than you can when only dealing with the surface of your conscious mind.

"I can't precisely tell you what just happened in the shop back there, but I can tell you to pay special attention to how the music in your mind coincides with other types of communication. Over the coming weeks and months, you will discover new ways to express yourself, even when you are not playing the mbira. I suggest you write your observations down in that journal you write in so assiduously."

Lizzie thought about this and nodded. Not magic then. She was a bit ashamed of herself for having had that fleeting thought and was relieved that there was a rational explanation.

Once they came out of their mental exercise, during their physical workout she allowed her mind to drift as she went through the forms. They were so familiar that she didn't really have to focus on them. This would give her an ideal time to think more deeply about it.

The next several days passed in quiet contemplation as she continued to lay the foundation for her garden. The concrete that lined the pond was finally dry, and she finished the rock lattice. She compacted and shaped the dirt that had been piled behind the pond to create the base of the fountain into a small hill, and Elias helped her to set up the pump, which would circulate the water from the top of the little waterfall into the pond to prevent stagnation.

Between her workouts with Tarafau, her jogging sessions with Lacey, and her focused work in the garden, that remarkable visit to the music shop kept running through her mind.

She had taken to doing mbira concerts in her mental workouts, similar to what she had done back in her agent-training days.

In the garden, she had even engaged the tree and the plants around her, reaching out to them with her music but also listening carefully to their joyful accompaniment. The question she kept asking herself was, how did that happen?

She knew that orchestras practiced hundreds of hours on the pieces they performed. How was it she was able to bring together these spontaneous harmonious performances? She could understand how it worked with Ynni, as they were mentally linked, and it was a simple thing for Ynni to anticipate the music Lizzie formed instinctively.

But what about other beings? Of course, all the beings in her mental world were just extensions of her own mind, but in the real world, what had happened with the refugees? How was that possible?

She finally concluded that she would have to start trying new things in the waking world. It was the only way she could take this to the next level.

She knew her schedule was about to pick up, but the timing was good. She had gone as far as she could in the garden until the concrete had completely cured and the pond was ready to be filled. She had appointments with the other Earth guardians and was looking forward to it. It would mean a lot of traveling, and that meant a whole new aspect added to her current experience.

She had been spoiled by the miracle of the Alliance gate network and the instantaneous travel it provided across the multiverse. She decided to pick up some good books to read on the very long plane rides that would take her to each of the gates except the China gate. She looked forward to getting to know each of the guardians better and learning more about her duties as a freshly minted gate guardian.

The following days, her preparation taught her some new things about what was required to travel internationally. She already had a passport that would work for anywhere she wanted to go, but she needed to plan her wardrobe carefully, as each place had different climates. She was grateful for the luggage Gaston had given her early on as a gift. She would only be using the smallest suitcase and the matching carry-on bag, as in reality she could take her entire wardrobe with her in her MDP.

She had been taught during her training in Sanglarka that traveling with no luggage or carry-ons would look suspicious and might get her tagged for watching by various government agencies.

As she made her preparations, she continued to focus on her mental exercises, paying particular attention to discovering how to meld her music into her mindspeech projections, especially to those animal and vegetable, as well as humans who did not have mindspeech capacity.

One day, while visiting with Lacey, she noticed her friend seemed a bit down. Her usual erect posture and energetic nature were drooping like an unwatered plant.

"I just feel like I'm in over my head most of the time," she had commented when Lizzie mentioned it.

"I'm only an assistant professor and, although I do think I have what it takes to eventually make it into the professional ranks, while I continue to work on my PhD. I often feel like I'll never keep up with the workload of grading papers and classroom duties along with working on my doctoral thesis. I come home every day exhausted and wondering whether it's worth it," she confided.

Subconsciously Lizzie had begun to hum a cheerful mental tune of her own making that seemed to spring from her desire to help and encourage her friend. Lacey couldn't hear it of course...or could she? Although Lizzie had made no audible sound, as they continued to discuss her feelings of frustration and inadequacy, something began to change.

Lacey's comments became less self-deprecating, and the corners of her mouth began to turn up. She sat up straighter in her chair. Lizzie doubted it was anything she had said—they were just chatting over a glass of lemonade in the still-unfinished garden area—but by the time Lacey left to go home and grade papers, there was a renewed spring in her step.

"Maybe I'm onto something here," Lizzie sent to Ynni, who had turned her reflection back on. Ynni had been sitting on the grass next to them the entire time.

"Lizzie does something new? Mindsinging? Like linkling croon. Ynni likes this much muchly."

"Ynni, did you help me with this?"

Ynni nodded her head enthusiastically, the dark green fur that dangled from her ears swaying, her long mustache wiggling, and her large eyes highlighted with furry white circles crinkled in her chartreuse face, as if at a secret joke.

"Lizzie could always do this, but Ynni does like to help...yes?"

Chapter 8: Guardian and Friends

(J*enny came to with a start. She had been deep into Lizzie's world when someone kissed her gently on her forehead.*

She had been so engrossed that she hadn't even heard the door in the hallway open behind her. She looked up with surprise and delight at the big grin on Burt's face. His tousled brown hair and those glorious eyes made her heart thump in joy and delight.

"I didn't know you'd be dropping in today," she squeaked in delight.

"Chidwi and Tidbit were kind enough not to alert you. I wanted to take you out to eat and catch up. I know you want to get back to the journal, but it looks like you're well into this last one, and I need some face time with my beautiful wife. Put on some glad rags and let's boogie."

Jenny happily complied, looking only slightly reluctantly at the journal as she placed it on the table next to her reading chair.

"Casual?" she asked hopefully.

"You could look gorgeous in cutoffs and a t-shirt, but yeah, let's do casual. I'm not exactly dressed for a ball, after all."

She laughed and donned some slacks and a summery short sleeved gingham blouse and ran her fingers through her cap of honey-blonde curls.

"Come on, kiddo, you can't do anything to improve on perfection, after all," Burt chided with a grin. "My wife turns heads everywhere she goes."

He drove them out to Santa Monica to one of their favorite seafood restaurants overlooking the ocean. It was so nice to spend time as just another couple enjoying a romantic lunch together, with no hint that they were interdimensional warriors and guardians of the multiverse.

Their time together was even more precious to Jenny when she considered how little time Lizzie had gotten to spend with Reloi. If she had learned anything from her aunt, it was that life was uncertain and it was important to make the most of every priceless moment. She and Burt were still young, but so had Lizzie been when she found Reloi.

Afterward, she and Burt strolled down the beach, enjoying just being together. Here on the beach with the noise of the surf serenading them, they could talk shop away from potentially prying ears in the restaurant.

"Bob and Merv are working at hyper-speed with the Mookookie to explore the potential of the MDP network and how we can use it in the coming conflict to potentially slant the odds in our favor. Cornelium is working on some new weaponry for the space fleet that may allow us to remove the Inseni troops from the planets they have conquered without harming the indigenous population.

"Liliath has called a major meeting later this week for the entire Alliance. You and I are invited, but we will not be attending in person. They are taking no chances with you. Even with all the security in place here on Earth and within the Alliance in general, and even with the entire city around the headquarters building on high alert, they don't want to take a chance that might allow someone to get to you.

"So, for now, you and I will be attending virtually in the gate office. You can even come in your jammies, if you'd like," he added with a chuckle and a wink.

On the long drive home, Jenny recounted some of Lizzie's more exciting revelations from the journals.

"Not only has she endured some very difficult times, but she taught me a lot about what I missed in the crazy rushed training I've had. At the moment, she's creating the garden in the backyard, but I have a feeling I'm in for a bumpy ride going forward. I admit that although I have been itching to get back into action, I think this quiet time with the journals is preparing me for what comes next.

"Thank you for being so patient with my process. It means a lot to me that you're so supportive. I'm not sure what you expected out of married life, but I'm pretty sure neither one of us expected this. I don't know what's ahead, but for now, I'm glad we made the decision to go forward. I'm pretty happy right now, and 'now' is sometimes all you get...."

Burt looked at her quizzically. "Now? We have forever in whatever dimension we find ourselves. You don't honestly think I'll let you go anytime short of eternity, do you?"

Jenny reached her hand across the console, and Burt grabbed it and squeezed it tight. "It's a deal," she said, looking across at the man she loved, "just for eternity and then we'll see."

He laughed, and the sound of that delighted laugh pursued her even after he said his goodbyes with a fervent kiss before disappearing through the gate office door.

She settled into her reading chair with a contented sigh and Chidwi, who had been hanging out in the garden while they were gone, hopped up on her favorite spot on the back of the chair. Tidbit looked up lazily from his spot on the window seat.

"Did you have a good time?" he sent, the end of his tail twitching contentedly.

"Glorious," she replied. "It was nice to take a break."

She grabbed the journal. "Back to it..." she said, picking up where she had left off.)

As Lizzie stepped out of the taxi, she waved to Melinda Mensch, who waved back in greeting.

"Good to see you back. I'll bet you're excited to get back to your garden! Elias says the concrete is cured well enough to get the fountain up and running. He thoroughly mulched the hole where your tree will be living and by now the compost is well established in the soil you put into the garden beds. When will you be picking up your other plants?"

Melinda had been happily engaged with the garden whenever Elias had come over to help with the heavy work. This impressed Lizzie since, in addition to her duties at the local library, she was also an accomplished watercolor artist, with work in many galleries up and down the Pacific Coast Highway.

Most of her art consisted of seascapes. When she wasn't working, she would head out and spend her time sketching. At home she would turn these sketches into amazing portrayals of the various moods of the beaches along the California coast.

"I've arranged for some of the plants to be delivered in the morning. How's the latest painting coming along?"

"Not bad. I'll be going out Monday to make a sketch of a flotilla that will be coming into Morrow Bay; full-on traditional sailing ships."

"Enjoy. Sounds exciting." And with a cheerful wave she grabbed her suitcase again and shouldered her carryon bag.

She sighed happily when she finally set her luggage down in her bedroom. It had indeed been quite a trip. This latest one had been in the Australian outback. She'd not only learned more about the gateways, but she'd been given the opportunity to bump around in the rougher areas, seeing wildlife and terrain that were nearly as alien as some of the dimensions she had visited during her agent training.

For now, she had two weeks before her trip to China. At this point she had visited the Puerto Rico gate, the Czechoslovakian gate, and the Indian gate. Each time she thought she had seen it all, she found that she had finally truly gotten her wish. She was no longer in a mental space where she was fidgeting over the languishing pace of her instruction.

She had gone so far beyond that, and once again it was all she could do to keep up with the flow of new information. She was in constant correspondence with the other guardians, her podmates, and the Grid refugees on four different planets, as well as the Fanilians.

Add to that her requirements to continue to build strong relationships with her neighbors and to eventually get involved in other community activities, and sometimes she felt mentally out of breath.

As she went out into the backyard, she gazed at the foundational work that had already been done. At the moment, it looked nothing like the vision she had for it.

The mound of earth behind the empty concrete pond lined with the empty rock lattice, and the big hole slightly off from that, edged by the garden beds, looked a bit forlorn. Tomorrow the plants would start arriving, and her work would be cut out for her. She knew that Lacey would gladly chip in when she wasn't working or grading papers, and that Elias and Melinda would be happy to help over the weekend.

As she continued to explore her new talent for what Ynni was now happily calling 'mindsinging,' she realized this was another way for her to contribute to every personal interaction. She had done it on the airplane when there had been a fussing child seated behind her. She had done it while standing in line at customs in the airports. So many very tired passengers surrounded her, and many were more than a little cranky.

Each time she brought up the most soothing music her heart could make, and each time the people around her not only calmed down but became a lot easier to deal with.

She wasn't sure how far she could push this, but it seemed to work in close proximity. She wondered what applications she could make of it not only in her duties but also in her personal life with her family and others.

The next morning, she, Elias, Melinda, and Lacey were waiting in front of her house when the delivery truck pulled into the driveway. With help from the burly delivery guy, they hauled pallets of strawberries and several types of herbs through the back gate to sit next to the staging area. That morning, Elias had filled the little pond and attached the hosing to the pump that would create the small cascade that would circulate the water in the pond. They had buried the long electric cable that led to an outside outlet. As soon as they flipped the switch, the water would start to flow.

Elias had used colorful river rocks to line the trough that would contain the little waterfall. They would plant several water-loving herbs along either side of the water flow. They had already established water lettuce in the gravel at the bottom of the pond, as koi loved nibbling on the plants, and this would supplement any other fish food they were being fed.

They went to work, chatting as they gently settled the plants into the beds they had prepared. Lizzie placed each of the strawberries into the little clefts between the rocks that formed the lattice for her aquaponic experiment.

Elias had been skeptical, but when she explained how it all worked together, he admitted he would be very interested to see how it went.

They wouldn't be putting the koi into the pond until the water had been given a chance to thoroughly oxygenate after they turned on the waterfall.

After only a short break for lunch provided by Melinda from a local hamburger stand, they plowed on accompanied, unknowingly to them, by the mental harmonizing of Lizzie and the invisible Ynni.

By the time the last plant had been given a new home with the exception of Windsong, and they had watered them all thoroughly, they were all ready to retire to their homes and take a break. Lizzie thanked them profusely, but each of them replied that it had been fun and that they could hardly wait to see it all begin to grow into what Lizzie had envisioned.

Monday morning, after a restful Sunday, Lizzie headed again through the gateway to Fanilia with the little yew tree. She was greeted by the Gate Guardian and immediately escorted to her transport. She had messaged him the day before regarding what she had planned to do.

She approached Bonwen with Tarafau carrying the tree in its pot.

"Bonwen, I wanted to bring Windsong to you one last time. Tomorrow I will be planting her in her permanent home. I don't know how I can thank you for your help with Windsong. As you can see, she is already putting out new leaves and shoots."

"Lizzie Japhet, you saved me. You saved Fanilia. There is nothing we wouldn't do for you. At any time, you can come and ask for a boon; and if it is within our power, we will accommodate you.

"Your little friend will be a delight to you and all your posterity for hundreds of your years. She tells me she looks forward to singing with you and Ynni for many times to come."

"Thank you again, Bonwen," Lizzie sent, blushing deeply without apology to her agent instructors. If she couldn't show honest emotion here, she couldn't show it anywhere.

"Go with joy, Windsong," Bonwen sent, as, once again Tarafau lifted the pot holding the little tree. *"Flourish in your home soil."*

"I will miss you," Windsong sent back. *"But I look forward to a permanent home for my roots."*

When Tarafau finally eased the little tree through the door of the gate office and out into the California sunshine, the little tree sent a happy sigh.

"Ah, I will love it here," she sent to Lizzie and Ynni.

The next day they carefully set her roots into the hole Elias had dug for her while Lizzie had been in Australia. Lizzie and Ynni gently spaded dirt into the hole around her roots, harmonizing as they did so, a song of planting and growing.

Lizzie could feel the joy emanating from the little tree as they sang her into her new home. They gently tamped the earth around the slender trunk and watered her carefully, just enough to get her started.

The next day Lizzie and Lacey picked up the pair of koi she had ordered from the fish shop. They placed the plastic bag containing the koi into the pond with the waterfall turned off. The bag with the two fish would sit there for 24 hours until the temperature of the water in the bag matched the temperature of the pond.

The next morning Lizzie felt like jumping up and down with joy when she turned the two koi loose into the pond, fed them, and turned on the waterfall.

Over the following weeks, each time she returned from one of her "business trips," she was amazed to see the growth of the plants and the little tree.

Lacey, who had volunteered to feed the fish and water the plants during her many absences, said she had never seen that kind of growth in a new garden before.

"I think you have the greenest thumb of anyone I've ever met. Didn't you tell me this was the first time you ever started a garden?"

"Well, I did work in my parents' garden as a kid, but this is the first time I've had a garden of my own," Lizzie admitted.

"Maybe it's beginner's luck, but I have to admit I've been impressed with your attention to detail. I wish the rest of my students were as diligent," Lacey said with a sigh, shaking her head.

That night Lizzie and her three neighbors ate out on what Lizzie would eventually make into a formal patio. Melinda had prepared lasagna with a big salad, and for dessert she proudly carried in a large cake with "Welcome Garden Friends" written in icing on the chocolate buttercream frosting.

Four friends, just enjoying a small celebration together; Lizzie had a hard time believing it. Nothing in her life before Gaston had inveigled her into joining the Alliance would have ever prepared her for this. She found herself wondering how much more her life could possibly change.

Chapter 9: Toeing the Line of Integrity

(*J enny paused. She noticed that Lizzie had spent a great deal of time describing settling into the house, setting up the garden, and getting to know her neighbors. This was a definite shift from the Lizzie who had started her journey as a socially awkward young woman whose entire focus had been learning how everything worked and answering all the questions churning constantly through her mind.*

Being so internally focused was now shifting outward. Jenny herself would never have described herself as a "social butterfly," but she had never lacked for friends and had spent many a happy hour with buddies from her hiking club or hanging out with her peers.

She found herself wondering if the other members of Lizzie's family had noticed the changes and how this would affect the rest of her story. She also wondered how she herself was being changed by her own experience.

She began to see how few people had ever really known Lizzie, including her own family. She had heard Lizzie described as "dotty," "eccentric," and even "odd," which told her that she had never revealed much to those around her.

Bob Reid had probably known her best, and even he had only the smallest inkling that she was so much more than she had appeared to be. She was now glad she had agreed to allow him to read the journals when she was finished. For now, she turned the page and read on.)

Lizzie finished up her morning correspondence with various Earth gate guardian friends, the refugee group, and the Gate Guardian on Fanilia. She would write some letters to family members and call her mom later in the day, but for now she had completed all her communication tasks. It almost felt like checking off her homework assignments in college, back when that was her entire focus.

As she prepared to head out to the backyard to check on how her garden was progressing, the doorbell rang.

Puzzled, she opened the door to find an unknown young man in coveralls and a ball cap.

"Lizzie Japhet?" he inquired with a merry grin. He was a bit short and met Lizzie's eyes cheerfully. "I've got a delivery for you. May I see your driver's license?"

Puzzled, Lizzie answered, "Just a moment," and turned and left him on the doorstep.

She went around the corner into the hallway and extracted her wallet from her MDP. She did have a driver's license but had never owned a car. She had mostly preferred getting around on her bicycle or using the transit system to get around, although now the closest bus stop was miles from her neighborhood, and there was nothing close enough to merit a bike ride.

Lately she had either gotten a ride with a neighbor or called for a taxi to get anywhere beyond the neighborhood. Still wondering why this young man needed to see her license, she headed out to the front door and showed it to him.

"Yep," he said, turning and beckoning to her. Over his shoulder, as she followed him through the little alcove between her neighbor's garage and her own, he said, "Just needed to make sure I delivered this to a licensed driver; company policy."

As they moved under the archway that opened out onto the driveway, Lizzie gasped.

In her driveway was a tow truck, and attached to the hoist was Gaston's car!

"I understand he wanted this to be a surprise. We've been storing it per his instructions... something about giving you a chance to settle in or some such," he said, grinning at her obvious shock.

"For me? I, uh, don't know what to say."

He strode to the truck, opened the driver's door, and removed a clipboard with some papers on it.

"Don't say anything, just sign here to say I delivered it and stand back," he said chuckling. "This is so much more fun than repossessing a vehicle."

She just nodded, signed the document where he indicated, and stepped back. He got in and activated the winch. With a loud whir, the front of the car slowly lowered until the front tires finally touched the ground. The winch continued to lower until the cable was no longer taut and straight.

The fellow hopped out of the truck, disconnected the hook from somewhere from under the bumper, and grinned again. He handed her the registration documents and jingled a set of keys as he handed them to her. "Go ahead," he said as she took them from him, "Start her up and back her out of the way. I'm off to a wreck on the Interstate."

He hopped back up into the cab of the truck as Lizzie, still stunned, got in, put the key in the ignition, and carefully backed the car out onto the street, parking it, for now, in front of her house.

He backed out and waved before he took off on his way out of the loop to disappear down the road.

She sat there behind the wheel of Gaston's treasured Bel Air with no idea what this could possibly mean. She had been sure that Gaston had sold the car before moving to Sanglarka. Obviously, even if he could have shipped the car to that remote location, there was literally nowhere to drive it. The mountain lodge overlooked a beautiful valley with no roads or access to anywhere else. This was why it was such a perfect location for Earth's Alliance headquarters. It wasn't on any maps that she was aware of, and they didn't even have a telephone. They raised all their own food and often received supplies from the various other gate guardians across the planet.

Just as she realized she should probably park the car in the driveway instead of sitting there in a stupor, Melinda Mensch passed her and pulled into her own driveway in her little blue sedan. She beeped her horn as she passed and waved.

Lizzie slowly backed up the car and parked it in front of her garage door. Her property now looked like all the other houses in the neighborhood. Except for those who had only one car and worked during the day, there was a car parked in nearly every driveway up and down the street.

"Isn't that Gaston's car?" Melinda asked as she strode across her own driveway towards Lizzie.

"It was. He doesn't need it where he is now, and I guess he decided that I did. I had no idea he was going to give it to me. I have to admit I've never owned a car before. He always kept it in such good condition. I don't even know where to find a car wash," she concluded, with an embarrassed half smile. "I know he always had his students clean it for him at the university. Maybe I can get some kids in the neighborhood to do it?"

Melinda laughed. "I know a boy down the block who does some others on weekends. I'll give him your name. In the meantime, I guess this means we can take turns driving to the grocery store now, right?"

"Sure, that sounds fine. I'm going to need the practice, I suppose."

Melinda laughed again. "Well, I guess I should get inside. My 'soaps' are starting up, and the doctor is about to propose to that adorable starlet who just had her appendix removed." She waved again and, still chuckling, turned back to her house.

Lizzie walked around the car. Everything, including the chrome bumper, was shined to perfection. It probably wasn't going to get much use, she mused. She only went to the grocery store once a week and almost never went anywhere local, not when she could travel across the multiverse in a single step. But she also realized that this was Gaston's way of giving her more of the appearance of some kind of normality.

Perhaps she would take a spin down the Pacific Coast Highway sometime, or maybe even visit the redwoods up north at some point. But really and truly she was grateful every day that she didn't have to get on the freeway to get to work, like so many of the graduates of her college would be doing right now.

The Bel Air was a beautiful car, much admired by all the male students of the university. But although it was kind of Gaston to give it to her, getting a car hadn't been on her to-do list at all. She realized she would have to look into picking up some car insurance; one more thing to put into her schedule.

She patted the car absently, as if it were some kind of faithful dog, and headed back into the house to get some lunch. Then she paused thoughtfully. Maybe just this once she could splurge and take some time out. Maybe now was as good a time as any to get in some driving practice. After all, she didn't have any scheduled obligations at the moment.

She decided to change into something besides her usual jeans and dress a little nicer, black slacks and a blue conservative blouse and her black low-heeled loafers. Now she looked just like any normal businesswoman having a day off shopping.

She decided to head to a department store a few miles away that also had several restaurants surrounding it, so she would have something to choose from. She wasn't really sure what she would be shopping for, but she kept plenty of cash in her wallet, which reminded her to grab a handbag to put her wallet in, as it would have caused quite a stir for her to pull her wallet out of her MDP.

Ynni watched all of this with rapt attention. *"Lizzie is going someplace?"* she queried, her furry chartreuse head cocked inquisitively to one side. *"Ynni come too?"*

"Of course, Ynni, but you will need to keep your reflection turned off and stay on my shoulder, except in the car. In the car you can sit anywhere you would like except on my shoulder, as I will be driving and will need to concentrate. Okay?"

"Okay." Ynni agreed.

Tidbit looked up from the window seat. *"I guess I'll go out and check out the neighborhood while you're gone."* And he hopped down to follow them out the front door.

As Lizzie watched him saunter down the street past the Mensch's house, she tried not to think about how nervous she would be, getting behind the wheel of the spotless car. She thought maybe her first stop should be the first insurance business she saw along the way. She didn't think she was a bad driver, but she was definitely inexperienced. She had learned to drive in her dad's car back in high school, but she hadn't seen the need of adding a vehicle, gas, and maintenance to her small student budget in college.

Sure enough, as the winding road in the foothills gave way into the suburbs, businesses lined the roadways, and she actually did see a place that advertised car insurance on a wooden sign on the street.

She made quick work of buying the first insurance package that was offered to her. She didn't feel like quibbling about price when her income was more than adequate for her needs. She tucked the documents into the glove box along with the registration she had put in there earlier and headed only a few miles farther down the street to the big department store in the shopping center that served that community.

It was not terribly upscale, nor was it trashy. The selection of goods was probably pretty mundane, as these things went, but it would do for her first venture out. She didn't want to travel any farther from her house than needed, this first trip out.

With Ynni perched lightly on her shoulder, she wandered up and down aisles of displays, Ynni making mental comments as they passed by merchandise, she wasn't familiar with. She didn't really have anything in mind but considered that perhaps she might buy a gift for her dad, whose birthday was coming up. That would give her an excuse to visit her parents.

The thought of driving all the way to San Diego was a bit daunting, however. She preferred going on the train, as she had done while she was in college. They had places at the train station where you could park your car for a day or two for a small charge; or better yet, she could still hire a taxi for those kinds of jaunts.

She wandered into the men's clothing department and decided that maybe a nice cardigan would be just perfect. As she strolled around a display of various folded sweaters, noting that a blue one would match her dad's sparkling periwinkle eyes nicely, she heard a disturbance behind her in one of the open areas of the store.

"Somebody help me!" she heard a woman's pleading panicked voice. "He's too strong for me!"

Lizzie didn't hesitate. She ran to find a woman kneeling on the floor beside a man who was thrashing in her grip.

"Let me go, woman!" he growled trying to wrest his wrists from her grip. "Get off of me!"

The woman, dark-haired and middle-aged, had one knee on his midriff. Her hair was askew, and one long strand had fallen across one of her eyes.

"He says he's going to kill himself! Please help me!"

"Take one step closer lady, and I swear I'll kill you both and then take care of myself. I'm done with all of this. Get her off me!" he growled again, his low voice vibrating with emotion.

Lizzie knelt beside the woman. She felt Ynni jump from her shoulder perch, and she hoped she was staying a safe distance away. She reinforced the woman's desperate grip and looked from one deeply emotional face to the other. What to do? She noticed the commotion had gotten the attention of several people who were converging on the spot. The store hadn't been crowded, it being a workday, so most of the shoppers were women, and they had been somewhat sparse.

"*Sing!*" came Ynni's forceful mental voice. "*Calm them.*"

Lizzie took a deep calming breath, continuing to hold firmly onto the two people, as the man continued to try to writhe himself away. Into her mind came one of her own compositions. She tried to imagine herself with her mbira, sitting peacefully under that lovely tree between the pods at the agent training center, her podmates smiling around her.

The seconds seemed like hours as she focused one hundred percent on just making the music she found in her heart. The mental hum inside her head was so much more than that. She could hear Ynni also mentally crooning in harmony and somehow, she could also hear Gi's harp weaving a melody of peace and hope.

She didn't know this man's story, but he was obviously distraught and disturbed. The woman seemed to be a total stranger to the man, but she couldn't even be sure of that. Instead of wondering, she stepped up the mental volume of her music.

The crowd around her had been murmuring agitatedly and she thought she heard someone tell someone else to call the police, but she ignored it, dwelling only on the music that spoke of things getting better, of better days ahead, of winning the battle that was playing out before her.

Slowly, what seemed like ages, the man's struggles slackened. The woman beside her was panting, but her breathing began to slow. Around her the murmuring of the crowd decreased. She began to feel Ynni's tiny hands patting her back.

"*It's okay, Lizzie. It's okay. You can stop now. The man will be all right, and the woman beside you is wearing out. You need to tell her to stop.*"

Lizzie realized she had closed her eyes to concentrate. She opened them now to see the man lying still, his eyes closed and his breathing slow and rhythmical. The woman still clutched his arms tightly, but Lizzie understood in that moment that if she didn't let go, she would probably collapse onto the man.

"It's okay, ma'am," she said softly to the woman. "You can let go. He's calm now."

The woman looked up, tears streaming down her face. "Do you think so? I'm afraid he might be pretending to get us to leave him alone."

"No, miss," he said in a soft low voice. "Life is bad, but maybe it isn't so bad that I need to leave it. You can let go. I promise not to do anything drastic."

Reluctantly the woman slowly let go of his wrists and sat back on her heels.

"I don't understand," she said. "Why the sudden change?"

"I don't know myself," he replied, shaking his head, grey hair tousled, and his face still flushed from the struggle. "One minute I thought I was losing my mind, and the next it was like it all melted away. Never felt anything like that in my life before.

"One minute I was angry and feeling like the world needed to come to an end, and the next my head was clear and I realized that as bad as things are, I need to keep trying because life can be good. I feel warm all over." He looked up at the faces around him.

"I'm sorry if I upset you folks. Honestly, I'm not usually this way. But I've had one heck of a month, and it was feeling like the whole world was out to get me. Lost my job. Lost my home. My wife left me, and lately I've been feeling really helpless and useless. I'm sorry..." he said again trailing off and shaking his head.

Most of the people in the crowd began to move away as if to ignore what had just happened. But one man held out his hand to help the man up to his feet.

"My name is Gerald, and you are?" he asked looking directly into the other man's eyes.

"I'm Max," he said, not looking away.

"I run a landscaping company, Max. You look like you're strong. Are you willing to get your hands dirty for a hand up? I was about to hire a couple new workers for a new area we're opening up."

"Yes, sir," Max replied in a low trembling voice, fixing his eyes on Gerald's face. "I grew up working in an orchard in Orange County. I can handle anything you need done, I think."

"Well, then, come with me. We'll get some lunch. I imagine you haven't had a square meal in a while." Gerald turned to Lizzie and the other woman.

"It took quite a bit of courage for the two of you to step in like that. I've been in some rough spots myself over the years and it was someone like you two who gave me what I needed at the time. So, thank you."

Max nodded his head, his hands clasped before him. "Yes, thank you both. I hope I didn't hurt either of you, but I have to tell you, you both have quite a grip for a couple of finely dressed ladies. God bless you both."

Gerald nodded again and clapped Max on the back, and then they turned and walked away.

Lizzie looked at the other woman and then extended her hand. As she shook her hand she said, "That was really very brave of you to tackle such a big man all by yourself. What made you do it? I'm Lizzie, by the way...."

"Marge," she acknowledged with a nod. "He was raving and waving his arms around. My self-defense classes kind of kicked in without thinking. All I could think to do was to restrain him, but he's bigger than I am. I was about to give up when you pitched in to help. Thank you.

"I still can't figure out how he just changed in the middle of our impromptu wrestling match. It was like someone hit a switch and he just kind of melted. Funny thing about it was that I also felt calmer and like everything was going to be okay all of a sudden, and for no reason I can figure out."

Lizzie didn't know how to reply. She felt Ynni leap back onto her shoulder and felt her tiny arms around her neck in a reassuring hug.

"Lizzie made deep music. Music is like magic, but not magic. Lizzie's music is different. And Ynni helped," she finished with pride in her soft mental voice.

"Indeed, I might not have done it without you," Lizzie conceded.

Marge stepped into the apparent silence. "Are you from around here?" she asked conversationally.

"Yes, I live in the low foothills." And she pointed vaguely in the direction of the little neighborhood on Infinity Loop. "I'm not around much. My job takes me out of town a lot. I just came here to buy my dad a sweater for his birthday and to get a bite of lunch, then back to work in my garden."

She realized that was probably more information than she needed to have provided, but she was still a bit nervous, and her cover story always seemed to be at the top of her mind, ready to be given at a moment's notice.

This was one of the things the other gate guardians had drilled her on every time she met with them for a couple days training.

"Oh, really? I'll bet the view is nice up there. You have a garden?"

"Oh, not much of one yet. I only moved into my house a few months ago, and the backyard was all just lawn. Right now, the new garden is all just a bunch of seedlings along with some seeds that are only just beginning to sprout. It will take a bit before it looks like anything much."

"Be patient. New growth is worth waiting for. Just do your part to give it a good space to grow in, and you may be surprised what comes of it. Well, we'd better get out of here. I expect the police are on their way, and I'd just as soon not be here to explain when they get here. Hope you find a nice sweater, but maybe you might want to try the men's shop down the street instead?" Marge said this with a mischievous grin, waved, and turned away.

Lizzie agreed that this was a case of not waiting for the axe to fall. She went back out into the parking lot, got into her car, and for several minutes just sat there. Ynni had decided that the passenger seat was her special place in the car and scrambled off her shoulder.

Suddenly Lizzie realized that her hands were trembling as she rested them on the steering wheel. This wasn't quite the outing she had had in mind when she had decided to take the Bel Air for a spin.

She sat there, taking calming breaths and reviewing the incident to try to figure out what had happened and the role she had played with her mental music.

She knew there were those who claimed clairvoyance and mind-reading abilities, most of whom had been discovered to do what they did through clever trickery for the prospect of conning people to give up their well-earned money for something that had no value.

However, was it possible that there might be others around her with talents they didn't know they had? Obviously, the Alliance had figured out how to tap into mental abilities in ways she still didn't quite understand. Would there be a future time when Earthlings would learn to communicate without words in a way that made all communications clear and understandable?

Might this not foster a time of peace on her world?

As her mind raced, she recalled the words of Marge and viewed them in a different context. "Be patient. New growth is worth waiting for. Just do your part to give it a good space to grow in, and you may be surprised what comes of it."

Marge had been referring to her garden, but wasn't it the same with other things that grow? Like her mental gifts, and the talents she was expanding on? Like the people on her world who were still discovering their potential? She had never been a patient person, and this was definitely a different perspective that had never occurred to her.

Another thing came into focus at that moment. What had she done, really? It felt like she had forced her own perspective onto that man and the onlookers of his distress. That was powerful, and yet it felt somewhat uncomfortable to her. She had no desire to have power over another being.

So, what was the difference between power and influence? Perhaps she had only influenced him, reached out to him in a way that triggered something that was already in him, only deep down where he couldn't quite reach it.

She felt okay about influencing another person. After all, everything she was experiencing right now was a direct result of the influence of so many people in her life and the experiences she had been given as a result.

Ynni reached up and put a tiny, soft, invisible hand on Lizzie's shoulder. *"Lizzie would never harm anyone intentionally. Lizzie has a kind heart. Ynni will help you know when a thing is a bad thing. You can be calm now and be happy to help today, yes?"*

"Yes, Ynni. I'm just worried I might eventually use this talent to push someone into something they don't want to do. I strongly believe that the ability to choose your path is an important right of every being. It's one of the things that attracted me to the Alliance in the first place. I believe in that. I know the linklings do as well. I am glad I have you to keep me straight. I can see how it might tempt someone to have the last say about what other people think or do. It may be one of the great evils of the multiverse, I think."

Lizzie could feel Ynni's wholehearted agreement. She turned the key in the ignition with a sigh. *"Let's get some lunch, shall we?"* she sent to Ynni.

Chapter 10: The Other Side of the Coin

(J)enny *was a bit taken aback by this little adventure of Lizzie's, realizing at once how big a step forward Lizzie had taken. It definitely gave her something to think about. And Lizzie's mention of lunch made her notice her grumbling stomach.*

She found herself sniffing the air appreciatively. Obviously, Lizziebot had been busy in the kitchen. Sure enough, there was a nice bowl of soup with some homemade rolls ala Arvid sitting on the dining room table. She felt so terribly spoiled during this time of recuperation.

Of course, had she been living her old life as a professional ghostwriter, she would have never had the adventure that had led to her active participation in a battle for the freedom of an entire planet, and she would never have been given an AI-enabled robot of her very own.

Lizziebot often fussed over her like an old hen over her brood of chicks. It amazed Jenny how human the robot seemed to be. Between the Lizzie AI that Lizzie had made and the way Bob had integrated her into the robot he had created and the constant upgrades he sent to her through the Alliance network, Jenny was constantly astonished at some of the things she could do.

It was Arvid who had suggested they add his recipes to her protocols and the advances that Bob was able to make due to his exposure to Alliance technology were beyond amazing. Lizziebot could use mindspeech, for instance, and she seemed to be developing a personality of her own. Both Bob and Merv insisted she was not sentient, but the longer Jenny spent time with her, the more she began to wonder if something was happening here beyond what they had always considered absolute.

"Robots just run programs," Bob had insisted vehemently every time Jenny brought it up.

Nevertheless, Jenny treated Lizziebot like any other person she spent time with. She said please and thank you and sometimes fretted about using such amazing technology and what felt like a friend to her as a household servant.

She dismissed the temptation to continue to read the journal while she ate by telling herself she didn't want to accidentally spill soup on the precious pages. Lizziebot had also put out a plate of fruit and a tiny cup of water for Chidwi.

She had also put down some of Tidbit's special "cat food" and some fresh water for the cat who was not a cat.

They ate together, not speaking in mindspeech, but Jenny knew that Chidwi read her thoughts and could feel everything she was feeling, so it wasn't like Jenny was ignoring her little friend.

She had noticed that Tidbit had been especially quiet since their morning workout.

"What's up Tidbit?" she asked him teasingly. "Cat got your tongue?"

He purred loudly, just the very tip of his tail twitching, a sign of either amusement or irritation, depending on the situation. "I was just realizing that you only have five days left of your limited duty, and I have been trying to give you space to finish the journals.

"Remember. I lived them with her. I know what you have ahead of you and I believe what you are learning may be crucial to our success moving forward in the upcoming conflict.

"There are some points you will need to pay particular attention to. Chidwi and I can entertain one another, and I have some mental work to do as well. I may go out early tonight. I need to visit Sanglarka and headquarters before I go home to Amenia.

"Elizabeth is about to go on her first agent intern assignment soon, and I want to chat with her before she takes off."

Jenny was excited for Elizabeth. They had become close friends, and she was happy that Elizabeth would soon be an official agent of the Alliance.

"Sure, no problem. So, I guess I should get back to it. I think the koi are probably missing you. You haven't teased them for several days."

He emanated a mental chuckle, which made her smile. She thanked Lizziebot as she came to clear the table. She let Tidbit and Chidwi out into the luscious garden that had come from Lizzie's patient cultivation and went back in to sit comfortably in her cushy chair.

She opened the big journal and turned the page.)

Lizzie spent the next few weeks in what now became a routine, but she surprisingly wasn't even slightly bored.

Her morning workouts with Tarafau, both mental and physical, were becoming more and more rewarding as she continued to explore her newfound mental ability, increase her physical stamina, and improve her defense skills.

They had now resumed sparring, and Tarafau didn't spare her bruises and sore muscles. He never scored on her hard enough to cause any permanent or disabling damage, as he had incredible control of his quarterstaff blows, but he said she should consider the bruises an incentive to step up her game.

Her garden was beginning to look a lot less like a lot of nearly empty dirt and more like the beginning of something promising.

She had visited her parents and siblings a few times recently and usually spent her time there showing off photos she had taken of her garden and discussing tips and suggestions from her parents.

She was becoming fast friends with her neighbors and was beginning to see that maybe that particular part of her assignment wasn't quite so onerous as she had first believed it would be. She couldn't exactly describe herself as a friendly person yet, but she was beginning to see the value of creating relationships and a support network.

It had all started, of course, with her time in agent training, when she had bonded with her podmates in a way she had never done before in all her time on Earth. Now she found herself actually looking forward to her unplanned luncheons or working in the garden with her neighbors. And not just in her garden, but also helping them out with their own various gardening tasks. It was as if she had her own little gardening club that met on a regular basis.

On top of all that, she was interacting frequently with the Fanilians and the Grildites.

The Grildite council members in charge of organizing their future migration had included Lizzie in all of their work, meeting about twice per Earth week, although their own week-like structure didn't correspond exactly to the seven-day weeks as Lizzie experienced them.

The woman Peniel, who Lizzie would have called a chairperson, kept her up to date with everything as they planned, organized, and carefully orchestrated the colonization of their future home world. Lizzie became rather fond of her, as she was both humble and businesslike.

Two worlds were currently being explored that they would get to choose from. The Alliance had included two Grildite teams in the exploratory crews. These reported back on a regular basis, and Lizzie had been invited to participate as they began creating their new settlement.

At the moment, however she was on her knees, feeding the koi. They looked fat and happy and seemed to have grown at least an inch since being placed in their little pond. The fellow in the fish shop had told her this would happen. The pond held over 300 gallons of water, which would give them adequate room not only to grow but also to mate and produce offspring.

Fish tended to grow according to the space available to them. Since there were no predators and since Lizzie had also provided them with appropriate water plants to encourage spawning, she was told she would always have a nice little koi colony to provide her plants with the nutrients and fertilizer they needed for the best potential harvest.

She heard the doorbell and jumped up to find Lacey, her arms full of packages. "These were on your doorstep, and I thought you might want to bring them in. What have you ordered?"

"Nothing," Lizzie replied, relieving her friend of some of the packages in her arms. "I can't even begin to think what's in here."

The return addresses on the packages turned out each to be from various family members. She and Lacey laid the packages out on the dining room table. Lizzie could hear Ynni's excited mental hoots as she opened the first package, still puzzled as to why they were all here.

Just under the brown wrapping paper around the box that was wrapped with brightly colored wrapping paper was a card with her first name written on it in her mother's curlicued writing. She opened it to find a birthday card with a picture on the front ablaze with lit candles. "To my Lizzie on her birthday. I hope the coming year brings you everything you could wish for yourself. We are all so proud of you. Love, Mom and Dad"

Lizzie put her hand over her open mouth. "I forgot! I totally lost track of the time!" she exclaimed to Lacey as Lacey said at the same time, "It's your birthday?"

Her mom, her dad, and both of her brothers had each sent her a gift. There was even one that had come clear from Sweden from Gaston and the bunch at Sanglarka.

"We need to throw a birthday party!" Lacey exclaimed. "Wish I had known before now. I'll go talk to Elias and Melinda! I'll leave you to your gifts and I'll see you at suppertime. Don't plan anything or do anything. We'll bring the food and the party to you."

And with that she rushed back out the front door so quickly that Lizzie had no opportunity to say a thing to her. It appeared that, like it or not, she was about to have a birthday party. This hadn't happened in a long time. She'd never told anyone at school about her birthday and hadn't had a real birthday party since she left home.

She hadn't given anything so trivial as a birthday any thought at all during her agent training or her internships, due to the wild differentiation between relative time on the various planets. Now she wasn't at all sure how she felt about it, but she decided that her friends would be disappointed if they didn't get the opportunity to celebrate with her.

So, she tidied up the kitchen, clearing breakfast dishes off the sink, and tidied up the rest of the house, even taking a little pleasure from using the new vacuum cleaner she had bought from the nice door-to-door salesman the previous week.

Slowly but surely, she was beginning to feel like the little house on Infinity Loop was really her own. Her mom's gift contained a newly hand-crocheted afghan in earth tones that went well with her new living room furniture and the dark red tiled floor and coordinated beautifully with the patterned area rug that covered most of the center of the room. She immediately replaced the old afghan she had draped there when she first set up housekeeping, the one she had been given when she had left home to go to college.

Her brother had painted a waterscape that she now hung on the wall between the gate office door and the hallway. It depicted a beautiful sunset from the boardwalk of the Santa Monica pier, reminding Lizzie so clearly about the day she and Thumble had sat on the beach together as she sorted out her feelings about life and dealt with the issues that had since been resolved by her training and experiences with the Alliance.

Her dad had sent her a repair kit for her car trunk, as Lizzie had told him all about the Bel Air she had inherited from Gaston.

She had to laugh when she opened the package from her older brother. It was a complete set of garden tools with pink handles and a matching utility belt. He knew she detested the color pink as "too girly," but she would happily use it to remember him. He'd always been the goofball of the family.

Finally, she unwrapped Gaston's gift. In it were several things: From Arvid, some of his amazing fudge. From Livia, an apron, like the one she wore when puttering around in the Sanglarka kitchen. It wasn't frilly as was the current style in America, but was simple, made from a light denim. And from Gaston, a set of bookends that portrayed two black cats, each holding up some slanting books with their paws.

When Lizzie showed these to Tidbit, he sent a mental chuckle, his tail twitching in catlike delight.

Lizzie immediately installed the bookends on her bookshelf near her chair by the fireplace, stepping back to admire the effect.

Also included was a group photo in a frame with signatures of all the Sanglarka training team below each of them. Lizzie knew exactly what to do with it. She put it on her bedside table so she could wake up to all of those smiling faces every morning.

She knew this was probably instigated by Gaston, as he would have been the only one to know her birth date.

Although she had given little thought to her own birthday, she had finally put the Earth calendar on her tablet, to remind her about things like Christmas and Thanksgiving and her parents and siblings' birthdays, as well as those of her nieces and nephews, with alarms to remind her ahead of time. Otherwise, unless her neighbors said something, most of what was going on in her own world kind of slipped by her.

Now that she had her house in suitable shape for company, her gifts put away or properly displayed, she went back into the backyard. Ynni was squatting beside the koi pond. The fish fascinated her. Lizzie had discovered to her surprise that Ynni didn't swim. She didn't mind getting into water up to her little chest, but that was her limit.

That being said, water and its inhabitants fascinated her. She had loved it when Lizzie had taken her to the Apex for the first time and she had been able to observe the bud-crawlers in their open tanks. She had been full of questions to Tarafau as to how the lobster-like amphibious beings breathed underwater as well as on land.

She had been trying to communicate with the koi, Lizzie knew, and was puzzled that she hadn't gotten a response. Either the fish didn't appreciate Ynni's attempts at communication, or their brains were wired differently, and their mental language might have been alien to land-dwellers.

Regardless, Ynni continued to try, and Lizzie found herself impressed at the little linkling's persistence in the face of failure after failure. She noticed that Ynni didn't get frustrated. She simply kept trying.

"We're going to have a party tonight," she told her little friend. *"Elias, Melinda, and Lacey are all coming over to celebrate my birthday."*

"Birthday? What is this?" Ynni sent with a puzzled tone.

"Every year we celebrate the year we were born with family and friends," Lizzie explained, amused that Ynni hadn't heard of anything like this before. *"We receive gifts congratulating us on another year on the Earth. There is usually cake, and we eat and laugh and enjoy one another's company."*

"This sounds like a good thing, but Earth must be a difficult place if you must celebrate still living another year."

Lizzie couldn't help herself. She started to laugh. She had never quite thought about it that way before. One of the things she knew about linklings was that they had comparatively long lifespans. Diseases were rare with them, and they had no natural enemies that Ynni had ever told her about. They also had a very different view of the death of the body.

Linklings maintained that death was just a transition from one dimension to a different one with different rules, that strong relationships were permanent and continued beyond what Earthlings and others viewed as death.

Ynni started to croon to the fish, and Lizzie noticed that the fish actually became more active, making the water swirl above them. Tidbit sat by Ynni, watching with the catlike intensity that no human could imitate. Almost unconsciously, Lizzie joined in with Ynni, not vocalizing but creating one of her mental spontaneous compositions.

In her mind the music followed the swirl of the water, the patterns of the undulating fish, weaving-in the wonder she felt from Ynni and the deep interest emanating from Tidbit. She wasn't sure what she expected from their little concert, but she was a bit disconcerted when one of the fish leapt from the water with a splash.

Ynni stepped back and clapped her little hands with an excited chirrup, looking up at Lizzie.

"What was that?" Lizzie asked of the two onlookers.

"I think you may have made contact," Tidbit replied wryly. *"Either they didn't enjoy it much, or you may have overstimulated them. I don't know that leaping out of the water is normal behavior for this particular fish."*

Lizzie considered it. *"I don't suppose I'll try that again. I don't want to upset them. If they feel threatened, they'll never mate, and I'd really like to have a school of them, if I can."*

That evening, as she chatted with her friends over cake and ice cream in her dining room, she frequently lost track of the conversation, drifting into a whole maze of what-ifs and how-comes. Several times she had to ask someone to repeat themselves when it was obvious they had asked her a question.

"I just wondered what's got you so thoughtful this evening. Surely it isn't because you are getting old and distracted." Lacey laughed at her own joke.

"No, sorry, it's just that I realize I've learned a lot since graduating from college, and I guess I'm kind of wondering what comes next."

"Well, it isn't like you don't have a great job with a future," Elias put in with a grin. "Working for an international science research firm is a career almost guaranteed to give you plenty of opportunities for advancements in your field."

"True," Lizzie had to agree, although she didn't think *advancement* was exactly the right word. There were no ranks among the gate guardians. However, there were definitely opportunities to learn and new experiences to be had.

"I guess I'm just beginning to realize that I'm fully my own person. Not a kid anymore, and my future is entirely up to me. I haven't paid much attention to birthdays the last few years; and all of a sudden, I wonder how my parents must feel after watching me grow up. It's all kind of... well... big, if you know what I mean."

Her friends laughed genially. "We're none of us quite so old or experienced as to begin to imagine what's really ahead," Melinda put in, her eyes crinkling in the remains of the laughter. "Elias and I have only been married a couple years now, I'm still new to the librarian job, and I'm still deciding what to do with myself. You've really got a head start on all of us, I think." And the others around the table nodded in agreement.

"Look, Lizzie," Elias jumped in more seriously than the other two. "Hopefully, all of us have a lot of years ahead of us. The way I look at it, we need to just make the best of it. Melinda's right. You've got a big head-start on the rest of us, but you can still blow it if you don't pay attention to what you need to do right now—today—to ensure that your future is as good as you can make it. You get to choose, after all."

"Don't get so serious on us," chided Melinda with a fond look at her husband. "This is a celebration, isn't it? Anyone want more cake?"

That night after her guests had helped her clean up and had gone home, Lizzie sat pondering Elias's words. He was right. She needed to change her attitude. So far, most of the things that had happened to her since accepting her contract with the Alliance had just happened.

She hadn't planned any of it. True, she had thrown herself into the task wholeheartedly, but at this point she realized she had just been reacting to events as best she could. That wasn't necessarily bad, but she knew she should expect more of herself. If celebrating a birthday meant anything, it should potentially mean reviewing your life and making necessary changes, so by the next birthday, the part of the world she was responsible for would be better than it was today.

And with that she felt something shift inside her. It was time to take her future into her own hands instead of just letting it happen to her.

Chapter 11: If Not Now, When?

(Jenny noticed the next entry actually skipped quite a lot of time. Evidently Lizzie had been so engrossed in moving forward with her intentions that she had not spared a lot of time writing. Jenny could see how that might happen. She herself had pretty much neglected her journaling over the past several months.

But now, realizing the value of what she was learning from her aunt's memories, she decided to try to be more diligent in that regard. It was obvious to Jenny that even though you might not think what you do from day to day is important, people in later times might find it interesting. Technology and ways of doing things did seem to change a lot from one generation to the next.

She couldn't blame Lizzie for skipping over what for her might have seemed inconsequential, but she had enjoyed her aunt's reminiscences about things like getting a clothes dryer to replace the clotheslines or the differences between what for her had been high tech and the tech she was exposed to in the Alliance.

Jenny noticed that after a while, Lizzie had begun to take that technology for granted as it became commonplace in her life.

With a sigh for the missing years in the journal, Jenny resumed reading. It wasn't clear how much time had passed.)

Lizzie looked out onto the vast valley. It was shallow, with low foothills surrounding it and two intersecting lazy, undulating rivers cutting it almost perfectly down the middle. It was very early in the morning, based on the low-hanging sun. The sky, broken only by a few fluffy clouds, was more teal than blue, but that might have had something to do with the dark teal foliage of the plants and trees along the bands of the twin streams.

"I think this is a winner," Lizzie sent to the leader of the scouting party. He grinned in response, gesturing expansively with both arms as if to encompass the entire valley into a welcoming embrace.

"We think it will be the perfect place to put the settlement," he agreed. *"We've done a survey, and the lands beyond these foothills are also fertile and will do well for farming. We have considered doing some terrace farming in the low hills as well. Our scientists tell us that much of the native plant life is edible for our species and that the few seeds we were able to preserve from our home world may even thrive here."*

This was just a final survey before the Grildite colonists started arriving in a few weeks. They had determined that so far there were no large predators on this continent, which boded well for a new colony.

The gateway, at the top of the ridge they were standing on, although it was not yet contained into a gateroom, had been connected long ago. A team of gateway technicians would eventually establish a gateroom and gate office here, along with an official gate guardian who had been undergoing the training since they had discovered this particular dimension amongst the rare uninhabited planets available for colonization.

They had discovered only a few indigenous species of animals, small and mostly plant eaters. Lizzie was so grateful they were finally going to be able to give the Grild refugees a place to live and reunite after this time of separation. Undoubtedly, each of the groups which had been taken in on four very different planets had developed some new habits and traditions, even though their leaders had stayed in touch thanks to the technology afforded to them by the Alliance.

Events like this were actually uncommon. The Alliance members were not required to respond to a disaster like Grild. Generally, they extended aid to things that were much more localized and contained. Relocating the inhabitants of an entire planet, even as few as the thousands who had survived the destruction of Grild, was not only challenging but time- and resource-consuming.

Lizzie had been given special permission by the Alliance council to continue to serve as liaison between the Grildites and the Alliance until they were completely settled in their new home. This was a benefit both to the Grildites and to Lizzie. The Grildites got to deal with someone they were familiar with, and Lizzie got to do some healing of her own trauma caused by the destruction of the Grildite planet and so many of the friends she had made there.

Lizzie had never told anyone in the Alliance about her marriage to Reloi, however, or of the additional trauma she had experienced from the loss of someone she loved so completely. She realized that some of those who were close to her would wonder why she never could get romantically involved or consider marriage, but they would just have to wonder.

This very private and precious thing she would keep to herself like a treasure in the vault of her heart. Only Reloi's family was aware of her marriage, and she was happy to keep it that way.

As they viewed the lush valley before heading down to do the physical survey, plotting out the design of the city as they had laid it out in their councils, Lizzie felt her heart surge with gratitude that Reloi's people would be able to finally settle into a place that was apparently safe to start again.

She knew they had learned a lot from their previous experiences. She doubted any beings in the multiverse would be more careful and protective of their home environment as these people who had seen so much trial and difficulty due to the choices they had previously made and the consequences of a natural disaster not of their making.

They hiked down the hill into the valley, quietly chatting in mindspeech as they noticed different features of the land around them. At one side of the path a little waterfall spilled into a small stream leading down into the valley, where it merged with the nearest meandering river.

It appeared that fresh water would not be an issue. The plan the council had put together for the colony placed farms and orchards in the V-shape defined by the intersecting rivers. Previous explorations of the area had shown that there were several local underground springs as well.

One of the things the scientists planned on this expedition was to test the fruits of various trees and bushes in the surrounding countryside to see which ones were edible, as well as to note those that might be toxic to the Grildites.

Scouts had also been sent out to check for any wildlife in the area. So far, they had only noted small grey rodent-like creatures resembling squirrels, and some small hooved animals that were a lot like sheep, although the long straight hair that grew down their neck and sides was almost a light shade of lavender.

The architects and builders who had accompanied them on this trip were pointing and gesturing in an animated mental conversation, consulting their tablets as they conversed. It was good to see their enthusiasm.

By the time they reached the river in the valley it was well past time to eat, so Lizzie broke out their camping gear from her MDP. The Grildites were already familiar with this technology, so the Alliance had agreed to allow Lizzie to supply transport for all their necessary equipment and temporary shelter as well as food for this expedition.

It was a cheery group who set up their basic encampment, some working on erecting the tents and some preparing food for their first-ever meal on the planet which would soon become the home for all the refugees.

"I hear we won't be waiting for any of the permanent structures to be set up before we bring all of our people here. They all agree that, due to the long growing seasons in this climate, the sooner they start getting things planted and begin to work on the permanent structures the better. Every soul, down to the youngest capable children, will be involved in building this community," one of the architects confided to Lizzie.

"We will begin transporting the first groups to the planet in about a week. I look forward to digging in with this team and getting things ready for them. Will you be here to greet them when they start coming through the gateway?"

"I plan on it," Lizzie assured him with a smile. *"I've been looking forward to this for a long time. It's true, it could have taken a lot longer for the Alliance to find a suitable planet for you, but I'm glad it didn't. We will celebrate the day you come to your new home together."*

One of the workers who were setting up tents cried out in surprise. They all rushed to see what was happening and had to laugh when they discovered that the worker had uncovered a den of the little squirrel-like creatures, a mother and her babies. The little creatures didn't act as if they were frightened, just surprised, blinking up at the light and the curious faces looking down at them.

"The animals will need names," the worker remarked thoughtfully. *"Perhaps we will let the children come up with names for the creatures we discover as we go?"*

"A great idea!" enthused one of the educators that had accompanied the group. *"I shall take some pictures of them and send them to the council. It will give the children something to think about and anticipate between now and when we get here. We'll vote on the best ones and announce the winners as a part of our homecoming celebrations."*

They all nodded in agreement, and the worker who had been setting up the tent decided to move it to a new location so as not to further disturb the little creatures. Lizzie thought that perhaps if they started out from the beginning with this kind of treatment to the local fauna, they might have a more congenial relationship to the wild animals on their planet than many, including Earthlings, had experienced.

All in all, the work wasn't difficult, and it was pleasant working with people who were so focused on the positive aspects of their new home. Lizzie had been a little apprehensive, considering what they'd been through, that a lot of the negative side of that experience would bleed through to their attitudes of everything they now had to do to once again establish a home of their own.

They settled Lizzie in what they called the "headquarters tent." During the day, she met with various team members in the tent and also made the trip up the hill to the gateway to greet more workers as they began to come through to supplement the work parties.

Every day, groups erected more tents of various sizes for specific purposes. Also, there were already areas where stakes were inserted in the ground and then strung to outline the placement of the first buildings, where most of the community structures would be established. The large mess tent was nearly always occupied with groups coming off various details, grabbing a quick bite before heading off again to get back to work.

At the beginning of every day, they would gather in an area that had been roped off for that purpose. There, they would thank the Creator of all things for this new home and then receive their assignments for the day. At the end of each day, they would gather again to give thanks for another day of productive work and to sing and even dance, as tired as they must have been, to celebrate being alive and engaged in such an important endeavor.

So far there had been no serious injuries, just the usual things you might expect, someone tripping over a root they hadn't seen or hitting a thumb with a hammer, so the medics had little to do at the moment. They took turns going with Lizzie to greet newcomers and helping them settle in, usually putting them to work within a few hours after their arrival.

Now, when they trekked down from the top of the hill, the area was beginning to look more like a small town made of tents.

They had created paths and the beginnings of dirt roads based on the diagram they had from the council as to where the town square would be and how the buildings would be situated.

Before she left Earth, Lizzie had informed her neighbors back on Earth she would be on a long-term assignment and had taken a taxi to the airport, where she had boarded a plane for the closest gateway in Canada. In this way her neighbors would simply assume she was on another of her assignments for the mysterious research firm that was her cover story.

From there, she, Ynni, and Tidbit had gone through the gate to Alliance headquarters where Lizzie's MDP had been loaded up with equipment that would be needed for the project.

Lacey and Melinda had volunteered to care for her fish and her garden during her absence, and she had sent mail out to all her family to let them know she would be traveling for the next several weeks.

This meant that she was free to continue her work here until all the Grildites were established in their new home. Every few days, as needed, she visited Alliance headquarters to acquire whatever additional supplies or equipment was needed.

The Alliance had pretty much given the Grildites a blank check where their needs were concerned. Lizzie was gratified by their generosity. Even though the Alliance hadn't had anything to do with the Grid disaster, beings from all over the Alliance were contributing. It was this kind of behavior that reassured Lizzie she had made a good decision when she had chosen to become an Alliance agent.

On one such resupply trip, she had been greeted at the gate by Liliath.

"Welcome, Lizzie. How is the project coming along? I wanted to tell you that many of your podmates have been following your venture and are appreciative that you are taking the time to stay in touch. The council has been very impressed with your diligence."

Lizzie wasn't quite sure how to respond to that. She had been so engaged with her project that she hadn't thought much about what others might think about what she was doing.

As they walked down the hill to where the Alliance guards stood by the usual hovercar, chatting about the project, Lizzie realized it was unlikely Liliath would ride one of the little hovercars to the headquarters building, and she was right.

To her delight, as they got to the bottom of the hill before Lizzie got into the hover car waiting there, Liliath strode several paces away and launched herself into the air, her blue-green wings stretched full out and her scales sparkling in the bright sunlight. Lizzie knew that Liliath would probably beat her there, but this was quite a treat, even though her hair had been nearly blown off her head by the wind generated by those huge wings, and Ynni held tight to her neck, chirruping in delight.

Generally, she made the trip back and forth from the settlement to Alliance headquarters alone—well, not entirely alone. During this project Ynni went with her everywhere with her reflection turned on. Tarafau usually stayed behind in the camp to lend his great muscles to the work.

Ynni became a favorite of all the workers, from the architects to the road builders. Those working tirelessly in the mess hall made a point to always have some kind of treat for Ynni, whom they affectionately called "the little one."

It was Ynni who finally made friends with one of the little sheep-like creatures. It had started following Ynni and Lizzie around the encampment, making satisfied noises that sounded very much like the purring of a large jungle cat. Ynni informed her that this was Jupal, and that Jupal would be telling her herd mates about these new creatures and what they were doing.

Evidently, although Lizzie had not made a mental connection with Jupal yet, Ynni had no such problem.

Jupal informed Ynni that there were fish and other aquatic animals in the river and told Ynni about the various food-bearing plants in the area. Lizzie was grateful for this adorable native guide and gladly reported this information to those who were still scouting the area.

The builders had located a very rocky place on the other side of the foothills where they could quarry stones. They had been careful to scout first, in an attempt not to disturb any native animals, but so far the rocky site only seemed to have some little lizard-type creatures and some seemingly innocuous insects.

Lizzie was sure that at some point they would run into something that was carnivorous; but so far, according to Jupal, at least in this area, the creatures were herbivores.

Among the first structures that had gone up were bridges that spanned the river closest to the city in two places, to give the farmers and herders access to the great stretch of land beyond where the city was being laid out. It wasn't uncommon near the end of the day or when workers were on a break to see one or more of them standing near the railing of the bridge, looking out over the landscape.

Lizzie could see where this would be comforting to a people who had been stretched so far beyond their comfort zone. They were beginning to think of this as home; and as they stared out from those bridges, she could almost see their minds envisioning the potential for a future here for them and their families.

Lizzie wondered how long it would take for them to start exploring beyond the fertile valley they would soon be calling home. The valley itself would be almost roomy, considering the numbers that had been rescued from the Grid disaster, but even if they didn't multiply quickly, in a few generations they would definitely fill it at some point.

She knew the council was very busy with their current plans, but if she had learned anything about the Grildites, it was that they were accustomed to thinking long term, a habit they had gotten into during their last exile into the core of their planet where resources had been very limited and serious measures had to be taken to preserve them for future generations.

By the end of the first week, weeks on this planet being about nine Earth days long, they had assembled a credible tent city, the tents arranged on an orderly grid of roads which they would soon undertake to pack down in preparation for the rainy season which, by their calculations, was for now several weeks away.

The accommodations would be a bit crowded at first, but as more workers came through the gate and the first refugees began to trickle in, they simply erected more tents. Before long they would have a veritable tent city, bustling with preparations, as they built more permanent structures.

The Alliance had arranged for several agents to continue bringing in supplies via MDPs over the coming months to be sure they had plenty to make do with until their first crops came in.

The farmers and their families came through the gate before the crafters and merchants, so they could begin immediately to prepare the land for planting in readiness for the coming rains. It would be some time before they could establish their habitual aquaponics systems in the basements of homes that hadn't been built yet.

However, Lizzie knew that the council had already planned to build with that in mind. The farms would have to be running at full capacity, as it would be as much as a couple of years before all the refugees each had their own home, so for now they would have to manage with the tent city.

The first community building would be large, designed for gatherings of various types and also for emergency shelter during difficult weather conditions. This area of the planet was, although not quite tropical, definitely temperate. As far as they could tell, there would probably not be many days in the year when the temperature would drop below what someone would call cool.

Probably the best part of her job during all this activity was greeting the new members of the community coming through the gates. She would check them in and introduce them to their guide, who would take them to their assigned tent.

Each new family who arrived on the planet set up a tent for the next family who would come through. This meant that newcomers immediately had lodgings and responsibilities and they felt useful and engaged in the community right from the start. Lizzie was impressed by the council's foresight in organizing it this way. The looks of delight as each family took in their first view of the valley were something that would stay with Lizzie forever. They had been through so much, and now they were home.

She was aware that each one saw their own personal vision of what their new home would look like in the future, and she hoped with all her heart that it would become exactly what they hoped for.

"I know there is a lot of hard work ahead of me," one of them sent to Lizzie after breathing a sigh of satisfaction when they had finally wrested their eyes away from what for them was such a glorious sight. *"But we know we can do it. We're going to finally all be together again, so it will be worth every hour of labor. I hear the soil in the valley is rich, and we can hardly wait to begin plowing and sowing for our first crop."*

Lizzie willingly spent every waking moment at her task; and when the last family came through the gateway, the last seat on the council at their head, she gazed once again with them out on the transformation before her.

It was truly a small tent city now. She could see where the foundation for the main building of the city was beginning to peek out from the basement construction. They had discovered on the other side of the river a huge stand of what looked a lot like massive bamboo plants, and they had decided on this as a primary building material. The woody stalks were as strong as most hardwoods on Earth and were easy to harvest.

Jupal had affirmed via Ynni that these were plentiful and fast growing, often taking over large areas of land whenever they got a root hold. By harvesting these plants for building, they could leave the trees to grow and eventually perhaps set up plantations to grow the bamboo-like plants under controlled conditions.

In the meantime, Jupal had gathered many of her fellows because the Grildites had been kind and had willingly shared some of their food with the little creatures. When the Grildites had inquired through Ynni regarding potentially trimming their soft long flowing hairs to use for spinning and making cloth, the little creatures had agreed that this might be a good exchange for being fed and cared for by the Grildites.

It became clear that this kind of reciprocal relationship would eventually prove very helpful for her friends and would perhaps even improve the lot of the native creatures.

Lizzie found herself humming internally almost constantly during her time with the Grildites. The song in her heart was one of exultation and delight, and she began to notice that even those around her who were tired or feeling the strain of the enormous task before them seemed to relax and become energized after they had spent time with her.

She still had some misgivings about this interesting ability. On the one hand, she felt she could use it as a tool for healing and encouraging. On the other hand, she didn't want to get to the point where she used it unconsciously to try to force someone to her way of thinking. That felt a little too much like compulsion to her.

She knew she had to take conscious control of how she used it, and she was woefully ignorant of how to do that. She decided that when she got back to her duties at the Los Angeles gate, she would consult with Tarafau about it.

Chapter 12: You Do the Hokey Pokey and You Turn Yourself Around

(J)enny was startled when she heard footsteps in the hallway. Once again, she had become so absorbed in Lizzie's time with the Grildites and Lizzie's dilemma that she had totally tuned out her surroundings. It was Bob, Merv, and Burt, all three with silly grins on their faces.

"Hey there! Didn't mean to scare you, kiddo," Bob called out with a chuckle. "That must be some really exciting reading. We stood here for nearly a minute before we decided to troop on in. The look on your face!"

Jenny shook her head with amusement. They looked like a trio of mischievous schoolboys. Even Mervin managed to look like he was up to something sneaky, his hands thrust into his jeans pockets, rocking back and forth, barely constraining a laugh.

"Okay! What's up, you three? You remind me of the cat that ate the canary. Tidbit, Chidwi, why didn't you warn me?" Jenny couldn't restrain an answering grin, as stern as she was trying to sound.

Tidbit simply turned his amber eyes on her and blinked, one ear twitching, the cat's signal that they hear you but are ignoring you. Chidwi patted Jenny's cheek. "Chidwi didn't hear them either. Jenny was thinking very hard about Aunt Lizzie, and Chidwi was not listening for peoples in the house."

There was a touch of embarrassment in Chidwi's sending.

"It's okay, Chidwi," Jenny sent soothingly to her little friend. "I'm guessing they have something important to tell us?"

"Indeed, Jenny dear," Burt said, stooping to kiss her on the forehead. "Why don't you come out on the patio and take a break from Aunt Lizzie's grand adventures?"

Jenny laughed. Burt had never called her "dear" before and it sounded way too formal, considering his usual very casual style of speech. She decided he had definitely been hanging out with Merv and Cornelium too much lately.

They strolled out the French doors onto the patio facing the garden that meant so much more to Jenny now that she understood something of what had gone into creating it. Beneath the yew tree that was now over 50 years old, the koi, several generations beyond the original couple Lizzie had first imported into the pool she had so painstakingly created so many years ago, swam serenely.

Chidwi immediately scrambled up the tree and perched herself above the pond to watch the undulating orange, silver, and gold fish, and Tidbit assumed his favorite place near the strawberry plants at the edge of the pool.

The rest of them settled themselves around the patio table. Burt scooted his chair closer to Jenny's and reached out for her hand. Little things like this were so comforting, especially when they had so little time together in person these days. Jenny was pretty sure it would be a long time before they had any kind of what most people would consider a "normal" married relationship.

However, Jenny wouldn't have had it any other way. Although she looked forward to simple things like getting to hold her husband's hand, she knew that they each had important roles to play in the Alliance's task to free the dimensions from the oppression of the Insenium and, as far as was possible, to prevent it from happening again.

"So, what's so important that all three of you had to see me in person?" she asked, looking around the table after a significant pause from the impudently grinning trio.

"We may have found a substantial flaw in the gate system." Merv replied, still grinning.

"That doesn't sound like something to be grinning about," she began, but Merv continued.

"It turns out that there is another communications network embedded in the gate system that none of the techs knew about. We stumbled upon the encryption somewhat by accident while we were working on the security aspect of the gateways.

"We also discovered some records stored in it, in a completely unknown language that may be the key to this whole mess, at least from our end of it.

We posit that it may be the original blueprints and working notes of the gate technicians who created the network to begin with."

Jenny's mouth dropped open, feeling the hair go up on the back of her neck.

"So, doesn't the Alliance have technology to translate it?" she asked, realizing at once it was a somewhat obvious question.

"Unfortunately, no," put in Bob. "That was one of the first things I considered. Something is itching at the back of my brain that might be a clue, but I haven't made contact yet. That being said, this could be the breakthrough we've been looking for."

"We couldn't wait for the next evening contact with you to tell you about it," Burt said nodding his agreement with Bob's statement. "I know you're really focused on Lizzie's journals, but maybe, at some point, you may stumble on something that will give you a clue that you could pass on? We're all itching to solve this, as you might imagine."

Jenny sat back as Burt put his arm around her and squeezed. She leaned into him, her head spinning. She wondered what Lizzie might have said about all of this. That ever-curious mind of hers would be buzzing right now, she was sure.

"Okay, so I'll keep an eye out for any hints. In the meantime, what's your plan?"

"We've got the entire Alliance science lab working on the documents, and they brought in some linguistic specialists," said Merv "But so far, they're baffled. The linguistic writing system in these documents seems to be a combination of stylized hieroglyphs and something similar to the Asian pictographs of Earth.

"According to the specialists, all we need is what they call a 'key,' a few phrases whose meaning we are sure of, that could unlock the rest of the puzzle. So far, computer analysis has not revealed any obvious patterns."

Jenny considered this news. The guys were right, this had some real potential. It might not get rid of the Inseni threat, but it might prove useful. Knowing more about the gate system and how it worked might mean they could finally secure the system and also discover gateways in dimensions as yet undiscovered by the Alliance.

Burt gave her another squeeze as she tried to absorb all of this. He leaned over and kissed her once more on her forehead. "We can't stay, but we all wanted to be present to give you this news. Only a few more days of your recuperation *time and you'll be back in the thick of it. By all means, continue your time with your aunt. I have a feeling it'll be time well spent."*

They all stood, and Jenny followed them into the dining room. She hugged Bob and Merv and they turned to go to the gate office. Burt, however, grabbed her in a mighty hug and then kissed her in a way that nearly curled her toes.

"See you tonight?" he whispered into her ear... "Our place?"

"Our place," she agreed, looking up into the eyes that were the light of her life. "I'll be there."

She gazed after him longingly as he shut the door to the gate office behind him. "I'll be there," she repeated to the empty room.

"Now, I'd better get back to this," she said aloud to no one in particular. "I've got research to do."

She sat and opened the journal.)

Lizzie knelt, a little basket by her side as she picked the plump deep red strawberries from the plants that edged the koi pond. It seemed almost magical how the little seedling plants had become these lush adults, first flowering with tiny white blossoms and then shedding their petals to reveal the tiny green berries that had been the center of the blooms.

Now she had enough berries to eat, to share, and to freeze for later. She had enough strawberries to make jam but didn't have the first clue how to start. Maybe she would learn how to do that next season. For now, she had already filled her gallon-sized basket and would be happy to take some to the Mensches and Lacey later today when they all got home from work.

The strawberry plants weren't the only things bearing fruit at this point. Little glints of gold swam in the koi pond now alongside their much larger parents. There was now a school of koi. She had already made arrangements with the fish shop to bring her excess koi babies in the future; otherwise, the pond would become overcrowded, which could cause future problems.

She was feeling like so much of her life had become fruitful, just like her berry harvest. Over time, the Grildites had settled into the valley and now had declared a day similar to America's Thanksgiving to celebrate the day when the last refugees had come through the gateway.

Lizzie had enjoyed the full week of celebrations that had followed. There had been a memorial service for all those who had lost their lives in the disaster, and they had asked Lizzie to play for them. She had spun a song both of loss and of impending joy, looking forward to future reunions in other dimensions at another time. Reloi, with his spirit of sacrifice and love for his people, was woven through the entire piece, and as the last note had died away, there were mixed tears of sadness and joy on every face.

Now that she was home again, she had focused mostly on her garden and staying in communication with all of those she had connected with over the past few years, including the other Earth guardians. She was encouraged that she was feeling more and more at home with her friends at Sanglarka.

According to Gaston, he was enjoying his retirement, if you could call it that. They had immediately put him to work as part of the training staff. Evidently there were two new Earth agents preparing to go to the Alliance training center, and Gaston had been helping with their indoctrination regarding Alliance history. His many years as a university professor definitely suited him to the task, and he was never happier than when he was teaching.

"It is a beautiful day," Windsong commented to her as she arose and prepared to take the strawberries inside.

Lizzie turned and smiled up at the little yew tree that was branching out happily. Her deep green foliage seemed to become fuller and more vibrant every day. *"I agree, Windsong. I'll be back out in a few minutes to tend to the rosemary plants. They are getting a little bushy, and I can dry the clippings for rosemary tea. See you in a few minutes."*

Of course, Lizzie didn't really need to explain herself to a tree, of all things, but she had developed a fondness for Windsong's comments and observations as she worked out in her garden. She almost considered her as a fellow gardener. Windsong was often very insightful as to the needs of the plants that surrounded her, and Lizzie enjoyed her positive mindset.

It wasn't unusual for Windsong to request a little concert from time to time, and Ynni was especially fond of the thriving little tree and crooned happily along with Lizzie's tunings on her mbira on those days when there was time to just relax.

Windsong wasn't yet providing much shade, but her branches already extended over part of the koi pond and the koi had a tendency to congregate in that part of the pond on particularly hot days.

Lizzie separated the strawberries into three paper lunch bags and put them in the refrigerator. She puttered around in the kitchen, finding the homey tasks of straightening, organizing, and cleaning somewhat relaxing, something she would never have considered as a teen at home.

When it was time for Lacey and the Mensches to be home from work, she grabbed two bags of strawberries and went out the front door.

Her front yard was relatively plain, compared to what was starting to come together in the backyard, and she still hadn't decided what to do about that. Although Gladys, Gaston's wife, had put up the beautiful wrought iron trellis that led into the front yard, training bright red bougainvillea over the arch, the rest of the yard was just lawn and a few somewhat straggly desert plants around the edge.

She was considering turning the lawn into a rock garden instead to go with the desert theme when she got a chance.

She went first to Melinda's house and knocked on the door. They had a doorbell, but Lizzie knew that the sound of it irritated Elias for some reason, so she usually knocked at the door.

"Lizzie!" Melinda exclaimed as she opened the door. "Come in! Come in!"

"Sorry, no time to chat at the moment," Lizzie explained, holding out the bag of berries. "I need to take these to Lacey and get back to the garden. So much to do before I leave for my next assignment. Feel free to join me in the garden, though. I thought you and Elias would enjoy some fresh berries on your cereal in the morning."

Melinda flashed her a brilliant smile. "We certainly would. However, maybe I'll make some shortcake and we can really get fancy! Thank you. I may stop by later. Enjoy your garden. It's really come a long way since it was all just a bunch of seedlings."

"Thanks to you and Elias and Lacey," Lizzie admitted wryly. "Traveling like I do, I couldn't do it without you all. The strawberries are the least I can do to thank you."

"Not at all, Lizzie. It's good to have neighbors with similar interests, and we do so much better when we help each other than when we try to do everything on our own. Not to mention I'm already working on a strawberry hill for our yard in anticipation of all of your strawberry shoots. I've seen several of them the last few times I was back there."

Lizzie had told her she would share after learning how strawberries reproduce by sending out runners which create entirely new strawberry plants, roots and all, ready to plant. She had been warned by the man from the greenhouse that strawberries could take over a garden patch, if you let them.

Melinda waved as she shut the door, and Lizzie crossed over to her neighbor on the other side of her house.

Lacey's entire front yard was surrounded by an incredible assortment of various types of roses. According to Melinda, Lacey had won awards at the county fair several years in a row and was considered one of the experts in the area. She was even asked often to speak at local gardening clubs about the care and nurturing of roses.

As Lizzie rounded the end of Lacey's garage, Lizzie found her down on her knees in front of one of her prize-winning rose plants, carefully trimming and harvesting blooms in various stages. The wicker basket next to her was full of roses of many colors and types.

"Hey there, Lizzie! I was just thinking of you. I have quite a bunch of roses to share. I'm thinking that vase on the telephone table was looking a little lonely."

The vase she spoke of was one of the few things Gaston had left behind for Lizzie. It had belonged to his wife, and he had been pretty sure he wouldn't need it in Sanglarka. It stood next to the phone on the table by the loveseat and was usually empty as Lizzie generally didn't have the time or inclination to fill it and take care of flowers indoors.

But Lizzie grinned and nodded and held out her bag full of strawberries. "I'll trade you," she chuckled as Lacey opened the bag and inhaled deeply of the sweet aroma of fresh berries.

"Thanks! Just the thing! I was thinking of making some strawberry lemonade. I had some at a roadside stand a few days ago and it was delicious. Now I don't have to go to the store to get some. How is your garden coming along? I was over a couple of weeks ago while you were out on assignment, and I was amazed at some of the growth. You must have a green thumb, for sure."

"I'm pretty sure it's a combination of several green thumbs working together," Lizzie replied, somewhat embarrassed at the praise.

"I'll be on assignment again next week, so I'm trying to get as much work done in the garden as I can before then. I'll only be gone a few days, but I admit I spend a lot of time while I'm gone wishing I could be down on my knees in my garden. I never would've pictured myself doing this a few years ago, to be honest. I never much cared for gardening when I was doing it at my parents' house."

"While I'm gone, you and Melinda should feel free to gather any ripe berries. I understand this particular variety will produce most of the summer."

"Sounds good to me. Yours are so productive. Maybe I'll make a batch of strawberry preserves and share it out between the three of us," Lacey agreed smiling thoughtfully.

Lizzie couldn't help but smile again when she replaced the vase on the telephone table several minutes later, full of a riot of colored blooms in various stages.

For the next few days, she enjoyed puttering in the garden, sharing even more berries with her neighbors, and occasionally serenading the koi and plants with Ynni crooning beside her and Tidbit lazily watching the sparkling fish. She would soon be heading to Sanglarka for several days with the other gate guardians.

This was an annual event, allowing them to more fully connect, and it was a celebration of a sort. Each came prepared to elaborate on their various side occupations at the different gate areas and to discuss world events.

It was the hope of every gate guardian that a time would come when Earth would finally be prepared to become full members in the Dimensional Alliance, but they all knew that many advancements must be made before that time.

It wasn't about technology, not really. It was about the political and intellectual climate of the Earth in general. It was obvious to the guardians, as well as the Alliance itself, that Earth had not yet developed tolerance and acceptance of anything unusual that didn't fit into their own world view, especially where differences in ethnicity and personal beliefs were concerned.

There had been a trend towards speculative fiction that showed humans panicking at the very idea of beings from other planets in the universe. The radio broadcast of H. G. Wells' tale, "War of the Worlds," had caused widespread panic before the advent of World War II. Lizzie could think of few sources she had seen where even fictional aliens were portrayed in anything but a negative connotation.

Thinking back to the podmates who had become dear to her and the Grildites and Fanilians she loved as much as any of her Earth friends and perhaps more than most, she knew somehow that it could be a long time before her home planet would be open to creating relationships with beings from other worlds, much less from other dimensions.

It was with mixed feelings, therefore, that she packed her MDP, said a brief farewell to her garden, and had headed to the airport to grab a plane to the Canadian gate, and then on to Miriha's gate and then to Sanglarka; this was pretty much the only way anyone could get there.

Of course, she could have gone directly to Miriha via her own gateway, but she had learned early on that she couldn't just disappear for days at a time without anyone seeing her actually leave the house. It would have made her that "strange hermit lady" on the block, instead of that important researcher who went on long assignments all over the globe, which was not all that unusual among the many professionals who lived in her neighborhood.

She only made straight gateway trips when she would be gone for a day or less, in which case, she told her neighbors she had reports to write and needed quiet time; something they could understand under the circumstances, or at least considering what they thought they knew about her. This nearly guaranteed that they wouldn't bother her.

When she and Shepherd, the Canada Gate Guardian, finally arrived through the rose-trellis archway that led into Sanglarka, Lizzie sighed in relief. She'd been looking forward to this. Unlike her initial time in Sanglarka that had been specifically for training, these gatherings were usually only partially business.

When the guardians got together, each of them had the opportunity to report on their individual projects, and all of them had connections in other dimensions. They came from such disparate cultures that their reports were more like watching an adventure film.

In the large dining room and the lodge lobby, expansive transparent screens allowed each of them to display charts, graphs, and photos as well as films they had produced with the amazing alien technology provided to them by the Alliance. Lizzie hadn't yet used some of the tech that most of these were familiar with, but she looked forward to learning more about how and when to use it.

Gaston was so pleased to see her, Tarafau, and Ynni. He inquired about the orphanage, and Lizzie was happy to report that they had been able to add a new wing and expand the playground, thanks to the generous yearly endowment that Gaston had arranged for them before he had retired to Sanglarka, plus the additional funds she sent them from her own earnings.

She brought him photos of the children and told him about the new "adopt a grandparent" program they had instituted recently. He was thrilled. His wife, Gladys, had gotten him involved initially with the struggling institution early in their marriage, and he had been involved with more than one generation of children and administrators over the years.

Lizzie visited the children on holidays, as Gaston had done, bringing gifts to all and providing scholarships for ongoing education for those who had lived most of their lives in the orphanage.

The first evening after supper, Lizzie and Yaw entertained the other guardians in the lobby with an impromptu concert. Lizzie let him take the lead and, to her delight, she was able to easily harmonize with his music. Even though his tunings were different than hers, reflecting his African heritage, she could follow via mindspeech and anticipate where the music was going.

Ynni happily crooned her descant, never missing a beat, and Thumble danced enthusiastically. The trio ended to enthusiastic applause from the rest of the guardians.

"You've come so far," Yaw commented after the last note died away. "I think you and I should study this phenomenon together. I'm wondering if this accounts for some of the dancing of my primate friends. I never choreographed their dances, you know. But I've always wondered how they seemed to naturally understand what moves go with what music."

Ernst, the Swiss guardian, was fascinated by Lizzie's description of her garden venture, especially the way she had incorporated the aquaponic aspect in such a natural setting, compared to the very lab-like environment in the Swiss observatory's aquaponics systems.

From the beginning of this visit to Sanglarka, Lizzie realized that these few days would definitely refresh her and prepare her to continue in her duties with more peace of mind and confidence. It was kind of like being back in the agent training center with a lot less pressure.

During the mornings before breakfast, they assembled in the workout room for breathing exercises, followed by working the forms with and without quarterstaff. It was much like participating in a dance without music. However, Lizzie found herself creating music in her head as they moved in concert.

Lizzie was somewhat disappointed not to see Meta there this time. Evidently the two recent Earth trainees had been sent off to the training center, and Meta would once again be an instructor there. She dropped Meta a note via her tablet telling her that she missed her. To her delight she had received a reply within minutes from her former instructor and friend.

"This class of agents is a bit of a challenge, but once again the Earthlings are standing above the rest of the trainees in this new batch. Wish I could be there to see you in person. Let's plan on meeting up once I get these trainees whipped into shape," she wrote back.

It was true that the convenience of the gate system made visiting across the vast expanse of the multiverse easier than going to the grocery store. It was so easy to lose track of this, once you had gotten used to stepping from one dimension to another just by going through what appeared to be a common doorway.

The second morning, Arvid announced that after breakfast they would reconvene in the workout room for a round of sparring matches. Generally, having passed their agent training, few guardians had regular opportunities to spar with others, with the exception of the China Gate Guardian, whose cover story included running a *daochang*, similar to a Japanese *dojo*.

Lizzie was a bit nervous about this, knowing that her skills in the quarterstaff and hand-to-hand martial arts were mediocre compared to some of the more skillful in her pod had been. She also knew that Tarafau, as she had experienced personally, was highly skilled and guessed that many of her fellow guardians were probably much more adept than she was.

Arvid, who had been made the trainer for the physical requirements of the agents who came through here for training, paired them up, explaining that the sparring matches would be by elimination. Once you were tagged by an opponent, you would be seated on the wooden benches that lined the wall of windows that looked over the expanse of the Sanglarka valley and up into the magnificent mountains that surrounded it.

Lizzie was paired with Lela, the Irish Gate Guardian. She was somewhat shorter than Lizzie, but her blue-green eyes twinkled with amused confidence as they faced one another. Lizzie heartily wished she could feel the same but kept her face composed as she had been taught, trying not to give her opponent a clue of the way her heart was racing.

On Arvid's signal, the air was suddenly filled with the rhythmic clacking of quarterstaffs and the grunts and sometimes heavy breathing of those around her. Lizzie only heard it as background noise, however. She had been trained to ignore anything but the person facing her, looking for any clue that would give her an advantage.

Lela looked directly into Lizzie's eyes, focusing on anything that might telegraph Lizzie's next moves. Suddenly she pivoted rapidly, her quarterstaff sweeping low, intending to strike Lizzie's shins. Lizzie surprised herself by easily jumping the swinging staff and pivoted, bringing her own staff around towards Lela's midriff. Lela caught her blow deftly on her staff, their staves making contact with a loud crack. Without pausing, Lela whirled her staff from the side like a baton, meeting Lizzie's own staff with another loud crack!

They fell into a rhythm, striking and parrying, and striking and parrying again. It turned out they were closely matched; and by the time Lizzie landed a swirling blow to Lela's backside during one of her quick pivots, they were both panting.

"Ya got me!" Lela exclaimed, shaking her head with an unabashed grin. *"I concede the match! You move on!"*

They both stepped aside, watching the others until Ernst tagged Shepherd. *"Looks like it's you and me,"* Ernst sent to Lizzie with a wicked smile.

Lizzie only nodded and took her place while Lela and Shepherd sat down on the sidelines to cheer the others on.

Once again, Lizzie put on what she mentally called her "Cubes" face and prepared to spar. She was privately amazed she had made it through the first round of the match.

Lizzie found herself whirling and exchanging blows in this very challenging new dance. Unlike the forms, sparring was intense and required complete focus on every step, and the reactions had to be varied according to the style and skill of your opponent. Ernst was very good, due to his long experience, and she was strained to the absolute max of her own skill.

She was unsurprised, therefore, when he finally tapped her smartly on her elbow, her not-so-funny "funny bone." They bowed to one another, Lizzie trying hard not to rub her elbow. She didn't want to give him the satisfaction, but from his triumphant smile, she knew that she wasn't fooling him.

The following matches quickly whittled the combatants down to Wang Xiu against Arvid and Idoya against Tarafau.

These two one-on-one matches lasted much longer than the rest. If Lizzie had thought her earlier matches a dance, she was now in awe of the rapid exchanges and skillful ducks, leaps, and pivoting evasions she saw before her now. It soon became apparent that these were the masters from among the Earth guardians. However, the two aliens, as they faced their opponents, were obviously the more skillful.

Wang Xiu appeared to be flagging, and it became obvious that Idoya was also beginning to run out of steam. The two of them were defeated almost simultaneously and, as they bowed and backed away to be seated amongst the onlookers, it was as if everyone was holding their breath.

It seemed obvious to Lizzie that, although Arvid was clearly skilled, he now faced an opponent nearly three feet taller and more muscular than he appeared to be. Lizzie was sure of the outcome: there was no way Arvid could conquer an opponent so much larger and stronger than he was.

They bowed solemnly to one another. *"You and me, old cat,"* Arvid sent with a grin so that all could hear.

"Tiny little dwarf man, do your best. No one will fault you when you are defeated." Tarafau replied, baring his fangs in a wide smile. To Lizzie it almost felt like Tarafau was patting the dwarf on the head condescendingly.

Arvid nodded, his grin not fading a whit. *"Begin!"* he sent and swung his quarterstaff at Tarafau's shins and then, with a reversal so fast it was a blur, brought the staff around vertically directly at Tarafau's head. Tarafau reacted without hesitation, first jumping the low sweep of the staff and immediately blocking Arvid's attempt at his head with a loud clack!

Clack! Clack! Clack! The staves struck one another again and again in rapid succession. Lizzie had never seen anything like it. They whirled and circled one another, each looking for a likely opening, each looking the other directly into their eyes, watching for the tiniest flicker right or left that might give them a clue of the next move. If Lizzie hadn't known better, she would have thought their moves had been carefully choreographed weeks in advance, they moved so smoothly from one stance and swing to the next.

Finally, Arvid feinted and Tarafau's staff was there to meet a blow that did not come. Arvid whirled and leapt in the same fluid movement, his blow landing lightly on Tarafau's midriff. Lizzie would have sworn the blow would be hard and potentially harmful, but Arvid only tapped Tarafau with a renewed grin of triumph.

Tarafau bowed low to the little man. *"You win again, old dwarf. Someday...."*

"Yes, indeed, someday... maybe... perhaps," Arvid returned with a wave of his free hand. *"Keep practicing."*

But Tarafau was not offended. He clapped the dwarf on the back. From the force of it, Lizzie was surprised to see that the dwarf didn't flinch and was not moved from his sturdy stance.

"Well done, one and all. You've earned your lunch this day. Let's all get cleaned up and meet in the dining room. I understand Livia has prepared her amazing beef stew, and I can smell that the fluffy rolls she is baking will soon come out of the oven," Arvid said, smiling around at the group. *"See you in about thirty minutes."*

After a congenial lunch, each of the gate guardians gave reports regarding their stewardships. It was interesting to Lizzie to see how varied their interests and disciplines were, and the different points of view regarding their duties. They were all keenly aware of the world situation, especially following the two world wars and the ups and downs of the various economies of nations around the globe even years afterward.

Here they were, guardians of the access points to the multiverse, caretakers of the secret that one could simply step from one universe to the next as easily as walking through a door. Each of them, although they were smart and engaged in sciences and crafts of varying types, would have seemed ordinary to those within their communities. None of them were seeking fame or wealth. They were, for all intents and purposes, ordinary beings with an extraordinary secret to keep.

She wondered if any of them had ever been tempted to use the knowledge they had to give Earth an advantage of some kind, but so far it appeared that those who had chosen each guardian out of the masses had made good choices. She herself had definitely felt a longing to reveal aspects of the advanced tech to her world, wishing to change the future for the better.

However, after listening to her fellow guardians and after all her training, she finally understood. She had seen what advance technology could do to a people who were not ready to use it responsibly; and after that experience with Reloi's people, finally, finally... she got it. That temptation was gone, replaced with a resolve to simply do her part.

Chapter 13: Stone Upon Stone

(J)enny could relate to Lizzie's longing to use the technology of the Alliance to rid the Earth of poverty and to prevent the ecological destruction of her planet. After seeing what had been done in other cultures within the Alliance, she longed some days to shout from the rooftops, "Stop! Pay attention! Take care of our beautiful world!"

She knew, however, that other voices, other organizations on her planet, had been doing that for a long time. What was one more voice in the cacophony?

There were several years of minor entries in the journal at this point, denoting the passage of time, but nothing more than glimpses into the day-to-day duties of a gate guardian and the work Lizzie did within her community.

She had continued Gaston's work with the orphanage and to make regular trips to visit both Reloi's people in their new colony and the tree Bonwen. She was very involved with her garden, going out to sing to her plants and the koi that, by then, were a school of sparkling fish.

She also spent a lot of time with her neighbors, who over time had become close friends. She had even kept her promise to herself to interact more frequently with her family; and although they still thought of her as this somewhat eccentric and mysterious person, she finally felt more like she belonged than she had previously.

Jenny knew she had only a few more days before she would go back to her own duties as the Gatekeeper for the Alliance, and she only skimmed the one- and two-paragraph entries made by her aunt in what appeared to be a hurried hand.

The one thing she noticed as time passed for her aunt was the difference in her attitude towards the people around her

Yes, she was still Lizzie, still fully engaged in learning everything she could, but she had finally reached outside herself and was the better for it.

"I have a few more hours before bed," Jenny sent to Chidwi and Tidbit after she grabbed herself a glass of water. "Let me know if I go too late." She didn't want to be chided by Burt for not following the healers' orders.)

"I'll be back in about a week," Lizzie told Lacey as they knelt by the strawberry plants that edged the koi pond.

"I think the kids at the orphanage will love using these runners to start their own strawberry patch." Lacey said as she snipped another little strawberry plant from its trailing runner and placed it in a small seedling pot, carefully patting potting soil around the little roots.

Both Lacey and Melinda had already established significant strawberry hills in their own backyards from the runners Lizzie had gladly given them, and Lizzie had been at a loss to know what to do with this season's harvest.

"Thank you for taking the time to help me get them ready and delivering them to the school," Lizzie said, nodding in agreement. "I would be happy to do it myself, but I made arrangements for this trip several weeks ago, and if we wait too long, this bed will be completely out of hand."

"I love that you are continuing Gaston's work with the orphanage. How is he? Have you heard from him lately?"

"I got a letter from him this week. He's enjoying his retirement and says that if his arthritis would cooperate life would be perfect. The last time I saw him, he was slowing down a bit but seemed in good spirits."

Lizzie had told Lacey that Gaston was settled in a retreat in Sweden, which was true as far as it went, and that she sometimes got the opportunity to see him there. Lacey took it all at face value, not suspecting that Lizzie might have anything to hide.

They finished up, and Lizzie helped take a couple of flats of strawberry seedlings out to Lacey's car, loading them carefully into the trunk. She was thankful to get this last thing off her list before she left to participate in the colony's yearly celebration of their rescue from the disaster that destroyed their home planet so many years ago.

"Are you ready?" she sent to Tidbit and Ynni the moment she strode into the bright living room.

"Ready!" both mental voices came with enthusiasm. These trips to the colony were nearly always happy ones. This was pretty much the Grildite version of Thanksgiving in the United States. The difference was that it took up an entire week of feasting and performances, with a vast fair containing booths that displayed the crafts and goods made with the bountiful resources now available to the Grildites on their planet.

Ynni leapt to her usual perch on Lizzie's shoulder, and Tidbit strolled with his tail high like a little banner behind him. Together they entered the gate office and went through the door to the gateroom.

Soon after the Grildites had settled in their new colony, a new door amongst the many that lined the seemingly endless corridor had appeared. This door led to the gateway that spanned the multiverse to the Grildite colony. Lizzie, of course, had no idea of the actual distance. None of the scientists that studied the gate network had discovered any valid way to measure the vast distances between dimensions. All they could say was that the distances were beyond any known measurement, such as light years, and were indescribable.

But for her, Ynni, and Tarafau, it was but one step across the threshold from Earth to the new Grildite home world.

Upon their exit, from their vantage point at the top of the hill, Lizzie stopped to take in all the changes that had taken place since that first day they had come to set up the initial temporary housing for the colony.

Now, where there had once only been tents and the roped off outlines of future tracts of land set apart for the city and for the farmlands that had been planned by the Grildite council, a sparkling city sprawled.

The sparkle came from a particular plant, hard, woody and sturdy, much like bamboo that, when dried and cured, revealed its dense mineral nature. Evidently it required a highly mineralized soil to grow.

The result was that, when used for building material, it reflected little points of light. The Grildites had loved it so much that they didn't cover it with paint, but with a protective varnish they made from another plant that grew in abundance along the banks of the two rivers that flowed through the valley.

The city was like nothing Lizzie had ever seen before. The streets were laid out in concentric circles with side streets radiating out, dividing the area like a large pie. In the center of the circle was a huge plaza with a large building at one end. Lizzie knew this was the community center and the seat of the Grildite government, very similar to the community center they had built in their capital city inside their former planet.

At this time, the center green was covered in booths and community eating areas, not to mention a gathering area for the various performances and events that would take place throughout the coming week.

Beyond the city were some suburbs curving around the edges of the main city, and across the river were the farms and crafting holds that had been established.

Orchards, vineyards, and farms appeared to be thriving, and Lizzie knew that Reloi would have been very happy to see his people moving forward with such amazing success.

They were greeted by a group of school children in their festival clothes, each with an mbira in hand. These younglings serenaded them, dancing to the tunes they joyfully played the entire way down the hill onto the main thoroughfare that led to the heart of the city. Ynni crooned along happily, and Tarafau now strode beside them, grinning his catlike grin.

When they entered the city, the main street was lined with the colonists, all dressed in their holiday finery. Lizzie knew that much of their clothing came from spinning the fibers of the little lavender lamb-like creatures they had befriended when they first came to settle there.

They had been very careful in their settlement to only use resources that were renewable and to keep the production of goods to the simplest methods that would use the least energy and have the least impact on the world they had adopted and that had adopted them.

So far, they had not encountered any inimical life, neither plant or animal that would impact them in any negative way, but they had not gone much beyond their home valley to explore. According to the surveys done by the Alliance, the planet was nearly twice the size of Earth and had many different climate types and geological marvels.

Eventually, the Grildites would be established to the point that they could direct their attention outward, but for now, they were content to thrive in the generous boundaries of the lush valley, with its rivers and rich soil.

As they reached the center of the large circular city, Lizzie was impressed by the improvements since her last visit, months ago. She had watched this city spring up from nothing, and it amazed her how quickly the Grildites had transformed the area. Trees lined most of the roads, and most of the buildings were two stories or less. The main exception to this was the large community building, which was four stories high, a half-acre curved rectangle facing the large circular park.

Wherever possible for building and construction they used stone and the "lorpa," their name for the sparkly bamboo-like plant.

There was no doubt that the Grildites were an energetic and focused people. In the several years since that first day looking out on the unpopulated valley, they had built a flourishing community.

The rivers that intersected the valley were wide, and now there were several bridges across each of them, giving access to all going to and from the farmlands beyond. Lizzie loved standing on the bridges, as many in the community often did, looking out over the pristine water. Like the buildings, there were sparkles emanating from the depths of the crystal-clear, slow-moving water.

Lizzie had gone to the banks of the river frequently on her regular visits to take the river rocks that created the sparkling effect. It was her plan to make a rock garden in her front yard between the wrought iron bougainvillea arch and her front door. So far, she had nearly enough to cover the entire area. She had decided to baldly lie to her friends when they asked where she got the rocks. She figured she could tell them she got them on one of her trips to Africa or Australia.

In this particular case, she thought, what they didn't know wouldn't hurt them, and every time she walked through from her driveway to her front door, she would be reminded of Reloi and his people, not to mention that a rock garden in place of the lawn would require a lot less care.

The procession finally emerged onto the circular community park. As they rounded the left side of the circle, she found herself grinning like the proverbial Cheshire cat. The young people and their mbiras continued to play a joyful tune which could barely be heard over the cheers of the people, her people, she reminded herself, who lined the street.

A raised dais had been erected just in front of the community center. On the stand, the Grildite council was assembled in their festival finery, all smiling an honest welcome to Lizzie, Ynni, and Tarafau.

They beckoned for them to ascend to the platform, and each reached out to touch the cheeks of their guests in greeting. When they reached the end of the reception line, the current chief councilor, Ngalia, gestured for them to turn and face the crowd that had gathered before the dais.

As they turned, silence fell like the curtain on a stage at the end of a play. Looking into the earnest and happy faces before her, Lizzie felt deep emotion stirring in her heart, and she was unashamed of the joyful tears that spilled from her eyes.

"My people," Ngalia broadcast in mindspeech, *"we are gathered here to celebrate and to give thanks for our rescue from a disaster like none other. We welcome our guests, who are also the siblings of our heart, our rescuers and our advocates with the Alliance. Lizzie Japhet, her companion, Ynni, and her mentor, Tarafau, have continued faithfully over the years to labor alongside of us, to bring us to this point where every Grildite has a home and a contributing occupation.*

"None of us go hungry. None of us are needful of any necessary thing. This planet which is now our home is exceptionally beautiful and bountiful. Now let us spend the coming week giving thanks and strengthening our bonds of friendship and unity."

At this, a deafening cheer went up from the crowd.

Ngalia stood there for a long moment, smiling beatifically, and then gestured towards Lizzie. Lizzie took that as a cue that she should say something. She was once again grateful for mindspeech, because even if she could have spoken the Grildite language fluently, she knew that her emotions were at this point too strong for her vocal cords to obey her.

"My dear brothers and sisters, for such you are to me," she sent, as silence fell once again, *"I cannot tell you how touched I am to see you all here, whole, healthy, and flourishing in your new home. Today we are grateful for those who willingly sacrificed their own lives to make it possible for so many of you to escape the calamity which brought us here. We have all lost loved ones, but as we look around us, here and now, we can find great gratitude for those who survived.*

"Let us show our thankfulness for that sacrifice by accepting wholeheartedly the stewardship of this glorious planet which has become our home. I say 'our' since, although my home planet is ever so far away, I will always feel that this is my home away from home. We will rejoice and be glad today and every day moving forward."

Lizzie bowed her head to indicate she was finished and was nearly blown away by the new cheer that reverberated through the park. She felt Tarafau's arm go around her shoulders and realized that once again she was crying. Since when had she become so obviously emotional? She felt like Professor Baird would have shaken his head at such noticeable and publicly displayed emotion.

She looked up again and realized that she wasn't the only one with tears streaming down her face. Each of the members of the council, most of the people in the crowd, and even Tarafau had joyful tears on their faces.

"Come, you three," Ngalia sent, gesturing to the steps leading off of the dais. *"We have created new quarters for you in the community building. These rooms will be your permanent residence here any time you come to visit. After you have had time to freshen, we will return to the park, where you can mingle with us and find something good to eat in one of the food booths.*

"I know our people are anxious to show you some of their crafts and perform for your pleasure."

The suite they showed them to on the second floor of the community complex was spacious and beautifully appointed; two bedrooms, a sitting room connected to a small kitchen, and bathing facilities. They had decorated the rooms with art done by various students in the community, and all the furnishings had been skillfully constructed by the Grildites from native resources.

They thanked their hosts for such amazing hospitality and allowed that they didn't really need freshening up at the moment but would be happy to accompany them out to the celebrations.

Ngalia asked if first they would like to see the newest addition, a full-fledged aquaponics system in the basement. Lizzie agreed happily, and Ngalia escorted them downstairs.

It was beautifully appointed, not looking at all as sterile and impersonal as the aquaponics lab at the Swiss gate. The Grildites had gone out of their way to make it beautiful, with paintings on the walls and crystals dangling from the ceiling, reflecting the special lighting they were producing using the energy from the solar panels on the roof of the building.

Colorful native fish swam lazily among water plants in the tanks that were the foundation of the system. The trays of plants that sat atop each of the tanks were in various stages of development and appeared to be herbs, vegetables, small seedling trees, and even flowers.

"We are using this aquaponics station to grow the seedlings to plant at the various farms surrounding the valley. Each building in the city has a similar station. It lengthens the growing season considerably when we start our seeds this way," Ngalia sent with an obvious note of pride in her voice.

This, for Lizzie, was the crowning glory, something the Grildites had been working and hoping for from the beginning. It was like the final seal of their efforts to establish what they considered to be a complete community.

When they emerged out into the sunshine, the festivities were in full swing. Various booths were surrounded by people perusing the displayed goods, and the food booths were doing a brisk business, amazing aromas wafting around them. Children dashed in an out of the crowd, laughing and waving little ribboned banners behind them.

It was as fun as any of the county fairs Lizzie had ever visited, and from time-to-time Lizzie could hear the music of some impromptu mbira concerts rising above the conversations and laughter around her.

She, Ynni, and Tarafau were welcomed over and over again by the various clusters of people, and when they entered the central area where long tables and benches had been set up for the revelers to relax and eat and talk, they were besieged by a number of the food vendors with trays of delicacies prepared for the occasion. They hadn't yet set up an official system of currency, but for now they traded with little tokens.

It was similar to what Tarafau's people did, each token representing the time and materials invested into whatever product or service was for sale.

Ngalia had presented both her and Tarafau a small pouch of these tokens, but when they tried to pay for the food offered to them, it was flatly refused every time. Thus, their lunch had been a string of delicious samples of the food that had been prepared for the fairgoers.

They sat at a central table surrounded by the Grildites, holding simultaneous mind conversations with those around them. The other bench at their table had been taken up by Grildite children, each eager to talk about their most recent adventures.

After eating, they attended various performances that ringed the edges of the park in six different areas, just far enough away from each other not to interfere with the sounds coming from other performances going on at the same time.

Lizzie was impressed that one of the priorities in planning the town initially had been to create a central space for their people to gather for recreation and community events. She knew that over time the honeymoon stage of the community would pass and there would more than likely be some bumps in the road as far as their plans were concerned. But for now, she was content that they were safe and working and playing together.

At one point, a long line of youth, dressed in their colorful festival clothes, danced in and out of the crowd, accompanied once again by the mbira performers, each playing on a handcrafted mbira of their own. Lizzie was still amazed how this had caught on and was quickly becoming a cultural norm.

By the time the sun began to set, Lizzie, Ynni, and Tarafau were grateful to retire to their reserved suite. Before they did, however, they were told that tomorrow there was to be a community beautification project, and they were invited to participate after breaking their fast.

That morning they gathered in the feasting area, everyone dressed ready to work. Their work clothing contrasted with their festival clothing only in the texture, but the various shades of pastels were still evident.

Ngalia stood when all were assembled and raised her hands for silence. The crowd fell still, with anticipation written on every face.

"Today we will celebrate the entrance into our beautiful new world with two activities. All are welcome to participate.

"When we dismiss, each of you, including children, will go to the riverbank, choose a stone that attracts you, and carry it to the path, laying them on either side close together to outline the path. Later we will plant flowers as a border next to the stones, but today we are laying the foundation.

"After the path is fully lined, we will return to the riverbank and gather larger stones to create the stone towers. The construction of the towers on either side of the gate will be supervised by our engineers to ensure stability and a pleasing form. I will reveal the second event after our evening meal. You may begin."

At her signal, there was an immediate exodus towards the river. Children ran ahead of their elders with giggles and whoops, each certain that their stone would be the most beautiful and perfect of them all.

The adults were no less eager to participate, if not quite so energetic, although a few decided on a foot race to the river while the others cheered them on.

Lizzie was impressed by this community exercise, bringing them all together in a common task that would beautify and enhance their community in a way that all could participate.

They started from the base of the hill at the beginning of the path leading up, each laying their stones end to end. The effect was amazing. The stones were of such a range of colors as to rival a rainbow, and the minute points of light that emanated from each stone seemed as if they were lighted from the inside.

Again and again, they ran to the river and returned until they reached the peak just before the circle of turf in front of the gateway. This circle was also lined with stones.

"Time to eat and refresh ourselves. Then we will tackle the stone pillars," Ngalia announced when the last stone was laid.

Lunch was served by the various food vendors, who had each taken the opportunity to place at least one stone on the path before returning to their task of feeding the workers. Conversations, both verbal and mental, buzzed around Lizzie and Tarafau. Ynni had been very entertained by the children who kept bringing her morsels of food. Ynni responded with gentle pats of her tiny hands on the cheeks of her benefactors, to the delight of the children and the amusement of the adults surrounding them.

As soon as the tables were cleared, they immediately went to the riverbank, each extracting larger stones, based on their capacity to carry them. Tarafau, who towered over the Grildites, hefted a large black stone, nearly blazing with pinpoints of light. It was smooth and glasslike, resembling black onyx from Earth. Tarafau's muscles rippled as he levered it up into his arms, so Lizzie was sure it must have been very heavy.

They trooped up onto the hilltop, the engineers in charge directing them to pile the stones into various stacks so they could sort them in preparations to build the towers. They soon had an impressive collection of large stones all gemlike in the sunlight. The river had polished them as effectively as a rock tumbler, and they shone like hundreds of little beacons.

Tarafau's stone was set aside as it was the largest stone anyone had procured. The engineers then directed the arrangement and stacking of the rocks. The huge stone Tarafau had brought was not stacked but was reserved for the front of one of the towers. They had decided they would have a craftsman engrave the name of the colony and the date, based on their new calendar, of their first day on the planet. It would stand as a memorial to that celebrated day.

When the pillars of stone were fully assembled, nearly as tall as Tarafau, they all admired them for a long moment and went back down the hill in anticipation of the feast and the next event of the day.

The crowd was not quite as boisterous as they had been earlier. They had all put in some heavy labor; up and down the hill carrying stones, nevertheless there were looks of satisfaction on every face. Even the children knew they had done something important that day. Future generations might not fully appreciate the significance of this event, but today every soul in this community was nearly glowing with gratitude and a kind of shared relief that they had come this far.

Once again, Ngalia stood and raised her hands for silence.

"Thank you, each one of you, for your willing and enthusiastic participation in our project today. Now look up and see the fruits of your labors!" she sent and every head turned to look up to the hill behind them.

The undulating path that rose up the side of the hill was now illuminated as if by tiny fireworks. The minuscule glittering minerals in each stone were reflecting the light of the sun as it began to set, and the hilltop was ablaze as if pillars of light stood on either side of the gateway.

There was an "Ahh!" in unison as they viewed the results of this day's labors, and Lizzie could feel a surge of emotion emanating from the crowd, the unspoken mental joy and gratitude of this concentration of minds and hearts. This had been magnified by Ynni's gift of reading the minds around her and passing it on to Lizzie. It was so overwhelming that Lizzie found herself sinking back onto her bench with her head in her hands.

Tarafau laid a hand on her shoulder, and Ynni crooned and patted the back of her neck with her tiny hands.

"*And now,*" Ngalia continued after a suitable pause, and every face turned to hers. "*We have another gift to give to our people. Since we fled Grild, we have retained the name of Grildites. But this is a new planet, and an opportunity to leave behind mistakes and tragedies of the past.*

"*This new world is as yet mostly unexplored, and we have impacted it very little, but we know that over time our numbers will grow, and we will expand our borders. We have begun well, and it is our intention to take the stewardship of these resources seriously. This is a new start for us; therefore, as we leave the past in the past, we feel it important to give ourselves a new name.*"

The crowd seemed to hold its collective breath, every eye focused on Ngalia and her fellow councilors.

"*After much consideration, taking into account our hope for an abundant future, we have decided to give this planet a name and therefore to rename ourselves. The name we have decided on is Promisia. We will become the Promisians. This is based on the promise we now make to ourselves, the planet, and all who come after us that we will be thoughtful and diligent in our stewardship over all we have, all we are, and all we hope to become.*

"*Will you, the people of my heart, make this promise?*"

There was a mighty shout of assent, both mental and verbal, from the assembly. Lizzie could feel it to her toes. These people were committed, and they would do as they had promised. The Promisians were ready to move forward with hope and determination.

That evening, a very tired but excited community celebrated well into the night. The council had wisely scheduled the events for the following day to begin after lunch, and everyone slept in, waking ready to celebrate the dawn of Promisia.

Lizzie had been expecting some delegates from the Alliance to participate that day, but when she and Tarafau had walked up the stone lined path to wait by the stone pillars by the gate, she noticed her key did not warm as they approached it. That was highly unusual, as anytime Lizzie had approached a gate since she had been named a guardian, her key had always warmed gently against her neck.

Due to its relatively recent activation in the Alliance gate system, the Promisian gate had not yet formed the appearance of a doorway, which was one reason the pillars on either side were a helpful reminder of its existence. It had always been an apparently empty space from either side of the gateway, and that hadn't changed.

She didn't say anything to Tarafau about it, but as they waited for nearly an hour, she wondered if perhaps the incoming delegation had mixed up the time, which was easy to do. Coordination with times between dimensions was complex and often difficult. However, she knew she could just contact them via her tablet. She removed it from her MDP and, although it immediately booted up, a message came up on the screen, "No connection available."

This had never happened before. She had at this point become used to immediate connection every time she used her tablet to communicate with her friends and colleagues throughout the Alliance.

"Tarafau," she said, handing him the tablet, *"Am I doing something wrong?"*

"I don't know, Lizzie. I've never seen anything like this before." He handed her tablet back to her and pulled out his own tablet that he had been issued from the Alliance and as it opened, the same message appeared.

"This doesn't look good...." He put his tablet back into his own MDP and frowned. *"Maybe we can just go to the headquarters gate and fetch the delegation; and while we're there, we'll see why our tablets are malfunctioning. No reason to disturb the celebrations below."*

Lizzie nodded, stepped up to the gateway and walked through to... the other side of the gate, still on the hill overlooking the valley of Promisia.

She walked back through in the other direction towards a flabbergasted Tarafau, standing there with his eyes wide and eyebrows furrowed.

"Not good... not good at all," he sent in what would have been his catlike growl in vocal speech.

"What can we do? I don't remember them teaching me about what to do when a gate failed in any of my classes in agent training. I never heard any of the other gate guardians talk about a gate malfunctioning before."

"First, let's go see the council and explain what's going on as far as we understand it, and then I think you and I need to visit headquarters and let them know this gate isn't working."

In her initial panic, Lizzie hadn't remembered Tarafau's unique ability to travel the dimensions without a gateway. They sped down the hill through the celebrating crowds to the council building, where the councilors were gathered on the steps leading into the building, apparently waiting to receive the delegation formally before escorting them through the various events planned for the day.

Ngalia's silvery eyebrows rose practically into her scalp when Lizzie explained the situation. *"Does this mean you are stranded here?"* she asked once she had visibly calmed herself.

"No, we believe we can use Tarafau's abilities to come and go as we need to, and we can bring help as needed. But our communications are blocked, and we need to let the Alliance know what's happening here. I'm sure they will send gate techs to help us figure this out. I just wanted to update you before we leave. I don't think we need to let this go beyond the council, though. I don't want to interrupt the celebration, and causing panic will not fix the situation. At this point, there is no immediate danger to anyone here. So, let's keep this between us, shall we?"

The councilors agreed solemnly. Lizzie and Tarafau went up to their suite in the building and he laid his hand on her shoulder.

They emerged into complete chaos in the street in front of the headquarters building. Even the guards who normally stood in front of the huge glass doors weren't at their usual posts. Evidently something was happening here as well. They took the elevator directly up to the private council room.

There was no one in the reception area, so they went straight through the large double doors into the council chamber, where all three councilors were engaged in a conversation with a number of the more prominent delegates from the various dimensions. The room was packed; and as they entered, the First Councilor, Khol stood and motioned them forward.

"To what do we owe this visit?" he asked.

"We came to report that communications between us and the Alliance have failed, and the gateway on the refugee planet no longer connects to the gate network." Lizzie said succinctly.

Khol sent the mental version of a head shake, and there was a noticeable murmur from the assembly.

"Alas, that tells us that there is more to this than we thought. A day ago, every gate on the planet shut down, as well as the gate in the space station above us. Now we wonder if this is completely widespread or if it is just a connection between us and that dimension. There is only one way to check this. Tarafau, may we ask you to go to several different dimensions that you have coordinates for and check to see if gates in other dimensions are having this same issue? Our communications are completely down, with the exception of tablets connected through the planetary network. We have no way to communicate with the gate guardians.

"Please start with Miriha's gate, which should tell us something. If her gateroom is nonfunctional, it is likely that this issue is throughout the entire network."

Chapter 14: Between a Rock and a Hard Place

(*Jenny set the journal down with a gasp. As the current Gatekeeper, she couldn't imagine the entire gate network going down and began to understand for the first time just one of the reasons Tarafau was such an important key to her position.*

The idea that the gate system might be vulnerable in this way was not only startling but also concerning, especially considering that it wasn't connected to the portals the Inseni was using to invade the dimensions. What if the Inseni figured out how to shut down the Alliance gate system, giving them free reign to terrorize, enslave, and plunder in the multiverse? They must prevent this at all costs.

It hadn't occurred to her when she first began to read her Aunt Lizzie's journals that it might uncover such vital information to her success as the Alliance Gatekeeper, especially in the current conflict.

Now she realized that many lives and the eventual destiny of every dimension could potentially hang on her ability to understand these things.

So far, her lack of training in her position had been bothersome, but now it seemed somehow disastrous.

She had no time to waste. She turned the page.)

Lizzie breathed a sigh of relief as they entered the large green building off the town square in Miriha's village. She had wondered if the blockage in the gateway might somehow impede Tarafau in discovering what was happening.

Miriha was not up in her office beyond the curving staircase but was pacing the large lobby area before a knot of people with concerned faces. She looked up as Lizzie, Ynni, and Tarafau entered. Lizzie noticed that there were also linklings among the group.

"Lizzie! Tarafau! Is the outer gate working?"

"No," Tarafau said sadly, shaking his head. *"None of the gateways at headquarters are functional at this time. We came from Alliance headquarters to find out your situation here."*

"Ah, yes, your ability is an amazing gift to us right now."

Miriha shook her head sadly. *"Lizzie, Tarafau, I cannot tell you how glad I am to see you. The entire network has shut down. Every gate in the gateroom has disappeared. There isn't even a hallway. The door opens to a blank wall.*

"I have to assume that it is also the case at headquarters?"

Lizzie and Tarafau nodded, and Miriha sighed. *"Then I will dismiss you all,"* she said to the waiting townsfolk. *"Please go about your usual business. This doesn't really affect any of us here. Since Tarafau and Lizzie are here, we can assume that the power of the Alliance is behind the effort to resume gate operations. Be of good cheer, my friends. I will let you know of any future progress."*

She waved a graceful hand towards the door, and without protest the group filed out of the lobby, faces still somewhat concerned.

"Now," she said as the room emptied, *"Let us go up and I can show you the gateroom, or lack thereof, and then you should go back to headquarters and report. I will await further reports going forward. I would go with you, but I am not a gate technician. I doubt there is anything I can do about the current situation, but I will keep a positive attitude and hope for your success. I admit it makes me feel somewhat vulnerable and helpless, something I don't enjoy much,"* she added with a wry twist to her mouth.

After showing them the gateroom, which indeed ended in a blank wall behind the physical door, she put out both hands to each of them, reaching out to pat Ynni on the cheek with one gentle finger. *"Take care, each of you. All my good thoughts go with you."*

Tarafau simply nodded with an encouraging smile and put his hand on Lizzie's shoulder.

Their quick return to the council chamber didn't seem to surprise the councilors waiting there. Tarafau had transported them directly to the reception area.

After their report, Ben, the second councilor, in a soft warm mental voice sent, *"This is unprecedented. For now, we have to calm those currently stranded at headquarters. In the meantime, I find it strange that the network shut down during what you report to have been a high point of the celebration of the planet now called Promisia. Can you think of anything that may have coincided with that celebration?*

"It may be completely unrelated, but it is a place to start. We have summoned two gate technicians to accompany you back to that planet. In the meantime, we have every available scientist working on it from our end.

"Tarafau, it would be helpful if some of the Daringi could aid us in making contact with the other dimensions to explore any other possible conditions that may have precipitated this event. If, after you take Lizzie and the techs to Promisia, you could recruit some of your people to aid us?"

"Of course, Ben. I would be happy to get you some help. I believe I can get a few hundred to expedite your efforts, if you will get each of them guides to the various dimensions, as they will need coordinates. As long as the guide has been to a dimension, our people can get the coordinates from a mental picture of the place they wish to go," Tarafau confirmed solemnly.

At a gesture from the councilor, one of the guards who had been standing at the back of the room escorted them to the lab at the top of the headquarters building, where they were introduced to two gate techs, Invira and Lob.

Invira was a tripoidal being, three legs, somewhat lizard-like, covered with blue-green scales and hairless. Lizzie could not be sure of Invira's gender, but the mental voice sounded female to her.

Lob was humanoid but with lavender skin and extremely large eyes that peered out above a long white beard. His mental voice, as they were introduced, was deep and a bit gruff.

"We're ready," he growled. *"The sooner we go, the sooner we can be done."*

Invira smiled, fanged teeth looking somewhat ominous though well meant. *"Don't mind Lob,"* she nearly purred in retort. *"He doesn't bite, and he's very good at what he does."*

Lob looked up at her, and for a moment he almost looked like he was going to smile.

Tarafau did smile his catlike grin. Lizzie could tell he liked Lob. *"So, now, my friends, I will first take Lizzie, Ynni, and Invira and will return in a few* minutes for Lob. Once we are there, we will take you to the Promisia gate, and you can get to work."

In only a few moments they were all assembled in Lizzie and Tarafau's suite and trooped out to the huge circular community park. They cut right through the center, acknowledging greetings but not stopping to chat. About halfway through the park, they encountered Ngalia, eating with a number of Promisian citizens. She rose immediately, excused herself cordially, and without comment joined them as they proceeded to the path that led to the top of the hill, its rock-lined edges sparkling in the light of midday.

"Impressive," sent Invira, looking around as they strode up the hill. *"These stones are incredible. I don't think I've ever seen anything like them, at least not as plentiful as here. Where do they come from? Are they mined from somewhere?"*

"No," Ngalia replied. *"We simply picked them up from the riverbanks."* She turned and gestured behind them at the valley below. The twin rivers sparkled beneath them, outlining the city and thriving farmlands.

"These lands must be incredibly rich in minerals then." Lob remarked. *"It would be a good idea to do a mineral survey once you are thoroughly settled in here. I know you have made amazing progress compared to the number of years you have been on the planet."*

"We have created the beginnings of a scientific institute to study the planet as we have the leisure to explore more thoroughly, but for now our focus has simply been to establish a functional community," Ngalia explained. *"That being said, preliminary examination of the soil and water do confirm a high concentration of minerals, much more than in our previous home."*

As they arrived at the top of the hill, Lizzie once again felt no answering warmth from her key. She had hoped the stoppage of the gates was a temporary glitch.

"I will leave you here," Tarafau sent as they approached the two sparkling pillars on either side of where they knew the gate had been. *"I must go to my fellows to arrange for their aid to the Alliance. I will probably return in a few hours. I know Ngalia will see to your comfort and any needs you may have.*

"Once you know what other equipment or resources you may need, I will be happy to retrieve from Alliance headquarters whatever you need to get this done."

And without waiting for a reply, he faded from view.

"That never ceases to amaze me," said Lob, scratching at his beard. *"That such a talent should be intrinsic to a being without any technical assistance is beyond me. I would so love to study one or more of his people."*

"Well, for now, we need to study the task at hand," Invira retorted wryly. *"Ngalia, we'll need to set up a bit of a lab here. We promise to leave it better than we found it."*

"By all means," Ngalia said with a nod. *"We will provide you with any assistance you may require. At your request I will be glad to send our own scientists up to assist you and a few strong backs for any physical tasks you may require. I will leave you to it, then. Lizzie, will you be our liaison?"*

"Of course. I could use the exercise at any rate," she replied instantly. *"I'll bring you regular progress reports."*

Lizzie could feel some of the old excitement she had always felt when a new and difficult problem was put before her. Scientific discovery was still her passion, answering questions that no one had the answers to and pursuing that alluring sprite, Curiosity.

Invira and Lob set about removing equipment and supplies from their MDPs, along with a square, pavilion-style tent about a dozen feet across. Lizzie helped them spread out a canvas floor and erect several long collapsible tables. Lastly, after they had set up several stools along the tables and arranged the various pieces of equipment within the pavilion, they set up two solar generators on tall poles supported by a collapsible metal base that looked like the legs of a giant spider.

"The solar panels will track the sun across the sky, and the power generated goes into this battery stack," Lob explained as Lizzie looked at the structures quizzically.

The battery stack didn't really look like it should hold much power, but Invira patiently explained as they continued to connect the battery stack to several pieces of equipment. *"We keep charged stacks in our MDPs for field operations such as this. Even if they weren't connected to the solar panels, each stack would run the equipment for up to two days, depending on the length of the planetary days. Since the solar panels continually recharge the batteries, the power is virtually unending and doesn't depend on the resources available wherever we are working.*

"We automatically assume that a colony in these early stages of development might not have a ready power source for us to work with," she concluded with a satisfied smile as she plugged in the last piece of equipment.

Lob had picked up a small, rectangular, palm-sized device and had activated it. Tiny lights began to flash, and numbers and characters scrolled onto the small screen.

"This," he sent, noticing Lizzie's interested gaze, *"records a number of things regarding gate activity and the surrounding energy environment it resides in. There is yet so much we don't understand about how all of this works together, but over hundreds of years we have gathered a great deal of data regarding working gates, both the natural ones and the ones that are connected to the Alliance gate network.*

"So much of what the original gate creators knew has been lost, and so many records are missing, that even after centuries of study we still don't know as much as we would like about the origins and mechanisms of the gate system.

"As you can see on the readout, the scanner is creating a database of current environmental conditions. When the scan is complete, we will connect the scanner to the computer under the canopy and compare the data with everything we know about working gates.

"The analysis will take probably about two hours total, considering everything we have collected regarding every gate we have connected to the network over the last few hundred years under many different planetary influences and conditions. Working remotely like this, we don't have access to quite as much computational speed as we would at Alliance headquarters, but this should be adequate to at least give us a starting point.

"That being said, I detect some amazing aromas ascending from the valley. I doubt we need worry about anyone tampering with the equipment. Shall we go down and have a meal and then return and see what the readouts have to tell us?"

He tapped a button on the device, took it over to the portable computer on one of the tables, and laid it on a pad next to it. *"This will communicate the information to the computer while we eat."*

Lizzie led the way down the hill, where they were greeted enthusiastically by the Promisians.

By the time they had feasted and were feeling the effects of good food, entertainment, and cheerful conversation, Lizzie noticed Tarafau striding down the steps of the community building.

"Amenia and Elizabeth send their love," he sent to Lizzie as he approached, his wide white fanged smile shining brightly from his ebony face. *"All is arranged, and we have an entire brigade of over 300 Daringi on their way to the various dimensions attended by agents and council members."*

"By now, the computations should be well underway," Lob remarked to Ngalia as they passed her on their way back up the hill. *"We'll keep an eye on the readouts, then decide what steps to take next. I don't know if we will have any physical tasks until we've had a chance to examine the results."*

Once at the top, they gathered around the screen readout. Sure enough, numbers and words continued to scroll rapidly up the screen.

"I suggest we take some quiet time until the alert sounds from the computer," Invira recommended. She invoked a comfortable looking chaise out of her MDP and set it up just outside of the pavilion tent and suited actions to words. She stretched herself out, the silky tunic and breeches she wore settling themselves onto her long slender body, the tripoidal legs making only the slightest bump.

Lob nodded in agreement, but instead of a chaise, he simply laid a long blanket on the ground and lowered himself down on it with a contented sigh, his hands folded beneath his head, and closed his eyes.

Lizzie would have thought them to be taking their ease, if it wasn't for the fact that she knew that each of them was likely deep in thought about the potential solutions to the problem presented them.

She and Tarafau followed suit. Lizzie sat on the turf in her accustomed position for doing her mental exercises, but instead of wandering into her mental village, she simply waited there focusing on her breathing and completely relaxing every muscle from her face to her feet, one at a time, then tensing individual muscles while keeping the others completely slack.

She had no clue how long she'd been doing this when a soft chirp from inside the pavilion sounded. Every one of them was immediately alert, and within seconds they were gathered around the device.

Since the language of the device was not English and the Alliance network was down, Lizzie had to wait for Lob to interpret the results. The minutes stretched by as he scrolled through page after page of analysis.

"Ah, we have a definite issue here, and it seems that it's beyond anything we've ever measured before. There seem to be multiple levels of interference, and identifying which of them may be causing this problem may take some time. I will duplicate these results and ask Tarafau to please take these to the lab in Alliance headquarters, if he doesn't mind. Since the network is down, this is the only way we can keep the Alliance apprised of our progress. I will advise them not to try to work on the issue from their end as, unlikely as it may seem, it appears that this issue may well be emanating from the local environment."

Lob took out a tablet and transferred the data from the computer to the tablet and handed it to Tarafau, who immediately faded from view.

"Tell me, Lizzie. What were the circumstances that led to this dysfunction? I need a full and detailed report. Try not to leave out even things that might otherwise be considered inconsequential," Invira asked Lizzie as Tarafau faded away and Lob continued to peruse the data on the computer.

So, Lizzie recounted the days preceding the dysfunction and tried not to leave anything out. She knew she hadn't been on site for every minute of the two days preceding the breakdown of the gate, but whatever she could remember she told Invira, who was recording the interview on her own tablet.

Ynni, who had remained abnormally quiet most of the day, was very helpful during the interview, reminding Lizzie of little details she had forgotten or adding in things she had observed that Lizzie hadn't noticed.

After that, Invira physically walked Lizzie through her day and continued to take notes as they walked, starting in Lizzie's suite in the community building, down to the river, and up the stone-lined path to the top of the hill.

Tarafau waited for them at the top of the hill. *"The gate techs at every gate we can get to have been advised to not tamper with their gates at this time until we have had a chance to work on the problem from our end,"* he sent to Lob and Invira.

"So next steps are to interpret these findings," Lob told them. *"This may take many hours, but I would suggest that in the meantime we all stay here at the site. If anything becomes clear early on, we will want to be able to act immediately."*

Lizzie settled back down in the shade of one of the pillars on either side of the gateway. For some reason she couldn't put her finger on, she wanted to be as close as possible in case her key might unexpectedly warm, indicating gate activity. She removed her mbira and idly began to play one of her impromptu compositions.

Ynni immediately joined in, in her usual crooning descant. Before she realized it, the other three had gathered themselves before Lizzie in quiet contemplation of the music, Lob with his tablet on his lap in deep concentration, and Invira squatting on her three legs, tapping the rhythm out with her long, clawed fingers.

Lob referred back and forth between the tablet and the other small device that lay on the turf at his side.

Lizzie was never sure, after that, how long she had continued to play on the peaceful hilltop, but she became aware of the soft padding of many feet at some point and realized that a large crowd was gathering around the hilltop.

She looked up and saw the young members of the mbira orchestra standing before her. Not a word was said, but the query in their eyes was clear. Lizzie simply nodded and began to send the melody she was playing mentally, as well as through her plucking of the keys of her thumb piano.

Slowly but surely, each player joined in, some with the melody and others with improvised harmonies. Lizzie soon realized this wasn't just an instrumental chorus; something more intense was happening here. The timbre emanating from the hilltop was certainly greater with the entire mbira band playing with great heart, but there was even more to it than that.

It was as if Reloi were there. She felt his smile, and saw in her heart the spiky silver eyebrows raised in delighted surprise. And as she expanded her understanding, she felt and saw in her mind's eye the many people who had not made it out of the horrible disaster that had destroyed their previous home. More than that, they were all smiling, equally transported by the music being made that was so much more than notes on a score.

The minds and hearts of all beings present had become attuned to the audible and mental resonance of the music that flowed unimpeded from the participants in waves of crescendo, until every being within its reach was exalted beyond anything Lizzie had ever felt before.

And instead of the wrench she expected to feel as the sound finally faded gently away, Lizzie began to feel so connected to everyone around her that it was as if she could see into every heart and they into hers.

"What was that?" Lob asked, his usual steady deep mental voice shaking with emotion.

"I'm not entirely sure," Lizzie replied, looking deep into his eyes. *"It just came to me... something to do while we waited, I suppose. But, unless I'm mistaken, something is happening we didn't expect."*

She nodded toward the stone pillar to the right of the non-functional gate. There, at the base of the pillar, with the words "Promisia" and the date of the advent onto the planet carved into its surface, was the huge black stone Tarafau had hauled up the hill. It was glowing fiercely, beyond the reflection of the sparkles in its depths.

Lob and Invira turned from the glowing stone to gaze at their instruments with awe.

"The data dump is going crazy!" Invira exclaimed. *"I don't know what you just did, but evidently that stone is tuned to resonances our equipment has never registered before. Is the stone hot to the touch?"*

Tarafau immediately went over to the stone. Feeling no heat emanating from it, he reached out and touched it. *"It is as cool as the surrounding air. There is no heat that I can tell, although touching it makes me feel strange, somehow."*

He removed his hand and stepped away from it.

"May I recommend that we remove the stone back to its original position on the river? It may be nothing but a strange phenomenon, but my gut tells me this is no coincidence," he sent to the group.

"If the stone is making you feel strange, perhaps someone else should take it down the hill?" Lizzie asked, her brows furrowed in thought. All this technology... and the solution was music? *"Don't get cocky,"* she remonstrated with herself.

One of her heroes had been Einstein, who had said, "The only way to escape the corruptible effect of praise is to go on working." She knew that he had spoken at length about the role of creativity in science, and he had also been a very humble man.

She needed to remind herself that this hadn't been resolved yet and she still couldn't take credit, even if her hunch turned out well. She thought of all the teachers and mentors who had brought her to this point.

"Lizzie will do well," piped up Ynni from her shoulder perch. *"You will see."* And with that enigmatic comment, she hopped down and went to the stone and touched it.

"It sings!" she exclaimed. *"It sings!"*

Tarafau looked at the two scientists, standing with mouths agape at the readings rolling down the screen of their computer. Invira held up a hand.

"Wait," she said softly. *"Don't move it yet. I suggest we let the readings stop first. We may never get another chance to study this phenomenon. I suggest patience at this point."*

Tarafau nodded and turned to the gathered crowd of Promisians. *"We may have resolved this issue, but we won't know for sure until the research is complete. Thank you for your support in this. You may have given us the key. Go now to rejoice and continue your celebration. You have done well."*

The group, still looking somewhat awestruck and with no idea what the research was about, obediently turned and trailed down the stone-lined path to the town.

As they departed, one of them turned back. *"We will send people to help after you have eaten. I will send food up the hill to you, so your vigil is not interrupted."*

Lizzie thanked them and then, as the woman departed on her errand, she turned to Lob, Invira, and Tarafau. Ynni had perched on the stone, a look of contemplation on her furry little face. She often wished that Ynni's ability to read Lizzie's mind went both ways.

"So, what are your readings telling you?" She asked the two scientists hovering over the scrolling information on their equipment.

"They are telling us that we don't know near enough about the gate system and how it works," Lob sent with a resigned sigh. *"The limited records we have refer only to running the system. No records have survived that tell us how the gates were discovered or how they created the system that monitors and connects*

all the known gates in the multiverse. We can only assume that the process took thousands of years.

"*The Dimensional Alliance itself, as a known and formal organization, has existed only for the past few millennia, as you would measure time on Earth. And Earth itself has only been a known gateway planet for the past thousand years or so. Thus, the many legends of creatures like elves, dragons, and such on your planet.*

"*It would be one of the most phenomenal finds of eons to discover the records of the original founders of the gateway system,*" he concluded with a look of sheer elation on his face.

When their food arrived, they ate in silence, the scientists paying no attention to the food they put into their mouths, focused entirely on the readouts of their scanners and the computer that was assembling it all into a record that she had no doubt would be the study of scientists all over the multiverse for a long time to come.

Lizzie, on the other hand, was deep in thought. Once again, her incessant curiosity rose to the surface and the questions multiplied in her mind. Her awe of the vastness and the impossibility of learning everything she wanted to know loomed once again like an ever-receding horizon or a mountaintop beyond her ability to ever climb.

She was brought out of her reverie by an exclamation from Lob. He was practically dancing, rocking back and forth on his broad sturdy feet, his beard swaying with the agitation of his head.

"*It is done! Let us begin the experiment. We have concluded this scan and will start a new scan as you remove the stone. Let us hope that the resonance from Lizzie's music that seems to have triggered the stone proves to be the key we were looking for.*"

Tarafau nodded; the bright light from the sun above and the glow of the stone below glinting off his shiny bald ebony skull. "*Come,*" he said to the four workers who had assembled. With great care and gloved hands, they rolled the stone onto a sling they had created from many layers of a strong canvas-like material. Each of the corners had been knotted in a way to slide onto four metal bars, two horizontal and two vertical, to the sling, so the stone could not roll far in any direction.

Although Tarafau had been able to lift the stone himself when he had brought it up from the river, they had decided that no one should handle the still-glowing stone more than was necessary, so they rolled the stone directly onto the canvas sling. It wasn't too heavy for the four men who gripped the handles on each corner extending from the four corners of the sling.

With great care they began their trek down from the hilltop, turning at the base of the hill back towards the river where Tarafau had found the stone.

In the meantime, Invira and Lob continued to watch, fascinated by what their scanners were telling them.

"We can see the influence of the stone decreasing as they descend." Invira informed Lizzie encouragingly. *"I can't be sure how it's affecting the gate, but there is definitely something coming off of that stone that we have never seen before."*

Lizzie was trying so hard to be patient. It was nearly unbelievable that they should find the key to this issue in such a seemingly random event and so quickly. Somehow, she knew that even before the equipment detected anything she would feel her key warm. So, she moved from the tent pavilion to just in front of where she knew the gate existed. She hadn't really considered what an amazing piece of technology was embedded into the little key that looked so much like a random piece of jewelry until now.

She had begun to take it for granted that everything just worked. She had been so engaged in the people side of her responsibilities, it had almost obscured the urgent need she'd always had to know how and why things worked. She smirked to herself. She knew that both Gaston and Liliath would find that highly amusing, knowing her so well from the beginning of this incredible journey of hers.

And then, surprisingly, as suddenly as it had gone cold, her key began to warm. Its gentle glow was so welcome that she found herself grinning like Lob and wanting to dance. Ynni actually did dance in exuberance, crooning aloud merrily in the way she often did with her tribe.

Lizzie didn't have to say anything. Evidently all of Lob's and Invira's equipment had lit up and more data was pouring in to their great excitement.

"Try to go through to headquarters," Invira suggested, pointing at the gate.

Lizzie didn't need to be asked twice. She stepped up to the gate, thought her destination and as she stepped through, she found herself in the main gateroom at Alliance headquarters. There was a loud whoop from several gate techs who had been surrounding the gate with their various instruments.

"*It works!*" one of them exclaimed, jumping up and down in her excitement. The tiny elflike being ran up to Lizzie and grabbed her around one leg in a big hug.

She was surprisingly strong, Lizzie thought, but she gently pried her off her leg. "*Indeed, I think you should let the council know and start testing to be sure it's the entire network and not just an isolated incident; don't you agree?*"

Two of the group ran off, and Lizzie sent, "*I'm going to go back and let the techs on Promisia know we were successful. I don't want them to worry.*"

She waved and stepped back through the gate to arrive immediately at the top of the hill looking down into the valley.

Chapter 15: Rock Solid

(J*enny decided that she would need to do some more studying outside the confines of the journal, but for now she was beginning to understand why her aunt had given her specific instructions to read the journals, more than hinting that the information would be useful to her in her role as a gate guardian.*

Of course, Lizzie had no way of knowing that her niece would, improbably and sooner than anyone could have expected, become the Gatekeeper of the Alliance gate system.

With only a few days left to her in her recuperation, she somehow knew that completing the journals would be vital to her tasks going forward.

Lizziebot had brought her supper, and Chidwi urged Jenny to eat and then to take a walk before it got dark.

Jenny reluctantly complied, but her mind was still going over the events of Lizzie's journals so far. Jenny knew that these journals spanned over fifty years of experiences, and she knew that this final journal couldn't possibly cover every single year.

At this point in the journals, only the things Lizzie considered significant were included. Jenny had to assume that the time gaps were during periods when life was routine to Lizzie.

She sat down after her walk with anticipation. Lizziebot had left a snack plate of cheese, crackers, and iced peppermint tea on her chairside table. She smiled. She wondered at the precise and detailed programming it must have taken to fully incorporate Lizzie's personality and behaviors into this amazing construct.

However, she still also wondered how much of it was actually programming and whether or not Lizziebot was also evolving, along with her compatriot Fidget, into something more than any of them expected.

She determinedly put those wonderings out of her mind. She had a journal to finish.)

"*Now what?*" Lizzie asked the assembled gate techs and the Promisian council members. They stood before the stone on the riverbank. According to the messages now sent successfully to her tablet via the Alliance communications network, all gate activity had been restored.

According to the gate techs, the stone radiated a type of energy they had never encountered on any other world they had access to among the members of the Alliance. As far as they could tell from what their devices had recorded, the resonance of the music swelling up among the small mbira orchestra and Lizzie had initiated it in the first place. But it had been the resonances of the second powerful impromptu concert combining mind and voices and instruments that had enhanced the power of the stone to make it noticeable to their scanners.

Currently, it sat, still sparkling, but no longer glowing, surrounded by the puzzled crowd near the river where it had been found by Tarafau in the first place.

The gate techs had scanned up and down the river in an attempt to locate any similar stones, but so far, this stone seemed unique. They speculated it might have been some kind of meteorite that had traveled from somewhere else on the planet, perhaps over eons of time via the current of the river.

Lob had told the council there would probably eventually be a team of scientists assigned to explore beyond the valley to determine the origin of the stone; but in the meantime, the gate was safe.

So far, only two gateways had been discovered on the planet, and they intended to discourage any use of the other gate until they had worked out how to prevent this from happening in the future.

"*Our lab is constructing a special container for this stone,*" Lob continued. "*Once we have it contained, we will test to make sure the container blocks the radiation of the stone and arrangements will be made to keep it safe from affecting the gate network ever again. Since we aren't sure what it would take to destroy the stone or how it would affect the network if we did, the box is the best solution we can come up with for now."*

"We also don't want anyone else beyond this small group to know about the stone," sent Invira, *"so the final disposition of the stone will be top secret. The box should arrive here in a few days. In the meantime, we would appreciate it if the general public is kept away from this area."*

Ngalia nodded solemnly. *"It will be done as you say. We will station a couple of guardians to ward off the curious. In the meantime, we will keep everyone occupied with other distractions. The final assembly for our celebration is to be today after the midday meal. You are all invited to attend."*

"Thank you, Ngalia. We will be happy to come as soon as we disassemble the pavilion and pack our equipment."

Two of the councilors volunteered to remain there until Ngalia could arrange for a schedule of guardians for the area. They would not be informed of the real purpose of the watch they would be keeping, just that the area was temporarily unsafe, and that people should be warned to stay away for a few days.

"I'd like to go up with you to help with the packing," Lizzie sent to Lob and Invira. *"I have some questions..."*

Lob laughed. *"Liliath warned us about you and your questions, but we'd be happy to answer any that we actually have answers for,"* his furry eyebrows were raised, and the corners of his eyes crinkled. *"There is nothing we know that we can't divulge to you. That key around your neck is the only security clearance we need."*

At the top of the now-deserted hill, they set about packing equipment into cases and disassembling the tent. As they worked, Lizzie asked, *"What happened here today? All I was doing was passing the time while we waited for your equipment to complete the scan. Are we sure that it was something I did that triggered the stone to glow?"*

Invira shook her head. *"Sure? It would be arrogant of us to say for 'sure' what happened here without further testing, but I can give you the working theory for our assumptions, if you'd like. It all comes down to resonance."*

"Resonance? Like a tuning fork? Or do you mean the resonance that happens when a group of people walk in step across a bridge that causes the bridge to shake?"

"Well, there are many kinds of resonance, but it boils down to vibrations of various kinds, so you are right about your two examples. We don't fully understand all of the different types of resonance in the multiverse. The few we know about are mechanical, acoustic, electrical, optical, orbital, series, and parallel resonances. We have also theorized that there are mental and emotional resonances, which accounts for the mental abilities we find in many species throughout the multiverse."

"So, the music...?" Lizzie began.

"I don't think it was just the music, although we do know the audible spectrum of resonance can have a significant effect on anything within the reach of the acoustic waves produced by any instrument, device, or voice. What we experienced was on several levels, not the least of which was your own personal range of mental talents.

"The participants in your impromptu concert were completely ensconced in your mental sendings. I have seldom felt anything so powerful before. The fact that there were no actual words being projected didn't seem to matter. It was the intent that was important, in my personal opinion, and your intent seemed to be healing, uniting, and the projection of utter peace."

"All of that?" Lizzie was sure her mental splutter had a note of panic in it. *"From me? All I was doing was something I have done for a long time. Could this be dangerous? Should I stop? I've been worrying about how my mental music seems to affect those around me."*

Invira laughed, a somewhat disturbing thing, much like when Liliath laughed as her fanged mouth was open wide and her forked tongue protruded alarmingly. Lizzie had never noticed that Invira was ever anything but kind and gentle, but she could imagine that she would never want to anger the lizard-like scientist.

"My dear, do you think that your ability to influence emotions in others through your musical talent might someday produce a cadre of zombie-like creatures who will do your bidding and make you overlord of the multiverse? If so, perhaps you might want to rethink this.

"Influence is not force. Forcing someone to do your will is among the most evil of all evils, but influence is something every being does whenever two beings come together. It is natural for us to influence one another in our words and actions.

"Choice is a precious gift that we, as the Dimensional Alliance, have chosen to guard for every being we have the ability to protect in this way. However, we cannot control how the combination of personal experiences and opinions affect the influence we can extend to people around us.

"I intuit that you are the kind of influence we desperately need in the Alliance. Not one thing I sensed from you was constraining or intended to do harm. Do not restrain your influence, but train yourself to always use it to calm, gentle, heal, and give peace to those around you, and all will be well. Do not fear your gift."

Lizzie nodded thoughtfully, letting out a breath she didn't realize she had been holding. *"Then, I was resonating to the stone?"*

"You and your little mbira orchestra," Invira chuckled. *"You were all so in tune with one another and your little linkling friend's descant was something beyond anything I have ever witnessed. The vibrations you were putting out together, including the mental vibrations you were using to harmonize the whole thing, was intense and so strong our instruments actually recorded it."*

"So the effect was multiplied by the combination of all of our efforts then," Lizzie mused. *"I think I feel much better about that. It seems unlikely then that I caused this all by myself."*

She looked up to realize that Lob had placed himself directly in front of her, staring with his huge eyes into hers. *"Earthling Gate Guardian, I would give anything to abscond with you right now to our lab and never let you go. You have an intuitive mind for science. Our team would love to have you both to study and to partner with you.*

"I have a feeling that our leader, Mervin, would relate well to your ability to ask all the right questions."

Lizzie looked around. All the equipment, the pavilion and the furnishings had disappeared into Lob's MDP. *"We'll be going now but expect a visit from someone in the next day or so with the box. At that time, you'll receive your instructions."*

He nodded to Invira, who reached out with a hug for Lizzie. Lizzie had never imagined in her lifetime how many different types of beings she would receive hugs from. Having hugged dragons and many other types of beings during the last several years, however, she accepted the surprisingly warm hug from Invira and happily returned it.

One last wave from Lob and they disappeared through the gateway, and Lizzie practically floated down the hill to the celebration.

Two days later, a runner knocked on the door of Lizzie and Tarafau's suite. *"You are needed by the riverside,"* he sent, panting. *"The techs arrived and said to meet them there."* The young man had been one of the guardians of the stone Ngalia had stationed both at the gateway and near where the stone lay on the riverbank. They had not informed any of those assigned to these places why they needed to be there but had just given instructions to let Lizzie or Tarafau know if anything came up.

The two techs who waited for them there were a bit unusual. The one had salt and pepper hair and looked very much like an Earthling, wearing a lab coat over a t-shirt and a pair of somewhat worn jeans. The other could have been Lob's brother, the ubiquitous lab coat and a knee length tunic over leather-like breeches and well-broken-in boots. His beard was nearly to his knees, braids extending from the mustache on either side of a wide mouth.

Both of them were grinning from ear to ear.

"Well met, Lizzie Japhet and Tarafau," the tall one said in a perfect British English accent. "We've brought you a box." He extended a hand to shake. "Merv...by the way. Glad to meet you."

"Wow!" Lizzie exclaimed. "Your English is very good. Are you a British Earth agent?"

"Not quite," Merv said with a mischievous grin. "It's a very, very long story for another time, I'm afraid, but I had to come and meet you. Lob and Invira were absolutely raving about you. Good to see you again, Tarafau, old chap."

Speaking vocally felt almost strange, something she didn't do except in Los Angeles, as they also used mindspeech in Sanglarka. She felt more than a little overwhelmed by this tall stranger. Lob had said Merv was their leader, so he was the chief scientist. For Lizzie, this was like meeting a movie star would have been for one of her friends at home.

"Show us to this amazing rock of yours," Merv said when Lizzie didn't immediately respond.

The four of them moved down toward the bank, dismissed the guardian, and there at the water's edge was the large stone, like the onyx of Earth, with crystal sparkles reflecting the sun like stars in the night sky.

"So, all this fuss over a rock," Merv chuckled and grinned at the others. "Really, people, what next? But according to Lob, this stone bears a strong resemblance to the Earth stone hematite in that it has a strong magnetic influence as well as a peculiar resonance we still can't quite place. Turns out that the combination of those resonances responded to whatever Lizzie did that day on the hilltop.

"We analyzed Lob's recording of it, but according to Invira there is an added aspect based on the vibrations Lizzie was sending out mentally along with the sound waves from the music that small chorus produced. Unfortunately, it's unlikely we can reproduce the exact combined resonance at this point. We continue to examine the data. For now, however, this is the only solution we could come up with."

He invoked a box several inches taller and wider than the stone from his MDP and set it alongside the rock. He slid open a panel on the front.

"We'll need to roll the stone into the box and close it," he continued, "after which I will put it back into the MDP, which is the first test. Then we'll transport it up the hill. Once there, we'll test the viability of the gate. Hopefully, that test will be successful, and we can give the Alliance a heads-up of the next test. We will then open the box momentarily to see if the gate shuts down again, then close it again and test once more.

"Assuming we have the results we are hoping for, we will go to the next stage of our plan. Let us begin."

Tarafau reached down and carefully rolled the stone into the box, and Merv quickly shut the panel and touched his MDP to it, and the box looked as if it crumpled like a piece of paper and disappeared into the MDP.

"Well, that part worked," Merv said, pretending to wipe sweat from his brow. "We didn't know if the MDP would allow the box into the portal."

At the top of the hill, they followed Merv's instructions. The gate worked just fine with the box sitting right next to it. When they opened the panel, however, Lizzie felt her key go from warm to cold. They closed the panel and the key warmed again. Merv stepped through the gate and returned immediately.

"Okay, chaps, first stage completed." He reached onto his wrist. For the first time, Lizzie noticed that he actually had two MDPs on his wrist. She knew from her training that the MDPs were meant to be inobtrusive, but this was the first time she recognized that she hadn't noticed someone else's MDP.

Merv handed her the innocuous seeming bracelet. "Take it and put it on your opposite wrist, so you don't get it mixed up. You are now the guardian of the stone and the registered owner of this MDP. Should we put that title in capital letters? I dub thee, 'The Guardian of The Stone" He laughed at Lizzie's shocked disbelief as she slipped the MDP on her left wrist.

"Before you get a bit of a swelled head," he laughed, "you should know that one of the main reasons you got the job is because you are a complete unknown to pretty much everyone in the Alliance. An obscure gate guardian on an even more obscure planet in a non-member dimension is the last place an enemy might think of, should they get wind of an object that could shut down the entire gate system."

Lizzie laughed nervously. "In other words, this glorious appointment is mostly because I'm a complete nobody in the grand scheme of things. I can live with that. I'm in constant awe of the vastness of the multiverse and continue to feel like a speck on a speck within a speck most of the time."

For the first time, Ynni piped up. *"Lizzie is not nobody! Lizzie is very much somebody!"*

They all laughed heartily at Ynni's offended tone.

"So, Miss Somebody," Merv amended cheerfully, "Your task is to keep this stone from coming to the attention of anyone who might not have our best interests in mind. Basically, that pretty much means everyone, since even good people sometimes find themselves in difficult circumstances that might tempt them. Are we in agreement?"

"Indeed, I think that's a very good idea. There are too many repercussions that might stem from another complete shutdown of the gate system. I will do everything within my power to prevent that." Lizzie agreed wholeheartedly. "My oath on it."

Chapter 16: Farewells

(J)enny sat bolt upright in bed, sunlight streaming in through the gap in her bedroom curtains. She had been dreaming about what she had read earlier the evening before. Something about it was niggling her brain, but she couldn't quite put her finger on it.

That night as she had slept, she had done her usual check-in with the Alliance and had met Burt at their favorite mental place, the little pool on the Merced River. Then she had allowed herself to drift into real sleep.

She had been at the top of the hill overlooking a large fertile valley with a good-sized town and many farms. A voice in her head had continually repeated, "Remember, remember..."

She wasn't entirely sure what she should remember, although she knew that this passage in Lizzie's journal was definitely a bit odd.

A rock that could stop the gates from working? Really? She couldn't imagine how that was possible. Perhaps she was supposed to remember the power of Lizzie's talent with music, or the principles of resonance that had been explained by Lob, the gate tech?

At any rate, she dressed and prepared herself. She had only a couple of days to complete the journal, and she also knew she still had to get her walk in and do all the usual things recommended by the healers. The last thing she wanted was to flunk her checkup. She had an appointment to see them in two more days, and she was determined that her convalescence was complete.

She knew that every other member of the Alliance was anxiously engaged in creating multiple strategies to rescue the various dimensions that had already been invaded by the Insenium, and she wanted to do her part.

Since the entire Alliance gate system was her overarching responsibility, she was determined to perform her duty to the best of her ability, but she knew she *had a long way to go to live up to the legacy bequeathed to her by her aunt and Miriha, and she didn't want to let them down.*

These things went through her mind as she prepared for the day. Lizziebot had breakfast ready for her as she emerged from showering and dressing. She was so grateful for the little bot and still in awe of the technology that made it possible. There was no denying that Bob was a genius, and the 'boosts' the tech from the Alliance had given his bots were incredible.

She hardly even tasted her breakfast, getting out the journal and diving back into the increasingly spaced-out adventures. Now the time between entries was even longer, which made each one even more precious.)

"Again," Liliath sent. *"I think you are very close. Allow Ynni to melt into your thoughts. Let her guide you. I sense she may be the key."*

Once again Lizzie plunged deep into the chasm of her roiling thoughts. This was so much different from any of the exercises they had done previously. When she had been invited to spend some time with Liliath working on her mental abilities, she had been ecstatic; but due to Liliath working her tirelessly for the past week and giving her so many practice assignments, Lizzie had been able to rest only during mealtimes and at night.

She was now practicing how to use her abilities when she was neither relaxed nor potentially focused. Nearly every time she had used her abilities in the past, she had been calm and under no particular pressure.

Now, however, Liliath was doing everything she could to distract her, requiring her to delve into her own mind while experiencing pain, discomfort, and irritations of various kinds, like loud arrhythmic noises and bright flashing lights.

Liliath had been so impressed by the different ways Lizzie had been using her combination of music and mental sending that, after several years of analyzing her performance, she had finally decided it was time for her to take a hand in Lizzie's training. Even though Lizzie was "just" a gate guardian, with no other distinct responsibilities within the Alliance, Liliath believed that the time might come when those unusual abilities might be useful.

Besides, to Liliath's way of thinking, no talent should ever go unused or be undervalued.

As instructed, Lizzie reached out to Ynni, who was waiting patiently by her side. Liliath had told them not to touch each other during these exercises, as Ynni often would do when Lizzie was practicing, but to rely completely on their mental connection. Ynni was there, and a surge of joy answered Lizzie's tentative reach. Even considering the loud screeching Liliath had begun to distract her with, she felt the rock-solid stabilizing effect that Ynni always had on her. She immediately began to put herself mentally under that tree on the training grounds. In her mind, she was surrounded by her podmates and the music swelled up in her, drowning out the cacophony of Liliath's distractions.

Ynni's croon, both mental and audible, harmonized smoothly with Lizzie's extemporaneous mental tuning; and before she knew it, Liliath's irksome screeching had become a descant to her melody. For a few moments that could have been hours or days, they blended: linkling, human, and dragon, into a glorious uplifting crescendo.

"*Yes!*" Liliath exclaimed as the sound faded away. "*I knew you could do it. Open your eyes.*"

The potted plant that had been placed between them on the floor had gone from a dormant state to blooming profusely, the sweet scent of the blossoms permeating the air of the workout room.

"*This looks like what many of your culture would describe as 'magic.' What you are able to do with your mental music, even without an instrument, is beyond amazing. This ability appears to be very closely related to healing. I believe that you may be able to speed healing and encourage growth in any intelligent life, regardless of the level of intelligence. And you have just proved you can do it under stress. This could be a valuable asset over time.*"

"*Can I heal myself?*" Lizzie sent; the first question that occurred to her.

"*That is a question I cannot answer. Affecting the cells in your own body may be much more difficult, but this is something you can test at some point. In the meantime, I would like to suggest that you practice this at your home gate as you can. Continue the exercises I have given you, and be sure to allow Ynni more access to your mind as you do so. I firmly believe that, to a certain extent, it is a combination of the two minds that enables you to do the things you have done.*"

"*Yes, Liliath, I will. I have to tell you that, if I didn't know better, I would have thought this to be magic myself, or some well-done illusion.*"

"*Your time with Reloi was well-spent. He opened the door for you to believe more confidently in your talent. His influence has made a huge difference in how far you have gone with your mental abilities.*"

Lizzie simply nodded. Most of the time she could feel the warmth that coincided with any thoughts of Reloi, but she admitted that when she was tired, the sorrow snuck up on her like a snake hiding in tall grass. She gulped and straightened. Even after many years had passed, even after all the time she regularly spent with the refugees on Promisia, her heart still wilted a little when she thought of all the happy years they could have had together.

Nevertheless, she looked Liliath in the eye and simply sent, *"So true."*

She was kind of proud of herself that she was able to say that without a tear welling up.

When she arrived back at her house on Infinity Loop, she and Ynni immediately went into the back garden. The little yew tree was no longer small and insignificant looking, and the seedlings planted in and around the garden pool were lush and mature. The entire area made Lizzie feel a rush of soothing contentment and healing. She had taken to doing her mental exercises in the garden whenever she was home; and for the past few years, she had felt more and more linked to the little oasis she had created in what had just been a large lawn before she had been given the house.

Tidbit and Ynni immediately ensconced themselves by the tree, Ynni clambering happily up into the branches and Tidbit lying lazily at the edge of the pond where the koi swam languidly around to his fascination and delight.

Lizzie suspected that, for Tidbit, it was a form of meditation that allowed him to think deep thoughts. He had once told her that fish such as were found on Earth were not native to his planet, and the closest thing to butterflies were actually one of the five sentient races that lived there.

She reclined on one of the chaises on the patio and just took in the peace and quiet of the scene. The years since Gaston had retired and she had taken over the role of L.A. Gate Guardian had gone by so swiftly that it was hard for her to realize that she was now in her thirties and still felt like a novice. There was always something new to learn and a new experience waiting in the wings.

The current war with the Groga had mostly passed her by, as Earth was not a member planet, and it didn't seem to affect them in any way. She was happy to leave that to the Alliance and their many military experts. She was grateful that there had been no sign of these raiders in her own dimension, although increased security measures had been taken.

For her own part, she continued to be active in her local community, to stay more in touch with her family and to continue her studies in mental and physical training.

She did have some concern, however, for her mentor and friend, Gaston. The last she had seen him at Sanglarka, he had seemed frail and weary, if still his cheerful and kind self. She had continued his charitable project with the orphanage; and, although the administration had changed since the first time she had gone there with Gaston, they still asked after his health every time she visited.

The across-the-street neighbors' teenagers had since married and now only occasionally visited with grandchildren in tow, so the neighborhood was pretty quiet for the most part. Lacey was in the full flush of her career as an up-and-coming professor, and Melinda and Elias, still childless, were often away.

Elias's work now often took him out of town, and Melinda happily took leave from the library to travel with him. Lizzie had seldom seen two people more suited to one another. Elias was very sensible and down to earth, working as he did with the design and construction of mechanical things, and Melinda was in awe of his skills and would do nearly anything to make him happy.

Lizzie's own family had grown by several nieces and nephews, and the older of her nephews were preparing to attend college. She was relieved to see that none of them seemed to be enticed by the whole "flower children" fad that had swept the nation. She enjoyed the folk music fad that seemed to accompany it, but she shuddered to think of any of them joining a commune and walking around with vapid expressions.

She could relate to the desire of young people for a utopian society focused on peace, but she personally felt like they were going about it in the wrong way. She found herself grateful for the freedom to choose, and she wished that people with fervent beliefs and desires didn't seem to be equally focused on forcing others to agree with their outlook.

In the meantime, she was looking forward to some peace and quiet of her own, enjoying the environment she had created with the help of her neighbors.

It wasn't unusual, whenever her friends were home, for them to gather out in her yard for some lemonade or, in the mild California winter, some hot cocoa, just to take in the peace and quiet that exuded from the lovely garden they had created together. With her neighbors out of town, however, she could indulge herself in some focused work on the mental exercises Liliath had given her.

The next few weeks seemed to fly by as she tended her garden, continued her mental exercises, interacted with neighbors and family, and, in general, kept up the duties of a guardian on a non-member planet in the Alliance network: she made sure that no one ever took any notice of the little house on Infinity Loop or ever had any reason to think it was anything but just another house in a Los Angeles suburb.

Then one day, as she perused the notifications on her tablet, she jumped up and sent urgently to Tidbit and Ynni, who were both seated on the sunny window seat.

"We're leaving now! Let's go!"

They didn't question her. Ynni jumped to her shoulder and Tidbit followed her through the gateroom out the door to Miriha's gate. She practically ran through the grove and the town square and up the stairs with shoes in hand.

"I need to get to Sanglarka right now!" she sent to Miriha as she opened the door to the gate office. *"It's Gaston. They think he may be dying. I need to see him."*

Miriha asked no questions and made no comments but simply escorted them to the Sanglarka gate. Surprisingly, she followed them through. They hurried up to the lodge from the rose-covered archway and entered the lobby. In the first conversation area next to the fireplace were gathered all the Earth guardians, as well as Arvid and even Liliath, the draconic administrator of the Alliance agent training center.

"How? What?" Lizzie sputtered in mindspeech. *"Is that allowed?"*

"We can only do this kind of thing in one place on Earth. Sanglarka has some special provisions that don't allow anyone to 'notice' anything unusual

that happens here," Liliath replied, sounding almost amused. *"Trust me that it generally still has to be something of special import to prompt me to make this kind of visit to your planet, however. Gaston has been an exemplary agent and guardian and a good friend to me and all of us at the agent training center."*

Gaston sat beside the dragon in a special reclining chair of a peculiar design Lizzie had never seen before. His face was pale and drawn, and he looked older and frailer than Lizzie had ever seen him. He smiled wanly up at her.

"Glad to see you could make it, dear girl," he sent. Lizzie suspected that mindspeech was much easier than vocal speech for him, as his breathing seemed to be labored.

"How could I not come?" Lizzie replied in kind, trying to keep her mental tone light. She didn't want the twisting of her heart to show as she spoke to him. She could see that, although he appeared to be peaceful, it would not be good to upset him.

"I asked Grenheim to gather us a last time, as I expect I may not have much more time to say goodbye to the people I most care about. You have been the daughter I never expected to have, and I am so proud of what you are becoming. Liliath and the others report you are exceeding any of our expectations, and that is so gratifying to an old professor, like myself."

"So, I pass?" Lizzie bantered, still trying to keep it light.

"'A+,' my girl. You have always been one of my favorite students. Your endless curiosity and driving desire to learn new things has always been inspiring to me. Don't ever change, dear Lizzie. You have many new vistas to explore. I will be watching...."

He coughed weakly, but his birdlike gaze searched her face as if trying to memorize it.

Lizzie couldn't help herself. She knelt at his side and threw her arms around him, whispering into his ear, "I'll try to never do anything to disappoint you," she said.

He let out a deep sigh and, for a moment, Lizzie feared he had passed in her arms. She leaned back, looking into his eyes, still alight with that bright gleam that meant he was thinking deeply. Then, clasping Lizzie's hand gently, he looked around the faces of the people he cared about, all smiling tenderly back at him.

"It is good," he sent. *"I am content."* And as that last thought entered every heart in the room, his eyes glazed; and this time the deep sigh was final. His head sank onto his chest. Lizzie reached up and closed his bright eyes, and it now appeared as if he could have simply fallen asleep in his chair at the end of a long day.

"How old was he?" Lizzie sent to the group. *"I never did ask him his age."*

"He managed to make it to 89," Livia replied, *"and never wasted a single day of his life that I can think of. Even here, in his 'retirement,' he was earnestly engaged in everything we did. He left behind a legacy of so many students who benefited from his wisdom, both in his life at the university and within the Alliance. We will miss him. He has requested to be buried with his wife, whose body he had exhumed and transported to Sanglarka as soon as he first settled in here.*

Will you stay for the funeral? It will be simple, as he requested. We will inter him tomorrow."

Lizzie nodded numbly. She had known this was coming, but it still hit her harder than she had expected. Gaston had been about the same age as her parents, and she found herself wondering when she would be required to deal with their passing as well.

That evening, they had a supper together in the large dining hall, a smorgasbord prepared by Livia and Arvid.

The talk around the table that evening began as somewhat subdued, but over the course of the meal various individuals started sharing fond memories they had of Gaston and his brilliance and sense of humor. By the end of the evening, all seemed to be much more at peace. Lizzie certainly felt a little less at a loss, but her dreams that night were underscored with a sense of directionless wandering in unknown surroundings.

She awoke in her suite to the usual morning signal and immediately went to the workout room, where she was comforted to find the rest of the gate guardians and Liliath preparing to do their mental exercises. There was something soothing about the unity of their habits as they completed their meditations.

"We will skip the physical workout this morning. There is a light breakfast prepared, and then we will retreat to the cemetery behind the lodge for the

interment," Grenheim announced as they all began to stand from their seated places within the workout area.

"*There will be time for everyone to shower and prepare for the day before breakfast. We are not on a fixed schedule, but I do know that Liliath cannot stay too much longer today.*"

Lizzie wasn't sure what she expected, but breakfast was not the sad, introspective affair she might have anticipated. Most of the conversation, once again, was about happy memories of Gaston and his contributions to both the academic world and the Alliance, especially from the point of view of the gate guardians. His quirky teaching methods and his generosity were all mentioned at one point or another.

Evidently Gaston's passing had been well prepared for by those at Sanglarka. By the time they finished breakfast and trooped down to the little cemetery behind the lodge, Gaston's coffin had already been set up on a trestle table by the open grave.

"*It is always a sad thing to say goodbye to a beloved comrade and friend, however temporary,*" Liliath said, once they had all gathered encircling the grave and coffin. "*Nevertheless, it is also encouraging to know that his legacy was and is a positive one. He has influenced each of us in ways we may find nearly impossible to fully express. Thus, we can honestly say that our friend Gaston will never be very far from us. He lives on every time someone he has influenced does something to make the multiverse a better place.*"

There were solemn nods all around the circle. The four strongest men in the group at that point each grasped a handle on the coffin and gently laid it on some straps that had been placed on a framework atop the open grave. Grenheim then tapped a button that started a quiet electric motor which gently lowered the coffin to the bottom of the grave.

As if at some silent cue, each of the participants took a handful of earth from the pile of dirt next to it and dropped it into the hole. Lizzie followed suit, not even noticing the tears running down her cheeks as she walked away up the hill to the lodge.

Days later, as she returned to the home that had been one of the many gifts Gaston had given to her, she realized that she wasn't as sad as she had expected she might be. She knew Gaston would have wanted her to take what he had given her and turn it into something that would be worthy of his legacy. This, along with what she had received from Reloi, would propel her forward with a full heart and an ongoing determination to make a positive difference.

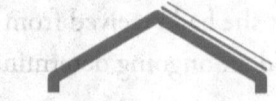

Chapter 17: Loose Ends

(*Jenny didn't even notice when Lizziebot came to clear away her breakfast. It was only when Chidwi tugged on one finger that she realized the dining room table had been cleared.*

"Jenny can come sit to read better?" Chidwi sent, looking up at Jenny from her place on the table next to her. Their habit was for Chidwi to sit on the table beside Jenny's plate setting, with her own breakfast of fruit and nuts, as sitting on the dining room chairs didn't allow her to eat comfortably.

Jenny chuckled. Between Lizziebot and Chidwi, she felt overly pampered, but she knew better than to complain about it. She knew it would hurt Chidwi's feelings, and Lizziebot had no feelings to hurt, so either way complaining did her no good.

She obediently went to sit in her reading chair, journal in hand, and settled herself to continue. Time was passing quickly for her on two planes—one in real time as her last week of recuperation was drawing to a close, and the other in relative time as she read the journal entries that continued to skip years at a time.

When she considered her aunt's long life, it was evident that if her journals had been a daily recitation of her life's details, it would have been more volumes than the box in her MDP could have adequately contained. This next entry, she realized with a shock, was several years later, and her anticipation built as she realized that her aunt was coming closer and closer to the time when her own story would be woven into the account.)

"What a mess!" Lizzie growled under her breath as another car slid between her and the car nearly directly in front of her, almost cutting her off on the crowded L.A. freeway. "That's it!" she shouted at no one in particular.

It was just her and Ynni in the car, and Ynni, perched on the seat near her, had started crooning worriedly.

"Sorry," she sent, repenting almost instantly of her outburst. *"But this is ridiculous."*

"Perhaps there are other ways to go where you wish? It seems that this is a distressing way to travel," Ynni sent in a worried tone.

Lizzie considered this. It wasn't like she couldn't afford alternative transportation. Taxis, trains, and airplanes were a lot less of a headache, as she didn't have to focus on driving and trying to keep herself from getting killed by some idiot who didn't seem to care about who they might hurt with their illogical driving decisions.

"You're right, Ynni. Let's go home."

And she turned around at the next exit and traveled home via side streets to avoid the freeway completely. It wasn't just a matter of temper. She was very aware of the changes in her local environment. The so-called "freeway" was often more crowded than regular city streets and had become increasingly dangerous for anyone who actually decided to observe silly things like speed limits and road safety.

From that day on, Lizzie became known in the neighborhood and to her relatives as a person who didn't drive but arrived at her destination in a taxi or other transportation. She knew it added to her reputation for quirkiness, but she didn't care. She was actually beginning to encourage the notion that she was a bit eccentric and somewhat "dotty," as she had overheard one of her teenage nephews comment about her at one of the family gatherings.

She continued to keep up the façade of being employed by a mysterious anonymous research facility and that her travels, although she sent them interesting photos from time to time from exotic locations, were strictly business related.

At some point, she knew, they would expect her to retire. She had long since decided that her cover story for "retirement" would shift to the idea that she had become so used to traveling and had made so many friends all over the world that it was a natural thing for her to continue to travel the world when she wasn't tending her magnificent garden or attending lectures by various scientists at universities around the world.

She also knew that she had been labeled as a "spinster," and that actually made her smile. She knew it wasn't an accurate label, but few knew anything about her time with Reloi, and none of her relatives on Earth would ever know she was anything but a confirmed bachelorette with no desire to marry.

She continued to visit Promisia and had long since extended her travels to other dimensions, as the Alliance had recognized her skill as an adept diplomat and ambassador. The assignments were generally brief, but as a result she had made many friends and contacts throughout the Alliance.

The Promisians were thriving, and they continued to take the stewardship of their planet very seriously. Ongoing exploration of their planet had shown them that they had vast resources and that the sheer size of their planet and arable land would allow them to grow a great civilization.

Lizzie often wondered if a time would come when future generations would forget their origins and the culture would potentially change. She hoped, if that ever happened, it would only be for the better, but her experience thus far with many different cultures had taught her that there were no guarantees; and all beings, when allowed to make their own choices, had both harmonies and dissonances in their history and potentially in their future.

Over the years, she watched various gate guardians come and go and eventually Grenheim retired, leaving Sanglarka to, it seemed to Lizzie, a woman rather too young to assume the responsibility of the main training gate on Earth.

However, she eventually had to admit that Lova was competent and, like Lizzie, had excelled in the training at the agent training center. Grenheim had stayed on for a time as a kind of safety net, but he soon realized that Lova was indeed fully capable of taking on full accountability for the task, especially with the support of the training team and the other gate guardians.

One day, as Lizzie was tidying up, she noticed a key ring lying far in a dusty corner at the bottom of the closet in the guest room. She realized with a shock that it was Gaston's old key ring. On it were keys to the house and to his office at the university, and two other keys she recognized at once: the keys to Professor Gaston's lab in Los Angeles where she had first gone through her "internship" with the professor while he was deciding whether or not to bring her on as an Alliance agent.

In all the time she had lived in the house on Infinity Loop, she had forgotten about that particular piece of property, which had been owned outright by Gaston and had actually been left to her in his will. There had been so much going on since then that she just hadn't thought about it.

An hour or so later, she thanked the cab driver and started by heading up the stairs to her old apartment above the lab office.

She was shocked to see how sterile and plain it seemed to her now. At the time she had not thought much about her surroundings within her living space, it seemed. There were no traces that she had ever lived there, except for the little wicker bed basket that Thumble had slept in. The rooms were dusty; and other than the furniture, there was nothing much in there.

Downstairs, when she entered the lab from the also-dusty office, she was prepared to find the same dismal dust on every surface. But to her utter surprise, once she entered the lab, there was no sign of dust. On the table in the area where she had done her first project for Gaston was a note.

> Lizzie: Please note there is a bit of alien tech within these walls you will want to dispose of before you decide to potentially sell this to someone. The sheet beneath this one has a map (a treasure map of sorts) that will point you to the various areas you never knew were available herein. Remember that you were not yet eligible for that level of confidentiality at that point.
>
> I suggest you dispose of this tech into your MDP until such time as you or someone else in the Alliance has need of it.

Taped to the map was a key that looked like the key you would use for a safe deposit box in a bank vault. Based on the map, she found in the film room a set of shelves. On one of the shelves was a metal box you might use to store sensitive documents. The key fit the keyhole nicely, and inside the box was a button. She felt a bit like Alice in Wonderland, fully expecting another note that would say, "Push me." She did push it, with a slight shiver at the thought, and the entire shelving unit swiveled out to reveal the door to a room Lizzie had not realized was there.

Inside the room was what Lizzie suspected had been Gaston's real office, whereas the one just inside the glass office door at the entrance was just for looks whenever he had something delivered or the facility was inspected for whatever reason.

It was similar in so many ways to the gate office that she almost expected to see another door leading into an impossible hallway. However, it was only a room—but filled to the brim with the kind of tech she expected to see at Alliance headquarters or Sanglarka.

Another note on the desk gave her instructions on how to disconnect the various pieces of equipment and finished out by instructing her to also go up the inner stairs of the main lab and disconnect all of the telescopic equipment that she knew was able to be raised mechanically above the rooftop at night. Evidently it had also been of alien construction and exceeded any of the simple telescopes one might expect to find in anything short of a major observatory or perhaps not even then.

The lack of dust within the laboratory was explained when she discovered the air filtration system. It was unexpectedly tiny, and Lizzie found herself wondering where all the dust went. She hoped she would learn more about all of the various interesting devices when she had time to decipher the ledger in one of the desk drawers in Gaston's cramped but legible handwriting. However, she discarded that idea when, to her delight, she found an Alliance tablet with another note attached to it:

> "Lizzie, I have created access for you on this tablet. Tell it, 'Professor, I have a question.' And it will open for you and reveal the secrets of the tech in this room. Please install this immediately into your MDP."

She happily did so, now impatient to get this task done so she could follow those instructions. She could see in her mind his mischievous grin as he wrote that particular pass key to the tablet.

Now, what to do with everything else? The other things in the "lab" ranged from aerodynamic experiments to things as simple as the necessary building supplies to make things like a loom for weaving simple things as he had given her as her first task during her apprenticeship. There were chemicals in one area, minerals and rocks in another, and various mechanical physics experiments featuring small ramps, immersion tanks, marbles, balls, and a number of toy cars, of all things.

From the ceiling hung skeletons of flying creatures Lizzie was pretty sure were not found on her planet. She decided that she would enlist the help of a few of her fellow gate guardians to disassemble most of the rest of the various displays within the large metal building and thoroughly clean the area before deciding what to do with the property.

She found her foot tapping with impatience as she waited for the cab to take her home. Although the MDP never felt heavier no matter how much anything weighed that was put into it, she found that all the new questions generated by her explorations into Gaston's lab were now weighing heavily on her mind.

Within a few days, Arvid, Yaw, and Lizzie returned to the lab in a rental truck. Lizzie tried really hard not to roll her eyes at the L.A. traffic, but they got there safely; and after Lizzie had checked out the deserted parking lot and the surrounding buildings to be sure there were no prying eyes, she backed the truck up to one of the receiving bays and rolled up the doors.

She had deliberately chosen to arrive very late at night so they could get the work done without any likelihood that they would be noticed by passersby. She didn't actually plan on putting all of the furniture and displays into the truck. Most of the usable things that weren't alien tech would go into her garage or potentially be donated to the university science department, but all of the sensitive equipment would be installed into the extra MDP she had received to store the stone in the lead box, including the alien skeletons. She had no idea if they would ever be of any worth to anyone but Gaston, but she decided that putting them into a dump someplace might cause some interesting conundrums for future archeologists.

The main furnishings of cabinets and drawers and worktables would be left in the building as part of the sale of the property.

They went to work with a will, and before the sun broke the horizon that morning, they had looked into every nook and cranny of every drawer and shelf of the entire facility, assuring themselves that they had not left a single clue that there had ever been any alien tech or of the real use of the lab left for anyone to find.

Lizzie's part had been to transfer each thing that may have been questionable to the MDP. Yaw and Arvid had seen to stacking the rest into the moving truck. When they finally returned to the house on Infinity Loop, all were tired, but Lizzie fixed them a quick breakfast and they unloaded into the garage, which was now overflowing with the detritus of the lab.

Yaw volunteered to take the truck back to the rental place, while Arvid helped Lizzie do some straightening and arranging of the piles of equipment and many boxes of supplies in the garage. It was still very early in the morning, and the neighborhood had not begun to stir when Yaw returned in a cab. After grateful hugs from Lizzie, he and Arvid headed for the gateroom to transfer from Miriha's gate to their different destinations.

Lizzie lost no time heading to shower, change clothes, and lie down for a quick nap. She knew she had a lot yet to do, but sleep was the first priority. This last chore on Gaston's behalf had closed a chapter in her life, and it felt good to know that none of the work he had done would be wasted. The college would be happy to get the various pieces of lab equipment and supplies, and she now had her own stash of alien equipment that she could make time to study and learn how to use.

After a refreshing nap of several hours, she realized that even once she cleared out the things she would donate to the university, she really didn't want her garage to end up being a workshop or a storage shed. As she thought about it, she realized she had a nice large empty space in her backyard about where the clothesline had been which might serve a new purpose.

She didn't hesitate. She knew that her friend Lacey had just returned from one of her visiting-professor lecturing trips, and she also was aware Lacey knew just about every person with any importance in the community.

She invited Lacey over for lunch in the garden area. After the usual niceties, catching up with Lacey's latest travels, she told Lacey about her storage dilemma.

"I don't really want your average storage shed," she explained to her friend. "I'd like a building that could be multipurpose, perhaps one side as a workshop and the other side for storing things that I don't need to clutter up my garage. I want it to look nice and not "sheddy," if you know what I mean."

"Ah, I get it." Lacey said, tapping the side of her head thoughtfully. "Functional, but not shabby and not run-of-the-mill. I think I know just the guy to make that happen. Do you want any security measures in place? This isn't the kind of neighborhood where that kind of thing is usually necessary; but just the same, I know your work is a bit hush-hush and you might want to take some extra precautions."

"That sounds about right." Lizzie said with a grin. She really appreciated having a friend who knew her so well. Lacey never got over-inquisitive about what Lizzie did for a living, and she never pressed her about it.

They made arrangements for Lizzie to meet with a contractor Lacey knew through the engineering department of the university, and Lizzie took her hand-drawn concept to the meeting. Since she kept it simple, the contractor agreed to a reasonable price, and Lizzie signed the contract and paid the down payment without a qualm.

Her stipend from the Alliance was more than generous, and she seldom had to pay out much more than for her groceries, taxi fares, or occasional clothing purchases, so her general expenditures were minimal, to say the least. Even her power and phone bills were covered by the dummy corporation the Alliance used to transact business in the United States.

However, the amount she had paid for the special outbuilding reminded her of another little item she had quite forgotten about in all the other things she had been dealing with over the past several years.

In her MDP were dozens of very full sandbags, filled to the brim with the gold sand of Linaria that had accumulated over the years. Every time she revisited that lovely planet to visit Bonwen and the Linarians, they gifted her with filled bags. The eccentricity of her delight at this amused them greatly. To them it was no more than useless dirt. You couldn't plant anything in it and they couldn't conceive of what she might possibly do with it. Nevertheless, it had almost become a standing joke for them to present her with several bags every time she departed from her visits.

Each of the filled bags weighed approximately 40 pounds; and considering that gold generally was priced by the ounce, she felt like there might well be a fairly large fortune residing in her MDP by now. Not exactly Fort Knox, but definitely worth doing something about.

The question was, "How do I turn all of this gold into money without calling attention to myself?"

As she contemplated this, she realized she needed to do a little research into how this happened on Earth and what she needed to do to disguise the fact that her seemingly unending resource wasn't of earthly origin.

Once again, Lizzie found herself spending a lot of time in one of her favorite places, her local library, specifically in the reference section. She researched mining, refining, and also the gold markets until she felt she had a fairly good handle on it, and then she decided on a little research trip.

Currently she knew that there were many active gold mines and refining facilities in Alaska, and she had always wanted to explore that area. It was springtime, so she wouldn't have to cope with the extremes of winter weather there.

She arranged for Ynni to spend some time with Tarafau and Amenia and her linkling tribe, as she had decided to take a trip to Alaska and follow up on her research. She had looked up everything she could find about mining regulations and operations and how gold was refined and distributed. She knew any further research would only be putting off the inevitable.

She informed her neighbors and family that she was taking a vacation to Alaska, without telling them the real nature of her trip. She packed a bag, considering that it would be suspicious if she traveled without any kind of luggage, and grabbed a taxi to the port of Long Beach.

She very much enjoyed taking the cruise ship from Long Beach to her port in Juneau. From there she had hired a guide to take her on an overland tour of the various mining facilities in the area.

Upon arrival, her guide immediately took her to an outfitter to be sure she had all the necessary equipment and supplies. He was short, for a man, and Lizzie could easily look directly into his blue eyes surrounded by bushy salt and pepper eyebrows. His unkempt greying hair was corralled by what could only be called a cowboy hat. Pretty much everything he wore except his boots and the red bandana around his neck was made of denim, including the worn and patched denim jacket.

"Well, missy, tell me again what you're lookin' for?" he asked as they went out to the barn where he stored his worn and obviously well-used jeep. He slung her backpack and his into the back seat and stepped up into the driver's side.

"I just would like to see any mines that are for sale in the area. It's a bit of a research project, but I am interested in buying a mine and hiring someone to look after it."

"Well, then, let's see...I know the Garner and Smith mine has been petering out. You say you don't care if it's productive or not?"

"Like I said, it's more for research than anything, although I'd like to hire someone who knows a bit about mining for various minerals to manage it."

"Gotcha," he said with a nod, and started the jeep and took off.

At first the roads were in pretty good repair, but as they left Juneau, there were a lot more bumps and potholes and fewer and fewer places to stop. They had brought tents as, he explained, "This time of year any inns or taverns will be pretty much full up. We might have to camp out in some of the places we'll be going."

As they traveled, she was able to get him talking about mining and some of his adventures as a gold panner and some of the mines he had worked in. His gruff exterior lightened up considerably as he mentally went back in time and could relive his adventures to a rapt audience.

Lizzie was in constant awe of the diversity of human experience. So many different paths any particular human could choose to take. She often wondered what caused any individual to make the career choices they selected. Handmade signs along the highway often said things like "We Dig Wells" or "Heavy Equipment Repair Shop" or "Homemade Preserves."

Then she considered that each of those people had made a choice of what course to pursue, and each of them made those choices for different reasons.

Her mind wandered to the places she had lived and visited and the multitude of professions that various people pursued. Librarians, welders, actors, seamstresses, store clerks, scientists, teachers, and plumbers, and the list went on in almost infinite directions, with an additional sub-stratum of offshoots for each profession.

She almost missed it when he finally paused his narrative to say, "Here we are. We'll stop here first."

They turned down a dirt road that entered into an area fenced off with barbed wire, similar to what you might find on any cattle ranch. The road continued past a lightly forested area until it opened out onto a flat cleared place in front of a row of fairly large log buildings with rough-hewn wood shingles, almost completely surrounded by several low hills.

He parked the jeep in front of the long-railed porch of the main building and they got out. He didn't knock but led her into the building, where a few men stood in front of a large stone fireplace looking over what appeared to be some sort of plans or maybe a map.

"Hey there, Arch! I just got your telegram this morning. This must be Lizzie?" asked the tallest of the group, dressed in what was almost a uniform, as Lizzie would soon discover; plaid flannel shirts, jeans, and well-worn boots.

Most of them wore rough beards of various trim lengths, and their hair was typically a bit on the shaggy side.

"Yep, Marshall. She wants a look at your operation and she's a-thinkin' about maybe buying a small mine herself. You know anyone who might be sellin'? I heard tell that Garner and Smith might be considerin' it."

Marshall cocked his head, thinking. "Hadn't heard that, but then I haven't left the site in a few months. I'll ask some of the crew and see what they might know about it."

He turned to Lizzie. "Well, ma'am, what do you want to see first?"

"I'd love a tour of your facility, not just the mines. I'm doing a bit of research on mine operations, since I will potentially be purchasing a mine at some point. I've read a lot, but I'm pretty sure that doesn't even begin to show the reality of your industry. I don't expect to learn everything about mining in a single trip. Of course, I will want to hire someone with experience to look out for my mine when I do buy one. So, let's take a look at what you've got, shall we?"

She caught a grin from one of the other men, and another one shook his head as if to say, "Greenhorn."

Lizzie didn't expect to get any real respect from any of these people, and she even hoped they would take for granted that she was just a gullible outsider. It would suit the purposes she would put the mine to if they didn't think that anything would ever come from it.

Marshall assigned the man who had grinned at her naivete to escort her around the premises and promised her a good supper when they finished at the mess hall, one of the other buildings in the small complex. His name was Gus.

The tour was actually quite well thought out. She discovered that Arch often brought tourists here to give them a taste of the mining occupation before he took them on gold-panning trips. In most cases, the tourists left the tour with some sparkly specks of gold in a small vial, and even occasionally a small gold nugget for their trouble, and an adventure they could brag about for years to come.

First, they toured the main building, the office where Marshall kept the records and charts related to the operations here. Maps on the walls depicted the various levels of the mines in the hills behind the mining camp. Various charts showed the different shifts of the miners and workmen in the business. The founding miners posed in faded sepia-toned photos framed on the walls, smiling and holding up bags which presumably contained ore dug from the mines on the property.

From there they did a brief inspection of the mess hall, which doubled as a recreation room for the workers on the property, and then took a quick peek into the bunkhouse with rows of beds, each with a footlocker, and a long row of hooks evidently for the coats and jackets of the miners.

Lizzie knew that her own operation was going to be much smaller, preferably, unless they actually struck gold, just a man and maybe his family to watch over the property and to give the illusion of it being a working, if not particularly prosperous, small mine.

They then entered the opening of one of several mine entrances, one at the base of each of four small hills just beyond the mining camp.

The mine was only dimly lit by what looked like old-fashioned gas lanterns. Gus picked up a large night watchman's flashlight at the entrance of the tunnel.

"Stay just behind me," he cautioned. "I'll stop at any point where there is something to see. Feel free to ask questions and I'll answer any that I can."

Lizzie saw almost immediately why he had given this instruction. There were a number of stretches between lanterns where it was pitch black other than the beam of light exposing the floor of the tunnel ahead of them. At one point, he had her stop and turned the flashlight off.

Lizzie was stunned. At no time in her life had she ever experienced such a complete and utter lack of light. She held her hand inches from her eyes and, try as she might, she couldn't catch the slightest glimpse of the hand she knew was so close to her eyes. When he turned the light back on after a few moments, it was almost painful to look at the beam of light that she had originally thought was weak and inadequate.

Lizzie was surprised to find there were places in the underground cave that were actually beautiful, something she had heard of but never seen in person. In one space, there was an actual cavern, not manmade, that contained colorful and glittering stalagmites and stalactites, like colossal abstract statues. She wondered, if it had been fully lit, if it would have been as spectacular as when the light of the flashlight had hit each in turn as they walked along the catwalk extended above the gap between one tunnel and the next.

By the time they returned to the surface, the sun was beginning to set. Lizzie felt more than a little wonder when she realized the lengths people would go to in order to mine precious minerals; and that those who did so spent much of their lives in nearly complete darkness.

The supper afterward was plain fare, a hearty stew with homemade biscuits, and it was delicious. The assembled workmen were a noisy and friendly lot, and they welcomed their visitors with the strong gripping handshakes you would expect from someone who did the heavy work required for digging minerals from the sides of rocky caves.

Evidently, they wouldn't be sleeping in their tents that evening, as there were a few basic guest rooms in the loft over the mess hall. Her room held just a cot, a washstand, and some hooks on the wall to hang clothing, along with a gas lantern on the nightstand next to the bed.

For Lizzie it was just fine. She even appreciated lying down on the thin lumpy mattress and snuggling deep under the heavy home-crafted quilt that had obviously seen better days. In no time, she drifted off to sleep. In her dreams, she was wandering down endless tunnels into wonderlands of colorful and somewhat haunting caverns.

They took off early the next morning after a great breakfast in the dining hall and rattled down the road to the next stop on their tour.

"I heard from a fellow at supper last night that there's a mine just a few miles down the road that might be what you're lookin' for," Arch drawled, as they exited the gate that led through the barbed wire fence.

"Sounds good. That was fun, and I think I have a better idea of what will work for my project. We may not need to go much farther, if I find what I'm looking for. It would be amazing if that were to happen, but I'm not going to hold my breath."

Like any good tour guide, Arch pointed out various landmarks, most of which were not buildings or monuments but rivers, mountains, and even certain trees. Lizzie listened as he droned on about the local history, and she could see that he knew his stuff. He had been recommended by the travel agency and evidently had a high reputation for doing enjoyable and informative tours of the area.

It was late afternoon, after a few stops for food and gas and personal hygiene, when they finally arrived at their intended destination. It wasn't quite as extensive an operation as the previous mining camp; it had only two buildings, and it appeared to have only one tunnel in the side of one of the hills that nearly surrounded the camp. The buildings were smaller and a bit more time and weather worn than the previous camp as well.

Arch had explained to her, when she noted the general shabbiness of the buildings at Marshall's operation, that miners knew that flashy buildings and nice furniture didn't add to their profits and the miners didn't care one way or the other, as long as they got fed, had a place to lay their heads at night, and, most importantly, got paid on time.

The old-timer who greeted them out in front of the small office was greying and stocky, with dark brown eyes framed by crinkles in the corner that showed he was inclined to mirth and optimism. His baggy jeans were patched and the cuffs were frayed, as were the cuffs of his well-worn flannel shirt. Lizzie liked him immediately.

His wide smile was enhanced by the two gold teeth in the front, obviously the only shiny thing about him. He extended a broad callused hand in greeting, shaking hers enthusiastically.

"Nice to meet ya, name's Gunther," he grinned, as she returned his grip firmly. "I hear you're thinkin' about getting' into the mining business?"

"Something like that. I hear you are thinking of retiring from it?" she returned with an answering grin.

"Something like that," he echoed and turning to Arch. "Where'd you find this one, Arch? This one has spunk!"

Arch laughed. "They don't grow on trees, m'boy," he answered, winking at Lizzie. "So, are the rumors true? You thinkin' of packin' it all in?"

"Yepper. I have a tidy sum stashed away and figured maybe to spend the time I've got left enjoyin' the fruits of my labor, ya know?"

"So let's show the lady around and see if this might be her cup of tea," Arch encouraged.

Gunther nodded and gestured for them to follow. As was obvious from the grounds of the camp, this was a much smaller operation. There was some mining equipment under a covered area with an arched roof and what looked like rolls of canvas that could be pulled down to form walls of a sort.

The main building was the inevitable office area, but it was only one room with a large stone fireplace.

The second building at one point must have been the bunkhouse separated into two rooms, one that doubled as a kitchen and dining area. There were a couple of outhouses just outside each of the buildings, with well-worn paths leading from a back door.

The office building had a small loft over the main office that was evidently Gunther's bedroom.

"I let all of the crew go a few months ago," Gunther said with a sigh. "We're still getting a bit out of the old girl, but the main veins were played out a long time ago. There are a few promising bits left, but I just don't have the energy or desire to dig any deeper. I say this just in case you're thinkin' you might get filthy rich with a little claim like this. Don't want to cheat nobody or give anyone any funny ideas about hittin' it big. It could still happen, but I'm doubtin' there's any new veins worth puttin' too much energy or money into."

"I appreciate your honesty, Gunther," Lizzie replied after that straightforward admission. "This is more in the nature of a research project, to be honest. I don't really need the money... just an appropriate location for my research. What other minerals might I find in these hills?"

"We've got plenty of zinc and some copper in the mines roundabout, and we occasionally find some raw jade, which is always just the icing on the cake. We've only opened up the one mine, but there might be more in the other hills. Most people are only interested in gold, however. We have all the equipment on the premises to mine pretty much any of it, depending on what you're interested in."

"If I were to get the property, I'd want someone to manage it, as I'll only be visiting from time to time. Do you know someone who is dependable and who would like a steady income? Bonuses, of course, for any big finds, you know."

"Ah, I see you get down to business pretty fast, lassie. Let's go into the nice warm office and see what we can figure out, shall we?"

Arch seemed a bit stunned by the rapidity with which they came to an agreement. Lizzie figured he probably thought he would have to take her to several mines. But Lizzie knew what she was about. The mine was only going to be a front to allow her to cash in all those sandbags full of gold at the assayer's office, a little at a time. Every time she returned to visit Bonwen they gave her more, after all.

Lizzie spent the rest of the week she had expected to use up touring mines acquainting herself with several potential candidates for the management of the mine. Based on Gunther's recommendation, she chose a man of middle years who assured her he would work the mine carefully. She had him sign a non-disclosure agreement as a matter of course. She did request that if he ever found any jade, she wanted to know about it, however, and that he would get a working wage, and bonuses for any significant finds. She hired Abram for the task, giving him authority to hire help as he needed it, and left for home with her bank account more than a little lighter, but with no regrets.

When she returned home, she arranged for an assayer and refiner, also requiring a non-disclosure agreement, to accept shipments from her via her 'office' in Juneau. He would transform the grains of gold into transactional gold bars and arranged for a broker to accept the gold and transfer funds from their sale into her account. Her office was mostly a shell with an answering service. They received shipments from her from time to time and then repackaged them to send to the assayer's office.

That being settled, she put it all out of her mind.

Chapter 18: The Carousel of Time

(J)enny now understood the origins of the incredible amount of funds available to her in the accounts willed to her by her aunt. She remembered the little note that had been appended to her instructions about the gold mines when she had first taken over ownership of Lizzie's estate. Obviously, money would never be an issue for her.

She had mostly ignored the occasional reports she got from the current managers of the mine but had noticed that they actually had opened up mines in the other hills on the claim and had found some rich veins of several kinds of ore. The mine was now profitable in its own right, the funds of which Lizzie had generously funneled back to the workers of the now-expanded operation.

The company office in Juneau still received the bags of gold as if they were being delivered from the mine in small enough quantities as to not call attention to the mine from potential gold-seekers. In this way it all simply looked like the mine was just one more normal mining operation. All this happened without Jenny having to think about it as the gold was shipped automatically from the private warehouse where it was stored.

The funny thing about that was that Jenny never really needed to worry about money anyway, since she also received a generous stipend from the Alliance. She now also understood the various charities that had received substantial ongoing yearly donations from the trust funds Lizzie had established for that purpose.

Lizzie had left such an amazing legacy behind her. Jenny determined that she would also follow up on these efforts to bless the world. She realized that since Lizzie couldn't affect Earth by sharing technological advances, she had put her energy and resources into making a difference for deserving people around her.

193

These philanthropic efforts extended to things like educational scholarships in the sciences, the orphanage that Gaston had supported, and a number of food banks and free clinics in various parts of the world. All donations were made anonymously, as Lizzie had not cared for any public acclaim, never wanting to draw attention to herself.

Probably some of her biggest donations had been for grants to companies and research facilities dedicated to alternate power and aquaponic and hydroponic projects. It was her way of contributing to what would head scientific exploration into the things that might make the most positive impact on her home planet without compromising her oaths to the Alliance.

There was an even greater time gap after the last entry she had read, and Jenny had to assume that things had been fairly routine for Lizzie for a long time.

Jenny read on.)

Lizzie sighed sadly as she strolled under the bougainvillea arch and entered her front yard. She hardly noticed the rock garden as she passed through to the door. She had, over time, in addition to her stones from Promisia, collected stones from many places around the Earth and from various places in the Dimensional Alliance planets she had visited over the years.

Her mind continued to dwell on her recent trip to San Diego to attend her mother's funeral. This was the second funeral she had attended this year. Her dad had passed six months before. Her mother never quite got over the loss, and it was almost as if she had given up when she had lost her lifetime companion. Her siblings and nieces and nephews had been there, some with their own children.

Since she and her brothers had been spaced years apart, their children had also been of a wide range of years from toddler to young adult. They had, of course, had opportunities to catch up on what was going on with each other, Lizzie carefully keeping up the fiction of her top-secret scientific research. Her brother George had gone into business for a large marketing firm, and her younger brother, Ed, into the military.

She wasn't quite so disconnected from her family as she once had been, but she really couldn't quite keep up with everything that was going on with them and their children.

It was comforting, therefore, to open the red door that led into the sunny living room of her little house. She knew Tidbit would show up the next day with Ynni, so for now the house seemed emptier than usual.

She headed, therefore, out to the backyard. There before her was the yew tree, now large and spreading its branches protectively over the koi pond, where the undulating fish sparkled in the sunlight under ripples caused by the water streaming from the little waterfall.

She settled onto one of the wrought-iron chairs next to the little glass and wrought-iron table that sat just at the edge of the shade of the tree.

"I'm home," she sent to Windsong.

"We missed you. Why so sad?" Windsong sent gently in return.

Lizzie wasn't sure she could explain but she sent out a jumble of her feelings and memories of the recent event. She knew the tree would have a hard time with some of the concepts, but words would have never expressed the deep reasons for her melancholy.

She had learned that her mental sendings didn't need to contain exact words, but strong feelings could also be sent, requiring no specifics. This still amazed her. Over time, her ability to communicate with the plants and animals around her had extended significantly, and she actually didn't think much about it anymore.

She didn't have a lot of time to ponder any of this, however, as a knock came at the door. Sighing again, regretfully she went to answer the door. It was Lacey. Like Lizzie, Lacey was no longer the young adult they had both been when they had first met, both just starting out their first adventures into their future occupations.

Was that a touch of grey at Lacey's temples? Surely not.

"Hey, neighbor, thought you might want a little tea and sympathy," Lacey said, by way of greeting, looking earnestly into Lizzie's face.

"How about lemonade instead?" Lizzie rejoined wryly. "I'm not really into tea, so much."

Lacey chuckled and nodded. "Haven't lost your sense of humor, at least. Lemonade will be just fine."

They went into the little kitchen and Lizzie rummaged around for the lemons while Lacey, who was very familiar with Lizzie's kitchen by now, got out the lemon squeezer, the sugar, and the pitcher.

In next to no time, they were seated out under the shade of the yew tree, two tall glasses of iced lemonade before them.

Lizzie inquired about what had gone on in the neighborhood over the week she had been gone. Lacey happily launched into the antics of a couple of teens down the street who had been washing cars to raise funds for summer camp and then told Lizzie about a new Chinese restaurant that had just opened a few blocks outside the neighborhood.

"The food is pretty good, and they have a delivery service, right to your door," she remarked. "I'd say it's at least as good as Lee's, and we don't have to fetch it ourselves. Their eggrolls are bigger, and I think I really like their wonton more."

"Oh, and you should know that the house across the street from you is for sale again. I keep wondering if there is something wrong with that house. I don't know that anyone has stayed there longer than five or six years since I've lived here."

Lizzie shrugged. "I don't know that there's anything wrong with the house. But I've noticed our neighborhood is awfully quiet compared to other suburbs. Maybe there wasn't enough excitement for them. With few exceptions, most of our neighbors stay to themselves a lot; not exactly snobby, but just not interested in getting very engaged with their neighbors."

"We do seem to have a lot of neighbors who travel a lot or at least aren't home all that much," Lacey agreed. "That's okay with me. It isn't like I'm going to be spending that much time at home over the next little bit. I've been assigned as a traveling lecturer representing the university on the topic of ethics. I'm still not sure why they chose me, but I think I'm going to enjoy it."

"Congratulations!" Lizzie said admiringly to her friend. "I think it's great that they've honored you that way. I'm sure you'll do well with it." She thought she knew how her friend felt. She herself was still a bit in awe of the fact that she had been chosen for her role as a gate guardian and all it implied.

"Sorry to hear about your mom, so soon after losing your dad," Lacey said, reaching out a hand to grasp Lizzie's. "I know it must be hard to deal with. If you ever need to talk...."

"Thank you, Lacey. I think I'll be okay. They both had a good run. And mom is with dad again, so I know they're both happy. I'm just glad I was able to reconnect with my family after I got the house here. We had drifted apart and now, even though I don't see them as often as I'd like, I'm at least in touch with my brothers and their kids. It took me awhile to realize how important my family is to me, though."

They passed the morning just chatting about various unimportant things, and Lacey finally excused herself to pack for her trip the following day. "It seems like you and I are constantly saying 'Welcome back' and 'Have a good trip,'" Lacey said with a chuckle as Lizzie showed her to the door.

Lizzie knew she still had things to do, so she sat down in her reading chair in the living room, took out her tablet and began to scan through her messages and the random bits of news regarding the Alliance. After having put down the Groga raids, the entire Groga population had mysteriously disappeared from their home planet, something that worried the Alliance council.

She had kept track of the situation, but, as an Earth guardian, she had no reason to be involved in any of it. Earth was not a member dimension after all, and it didn't affect anyone on her planet. Each agent and guardian within the Alliance structure had specific responsibilities and, although they were kept abreast of whatever was happening across the dimensions, she was content that this wasn't anything she had to deal with.

By this time in her guardianship, Lizzie had watched many chief councilors come and go, as those responsibilities rotated on a five-year (five Alliance years) basis. Although she knew the names of the current councilors, she had never met any of them in person at this point.

She continued to have yearly conferences with the Earth Alliance guardian council at Sanglarka, something she looked forward to, but even then, some of the original guardians she had known in the beginning of her guardianship had either retired or passed away. Probably the most wrenching of those was the passing of Yaw, the big Ghanaian, who had introduced her to the mbira. She would forever be indebted to him for opening up her recognition of the music that had since surrounded her everywhere she went.

The management of Sanglarka had been passed to the young woman named Lova. Grenheim was getting on in years; and, although he seemed as hardy and active as ever, he had admitted at their last gathering that he was definitely looking forward to complete retirement after having mentored Lova during her first years in his former position.

Livia, her hair now a bit wispy and bright silver, had confided to her that she was looking forward to doing some traveling with her husband to someplace warm and tropical that didn't involve anything to do with the Alliance or snow. "We need some 'us' time," she had said with a twinkle in her periwinkle blue eyes. "Not unreasonable, I would think."

Lizzie had to agree that it would be nice for them to not have to worry about all the rest of the guardians and any new agents that needed training. They had surely earned that time together. However, it definitely meant that once again, much was changing in her life.

Both Elias and Melinda had retired, he from the city planning council and she from the local library. Still childless, they now had time and funds to devote to travel and exploring, allowing Melinda to pursue her art in exotic locations, so Lizzie didn't see much of them these days.

Lacey had been right. Most of the people in her neighborhood seemed to be out and about most of the time. The fact that Lizzie had been able to make fast friends of her neighbors on either side of her house seemed to be an exception to the rule.

In the meantime, Lizzie had continued to work out daily with Tarafau and was happy to go jogging with Lacey whenever their schedules allowed it. Lizzie continued to commune with her garden and to play the mbira and occasionally, when she was alone, the strange alien musical instrument she had received from the Daringi council on Tarafau's planet.

She had been hesitant about that in the beginning, but she realized that anyone who heard her little concerts on the marvelous instrument that allowed a person to play an entire orchestra at once would assume she had the radio on.

It almost came as a shock to see strands of grey in her own hair. Her parents had both gone grey early on, and she wasn't sure she liked it. But she also wasn't going to go to the trouble to dye it to hold onto a more youthful look. If anything, she felt it gave her a certain status.

Not to say she was any less active in her pursuits in the Alliance. She still visited Promisia several times a year, and she couldn't stay away from Fanilia either. Both of these locations had dear and permanent places in her heart.

The Promisians had expanded their original colony slowly and carefully as they explored the various regions surrounding the large valley where they had initially settled. They had reestablished their school system, and they were still extremely focused on preserving the environment of their new planet to the point that Lizzie was amazed at how little impact the colony had on their surroundings. The concept of "stewardship" was foundational to their culture.

Visiting the Fanilians was always a delight. Lizzie was bemused at the role she had assumed as a messenger between Windsong and Bonwen, each always giving her greetings, ideas, and thoughts to share across the dimensions to the other. Every time she, Ynni, and Tarafau stayed there any length of time, there were parties and events they were asked to preside over like some kind of visiting dignitaries.

She continued to attend weddings and funerals within both her Sanglarka family and her own family, taking comfort and solace in the connections that bound them together.

One particular event that stood out in her mind had been the wedding of her nephew Ed. The curvy and vivacious brunette he married was bright and interesting to talk to. Donna was a bit of a homebody, looking forward to her role as homemaker, but she was also intensely inquisitive and well-educated. Lizzie knew she would learn to love this "niece-in-law" and looked forward to getting to know her better.

She always visited San Diego via the train, taking a cab from the station. She could have done it by plane, as the L.A. airport was convenient to her, but she enjoyed the calming nature of train travel and the scheduling of her visits was structured enough that she didn't have to make excuses for not staying "just a few more days?" As much as she had begun to love her family, these visits were still a little overwhelming for her after only a day or so.

She still had occasional assignments in the way of what would normally be considered "agent" duties, but that was always a welcome break in her routine. Her life had come full circle, it seemed, and she began to wonder if her adventures were indeed over and done with.

Chapter 19: And Then This Happened

(Jenny noticed that things had changed radically since the beginning of Lizzie's journey along the path of her involvement with the Alliance. Although she continued to do the duties she had been assigned and continued to hone her skills and keep herself physically fit, Lizzie had settled into a pattern that was comfortable, if not as exciting as it had been in the beginning.

Jenny found herself wondering if this would ever be the case for her. For now, it was a little more exciting than she would have hoped for, if she was completely honest with herself. As she continued to read she had a feeling that the last chapters of Lizzie's journals would reveal some things that she had often wondered about and that might concern her very personally.)

When the moving van and a little blue sedan parked in the driveway across the street, Lizzie peered out the front window to see who it was who had finally bought the place that had been occupied by so many families over the years.

There were three of them, a somewhat short, but stocky man, his petite blonde willowy wife, and a toddler who looked a lot like his dad in miniature. The wife immediately went inside to oversee the placement of their belongings, the little guy holding her hand as they crossed the threshold of their new home.

The man stood outside talking to the movers, gesturing, nodding, and pointing, then went inside to help his wife.

Lizzie wondered at this. There hadn't been any small children in the neighborhood in quite a while, and it was fairly obvious that this couple was young. The neighborhood was a bit on the pricey side as real estate went these days, so she could deduce that the young man already followed a fairly lucrative career.

She had just decided to go by and introduce herself after lunch and was in the process of putting together her usual salad and sandwich, when there came a knock at the door.

It was the young man, his little son hoisted on one hip with both hands around his dad's neck. "I was wondering, or at least my wife wants to know: when does the garbage truck come by? The movers didn't know, and my wife says we're going to either have a lot to put curbside or we're going to have to know where the local dump is. Unpacking, you know. I'm Bob Reid, by the way."

"Lizzie, erm, Lizzie Japhet. Nice to meet you, Bob. And who is this little guy?"

"This is Cleon Christopher Reid. He vacillates between Chris and Cleo," he responded with a grin under his brushy brown mustache.

"Well, the garbage truck comes around on Wednesday. Have your garbage cans and any boxes out on the curb before 9 a.m. and you'll be fine."

"Excellent. We're looking forward to getting to know our neighbors, and I had noticed that you were home. Thanks for the info." And he turned to leave, but Lizzie, with a sudden impulse, touched his arm and he turned.

"I know moving and unpacking can be pretty exhausting. I'll bet your wife has enough to do without fixing supper too. Why don't you all come over to my house tonight? I'll order in Chinese, and we can get to know one another better. The local Chinese restaurant delivers, and their egg rolls are excellent."

Bob's bushy eyebrows shot up in surprise, a delighted grin on his face. "Why, that's very nice of you. I'm sure it will be a relief to Carol, and once we're settled in we can return the favor. My wife makes one of the best tuna casseroles on the planet."

That evening the three of them showed up as soon as the delivery van from the restaurant pulled out of the driveway. Carol made a great deal over Lizzie's house and oohed and aahed over the garden with its happy little pond full of fish. Lizzie could tell they were going to fit right into the neighborhood, especially with Elias, Melinda, and Lacey.

Lizzie was fascinated to discover that Bob was a scientist and inventor, as well as a lecturer at the university on the topic of engineering and physics. He seemed somewhat young to be so advanced, but he revealed that he had gotten his PhD when most other students were still struggling to get their master's degree. He was very matter of fact about it, not bragging or boasting, just stating it as a simple fact.

Carol was a cheerful, bright young woman who had chosen the role of homemaker, even though her own degree qualified her for employment in the field of teaching. She wasn't at all apologetic about it. "I want to give Christopher the best childhood he can possibly have. Everything I've learned in school has prepared me very well to raise an intelligent little boy to become a good man."

And Christopher was indeed very smart. He had many questions about the garden and various things in her house, even though he was barely four years old. Lizzie thought she could understand how challenging it must have been for her own mother to bring up a child who was constantly asking questions. He was especially fascinated by the koi in the pond, and over the years he would gladly spend hours sitting next to Tidbit by the pond, watching the fish as Lizzie and her parents chatted about various things.

He loved helping her harvest the large, sweet berries as the white strawberry blooms turned almost magically into the red, beautiful fruit. There was always enough to share, and much of what he picked went directly into his mouth instead of being carried home for the family to share.

Within a few months of moving in, Lizzie noticed that the garage next to Bob's house was being demolished.

"What's up?" she asked, crossing the street to where Bob stood supervising the work.

"We've decided that a lot of my work can be done from home," he said. "I'm going to build a large workshop space for my 'tinkering.' I have some ideas that I think might do well in the marketplace, and I need to be able to work on it outside of the lab that employs me."

"Interesting. What kind of things?"

"Ah, that would be telling," he said with a mischievous twinkle in his blue eyes. "Really, I'm not sure that any of it will be worth much, but I need some private space to do it. My architect says he can make the workshop blend in nicely with the neighborhood, and I just got a big bonus for my work on a private government contract. I thought this would be the best way to invest the money."

That made sense to Lizzie, but it also piqued her curiosity, something she still hadn't completely conquered. As she watched the well-built workshop go up over the following months, she found herself imagining what kind of things he might be working on, and it nagged at her.

She controlled herself, however, and respected his privacy, as much as it pained her to do so.

Once again, her life settled into a kind of odd routine, including her continued visits to Promisia and Fanilia and her various community projects. She found that Bob and his wife were very willing to participate in many of these projects, especially the orphanage. She continued to build the façade that said she was an active professional engaged in private work for unnamed companies across the world. And, all in all, she found that her life, if not boring, was at least somewhat predictable.

That was until, at one of her visits to Sanglarka, she was given an assignment. It wasn't really new. It had been implied in her early training as a gate guardian that one of her responsibilities was to choose a successor, in case something was to happen to her or for when she was ready to retire.

She knew she was getting older; the grey had nearly completely taken over her short-cropped hair. She was still healthy and active, but it took her up short when Miriha had decided to attend the Earth guardian retreat and had taken her aside.

"It's time for you to begin the process of finding your replacement. I know you have no intention of retiring at any time soon, but the lifespan of mortals on your planet is relatively short compared to many of us; and even then, life is unpredictable. Have you given this any thought at all?"

Lizzie shook her head, somewhat shocked at this thought. *"I guess I knew in the back of my mind that this was one of my duties, but I had honestly forgotten about it. How do you suggest I go about it? I can't say that I have anything like a potential candidate in mind at the moment."*

"Begin to consider the people you know who are of a likely age and disposition to want to learn new things and explore new places and possibilities, with an open mind and no fear of hard work.

"Remember yourself when Gaston sought you out. What were you like back then? What were the qualities that prompted Gaston to test you for the position? Think back. It will come to you."

"If you say so, Miriha." Lizzie agreed, rather reluctantly. She still didn't get what had made Gaston choose her when there were so many potential candidates within the college community where he knew so many young, promising, and curious young people.

"In the meantime, we have an assignment for you. We would like you and Tarafau to do some research 'in the field' so to speak. There are rumors that there may be a previously unknown gateway in an area in Africa that we need to find, if it is there. Because of its location, with very little population, we will be giving Tarafau, once you get where you're going, special permission to resume his regular form during this mission.

"Will you be willing to accept this commission? Your experience on Fanilia makes you the best qualified to take this on."

Lizzie was stunned. Two subsequent bombshells in only a few minutes, but she didn't hesitate to nod her head.

"When do we leave?" was all she said in reply.

Chapter 20: Foundations and Beginnings

(*Jenny realized that she was about to explore the years in her early childhood, when, to her, Aunt Lizzie was more of a family legend than anything else. By this time, she would have probably been in junior high school. She knew she couldn't even afford to pause for a moment and told Chidwi she would be skipping her walk for now.*

Chidwi hadn't been adamant about it. Jenny got the feeling that the little linkling was as engaged as she was, sensing her excitement and anticipation. She was grateful for the quiet uninterrupted time to race towards the finish of the journals, so she turned the page.)

Lizzie wiped her face again. It was hot, humid, and even in the shade of the jungle foliage she got little relief from the heat.

They had been at this for weeks, combing through the area carefully, Lizzie almost constantly touching her key, hoping for that slight warming that would indicate the nearness of an unconnected gateway. Because of the remoteness of this area of equatorial Africa, there were no known human habitations anywhere near the part of the jungle they had been searching through, so Tarafau had been given special permission to come in his Daringi form.

It had been necessary to give her a companion in this venture who would be equipped to protect her and support her in her search. Ynni, however, would be spending this time with her tribe in Amenia's beautiful grove behind her garden.

On Tarafau's planet there had been similar jungle areas and, although the animals native to the African jungle were different, she felt confident that if anyone would be capable to get her safely through this assignment, it would be Tarafau.

Before she had left her house, she made arrangements with her neighbors regarding her garden and had taken the first steps in her search for potential candidates for an heir to her guardianship.

She had consulted with Lacey and established several scholarships for promising youth who were interested in the sciences, had inquiring minds, and had proven themselves to be reliable and diligent in their studies. It had occurred to her that, since Gaston had found her via the university, this might be a good place to start.

She had adequate funds to create full-ride scholarships for multiple students over the coming years, and she realized this was one way she could also encourage advancements in the sciences and technology without compromising the promises she had made to the Alliance.

But for now, like a good stew, her project would have to simmer over time until it became what she had imagined when she put the ingredients together.

"Do we have any idea how much more space we need to cover?" she asked Tarafau a bit plaintively. "If nothing else, I think we need to take a break. The Alliance doesn't expect us to find it on any particular timetable, and I need to find a place to sit."

Tarafau, although he almost always addressed her in mindspeech, spoke vocally, having spent so many years on Earth with Gaston that his accent was only slightly alien. "Our instructions told us that the potential gate was a possibility, not a fact. If they knew it was here for certain, they would have known exactly where it was. All we know is that some local legends and tales from explorers tell of events that may or may not be a result of gate activity."

Lizzie nodded impatiently. "I know, but how much farther do we need to go? I'm getting nothing from the key. Have you gotten any sign from the scanning device?"

Tarafau held the tiny device in his huge hand, making it look even less impressive than when Lizzie held it. It was about the size of a business card and nearly as thin. The readout consisted of numbers which indicated certain levels of resonance. If the numbers went up to a particular point, they would have potentially stumbled onto a gate.

He shook his head, the little shafts of light through the trees glinting brightly off his shiny, bald head. Instead of wearing his usual bright robes, he wore what might have been considered the standard safari-type outfit of a khaki material and sturdy boots.

The only thing that was at all alien about him was the points hanging down from his earlobes, the opposite of the points she always pictured as elvish. They had somewhat disguised this with earrings similar to the type the local native males wore. At first glance, he would have appeared to be a native guide.

From off to one side they heard a gasp and a rustle. Tarafau didn't hesitate; putting a finger to his mouth and gesturing for Lizzie to stay put, he went towards the sound and returned firmly grasping by one arm a young man, perhaps in his early twenties.

The man appeared to struggle slightly at being propelled up to Lizzie, a look of mixed defiance and curiosity in his blue eyes. His brown hair was tousled, and he was also dressed in standard safari gear.

"Lemme go!" he panted. "I'm not doing anything! I'm not going to hurt anyone! I was just taking a pee in the greenery! Lemme go!"

"I'll let you go," Tarafau said, looking down at the young man seriously, "but you need to stay put. We've got some questions for you."

With a sullen glance up at the huge black man and a sideways glance at Lizzie, who nodded encouragingly to him, he said, "Okay. I'll listen. I don't have anything to hide."

Tarafau smiled his catlike grin, and the young man's face went pale. He had noticed the fangs, obviously, and now Lizzie knew steps would have to be taken. This was exactly the reason that Tarafau had been restricted to his Tidbit form while he was on Earth, except at protected places like Sanglarka and very occasionally at the Swiss gate.

Lizzie shook her head. "Sorry about this, but we were under the impression that there were no humans living in this area."

The young man's eyebrows shot up at the use of the word "human."

"Um... well, no, you're right. There are no native settlements of any kind in the area, but I'm with my professor on an archeological dig about a mile from here. I was taking a break. I'll go now and leave you to... um... whatever you were doing, okay?"

"I'm Lizzie Japhet, and we're on a similar assignment," she said, hoping to ease the young man's obvious discomfort. "What exactly is your professor looking for?" It occurred to Lizzie that perhaps he might be exploring some local legend that might correspond to what she was looking for.

"Burt... I'm Burt Scout. And the professor heard something about an ancient burial ground that might provide a missing link... you know... origins kind of stuff."

"I see," she said, thinking hard. She noticed that Burt kept glancing nervously up at Tarafau and realized that this could be a very big problem.

"Are you an archeology student, then?" she continued conversationally, grateful for her training in keeping a straight face in a difficult situation.

"Nope, my major is in astronomy and... well, sciencey stuff," he said awkwardly. "Just taking a break. I needed something besides sitting through lectures on stuff I already know and doing the busywork necessary to get the letters after my name. To be honest, sometimes I think I could do a better job teaching the classes myself even though I should still be in high school, truth be told."

His eyes widened as he realized he might have said too much. "Not that it isn't worth it," he continued, now looking embarrassed. "I think that sounded like I'm a little full of myself, but it's the truth." And he looked down for a moment with an uncomfortable pause.

"I get that," Lizzie assured him. "I often felt the same way. What if I was to tell you there might be a better way to get your education and do some real hands-on work in the sciences?" A plan was forming in her mind, and she knew she might get in trouble in many ways for it, but she honestly couldn't think of any other way to fix this.

"Tarafau, I think we may be done here, at least for now. We should report immediately, and I think Burt, here, might like to meet our associates...," she trailed off with a meaningful look and sent in mindspeech, *"We'd better take him to the council. They'll know what to do about this."*

Tarafau simply nodded and put a hand on Burt's and Lizzie's shoulders, and they faded from sight, arriving directly into the reception area of the Alliance headquarters council room in the blink of an eye.

"Holy Roddenberry! What was that?" Burt exclaimed, looking up at Tarafau, his eyes almost popping out of his head.

"We just translocated from Earth to a different dimension. You have seen and heard some things you shouldn't have, and we need to know what to do with you," Lizzie told him matter-of-factly.

"Do with me? Seriously? Let me go back! Is this just a bad dream?" He looked up into Tarafau's grinning face, noting again the catlike fangs.

Burt almost wilted. "Not like I can do anything about it, I guess. But I don't think you folks play fair at all. Let's go," he said, looking completely resigned to a potentially terrible fate.

"We need to see the council on a matter of importance," Lizzie sent to the nearly humanoid receptionist. Burt, following her glance, saw the obviously alien face, blanched again, and shook his head.

"They say you may come in," the receptionist sent after mentally consulting with the councilors.

They entered the huge doors leading into the private council chambers. The current set of councilors were an elflike female named Milek, a humanoid female with pale yellow skin named Flah, and a dwarf-like man named Ingot.

"Welcome," sent Milek calmly. *"The receptionist said this was somewhat urgent?"*

Lizzie matter-of-factly sent a short description of their encounter in the jungle with young Burt Scout, who stood stiffly in the apparent silence, his mouth agape in growing astonishment and concern.

"I see," Milek sent, considering. *"I think it will be important for the young man to hear this conversation and to be able to respond intelligently. It is obvious that he is distressed and confused by the circumstances."*

She descended from the dais and walked directly to Burt, holding up a hand to indicate her peaceful intentions and placed a finger on Burt's forehead, looking gently into his eyes.

Burt shuddered slightly. *"You should be able to hear me now,"* Milek sent, the kindness and gentleness of her intentions sent along with the simple statement.

"Simply think what you wish to say, and we will all hear you," she added in the same soothing manner.

Once again Burt's eyes widened, but this time with amazement. *"Can you hear me now?"* he ventured.

"We can hear you," they all sent in chorus.

"Wow! This is pretty cool. Does this mean you aren't going to eat me or send me to some slave colony to labor in the mines on some distant planet?" he sent back, a hint of hopefulness along with the bit of glibness in his thought.

"We haven't eaten a guest in recent memory, and I don't think we have any mines that need tending at the moment. Actually, we were hoping you might be able to help us with a quandary," Milek sent again, a smile on her face.

Burt relaxed noticeably. *"I'm listening,"* was all he said.

"We are official representatives of the Dimensional Alliance. We represent universes throughout the extent of space as you understand it."

"Wait," Burt interrupted. *"Universes... with an 's'?".*

Melek smiled and Flah chuckled, her hand over her mouth. *"Yes, Burt Scout. We know Earth has learned much about the stars and galaxies that surround them, but there is so much more. Does that interest you?"*

"Yes! Are you serious? Is it my birthday?"

Fortunately, mindspeech translated his intention to the councilors, who continued to smile.

"I take it then, that we have caught your interest. What if we were to offer you the opportunity to be, after some significant training, a representative of Earth for the Alliance; a kind of ambassador, with the benefit to get the opportunity to travel the multiverse in ways that you cannot yet conceive and learn science beyond the realms of Earthly understanding?"

Burt's jaw dropped and he intently looked into the eyes of each of the councilors before him. They had all descended from the dais, standing within arm's reach of the young man. *"You're serious,"* he declared in absolute awe. *"You're really serious. I can feel it. What do I have to do?"*

Lizzie almost didn't restrain herself from rolling her eyes. He reminded her of herself so many years ago in the banquet room of the Swiss observatory containing the gate that would lead her to her new life.

"First off, you need to understand what you are committing to. Earth is not a member of the Alliance, but there are gateways there that must be guarded from the knowledge of the Earthlings until such a time as they are fully ready for membership. You will find out all about gateways very soon, but let's just say they are tools that allow people to transfer from one universe or dimension to another in moments.

"Because these gateways must be kept secret, for reasons you will soon be able to understand, we must have a complete and heartfelt commitment from every new agent of the Alliance from a non-member planet that they will never reveal anything about the Alliance or its activities.

"We will be able to recognize a dishonest or noncommittal response.

"Your choices are this—and I know we are not giving you much information to go on: you can either agree to the conditions of the opportunity we are offering you, or you can return home understanding that we will erase the memory of everything that happened from the time you found Lizzie and Tarafau in the jungle until we replace you in that spot, unaware of how much time has passed or anything you have experienced regarding the Alliance up to this point.

"Do you understand?"

Burt nodded solemnly.

"I do. And I will, Scout's honor," with a slight grin at his intended pun that obviously went over everyone's head but Lizzie's. Nevertheless, there was no doubt that he meant every word. It looked like a new trainee would soon find his way to Sanglarka.

Chapter 21: The Search

(J enny couldn't help but grin. She had heard the tale, of course from Burt before, but it was so much fun to hear it from Lizzie's point of view. It was amazing to her how two different people could have the same experience and remember it so differently. Now she realized she was getting very close to her own encounters with Lizzie, and she didn't even hesitate to turn the page.)

Lizzie turned the page of the magazine she was reading on the train to meet with her family at a special event that she had actually organized herself, unbeknownst to anyone in her family. Her great nephew Ed's younger daughter was about to receive a reward for a job well done, and Lizzie had been unable to resist taking advantage of the occasion to see the young woman in person.

The essay contest she had engineered specifically to include the school district where she knew her niece went to school was a test, similar to the tests Gaston eventually admitted to her that he had been creating for her, long before she realized she had gotten his attention.

She glanced out of the window, feeling a little impatient. She had considered flying but realized it would be a little out of character, considering the story she had so carefully crafted around herself, the old-fashioned maiden aunt, a little eccentric but fairly predictable in certain habits.

She would arrive at the train station in a few minutes, based on the landmarks they were passing, where a cab would be waiting to take her to her great nephew's home. From there they would go to Jenny's school, where she was to receive an award for a very interesting essay entitled, "Why Aliens Must Exist." Although Lizzie would not be personally presenting the award, an all-expenses-paid scholarship to Space Camp at NASA, she had been one of the contest judges, although her family didn't know it.

Like Gaston, she was careful not to give any clues as to her intense interest in the young lady. The fact that she was related had little to do with it.

According to answers of her casual inquiries about Ed's family, Lizzie learned Jenny was an intensely focused student, creative, curious, and a voracious reader. She had already skipped two grades in school, so she was much younger than the other students in her grade. Jenny's talent for writing had been emphasized in their conversations, which made an essay contest a perfect vehicle for Lizzie's needs.

She was greeted enthusiastically by Ed and Donna, when she arrived at their door, and they immediately left for the event after Lizzie assured them she had eaten on the train.

Jenny had not been apprised of the final result of the judges' decision, only that she had placed in the competition and there were to be awards given out. It was the week before the Easter break, which would give the winning candidates the opportunity to prepare for the camp, which would take place that summer. Only Lizzie, the school administrators, and the other judges knew the results ahead of time.

Jenny sat on the stage in the auditorium along with the other contestants, her classmates assembled in the seats below and chatting noisily. A section had been reserved for family, and they were escorted to their seats. When the principal stood and looked out benignly over the crowd, a hush fell immediately.

"Before we adjourn for a week of frivolity, there is one last thing we need to do. As you know," she said, scanning the crowd of students and the families in the first two rows, "an assignment was given to all students a few months ago to write a three-page essay on the science topic of their choice. This was part of a special competition sponsored by NASA throughout the entire San Diego school system. We are proud and happy to say that our own students scored very well, and two of the three finalists will represent our school.

"In addition we have a number of honorable mentions who also join us today.

"Today, the chief judge of the competition, Mr. Delaney from NASA's youth outreach program, will announce the names of the finalists. I am proud to say that the students on the stage all placed high in the final scores;

and although each will receive a trophy, only two will win the highest prize, a week at the NASA Space Camp, all expenses paid by NASA. I give you Mr. Delaney."

She gestured expansively to the tall red-haired man wearing a military style jacket, the front pocket emblazoned with the official NASA emblem.

He stood and approached the lectern to enthusiastic applause.

"Thank you, my young friends, and greetings from all the scientists and technicians of NASA. Someday some of you may find yourselves reaching beyond the edges of the solar system into the unknown frontier of space. Until then, however, it is important to nurture the interest and understanding of physics and the sciences. To that end, we encourage each of you to see if your talents may lend themselves to explore those opportunities.

"Today it is my great honor to present awards to the following students, beginning with the honorable mentions...."

He enthusiastically announced each name for six finalists, along with the title of their essay. These were given small trophies and a patch featuring the NASA logo, and they received a round of applause.

The next group of five received slightly larger trophies, a patch, and a scientific calculator for scoring in the next to highest category

Then finally he came to the awaited moment. The applause once again died down as Mr. Delaney held up his hands for silence.

"I now give you the name of the third-place winner who is not at this school, but who some of you may know. Mr. Grant Fulmer, whose essay was entitled, "The Myths of Potential Space Exploration," an insightful and instructional piece that has many of our scientists both nodding and shaking their heads."

There was brief polite applause, and he continued. "In second place, your own Mr. Lawrence Gedding." And before he could go on, a shout went up from a number of students and enthusiastic parents. Lawrence stood, blushing to come to the podium when Mr. Delaney gestured him forward. "His essay was 'The Importance and History of Measurement in Scientific Discovery," he said, and this time the entire auditorium exploded in applause and cheers of encouragement.

He handed Lawrence an official NASA windbreaker and a tall trophy and then motioned for him to step back a pace.

"Finally, in first place, Miss Jenny Japhet, for her essay titled, "Why Aliens Must Exist," which went far and above the implications of the title in insight and detail. We look forward to discussing it with this brilliant young lady."

Jenny, who, when she had heard Lawrence's name announced, clearly knew she had won the competition, sat there for a moment, stunned by the raucous cheers and standing ovation from her peers, the school staff, and her family members, before she stood and took her place beside Mr. Delaney. He hefted the large trophy for a moment, his eyes twinkling, then handed her first her own NASA windbreaker and then the trophy, and lifted her hand still holding the jacket high over her head. "I give you Jenny Japhet!" he exclaimed.

After the students were dismissed to their classes, the contestants and their families were invited into the cafeteria for a private reception. The cafeteria had been decorated with banners proclaiming each of the names of the successful participants, and there were several desserts spread on long tables, along with the obligatory punchbowl at the end.

The students were formed into a reception line where they endured the endless stream of congratulations from all the attendees. Finally, after starting at the end featuring the runners-up, Lizzie got to Jenny, just behind her mom who had given her a big hug and told her how very proud they were of her. When Jenny's mom moved on to speak with the principal and Mr. Delaney, Lizzie moved up to shake Jenny's hand.

"What a fascinating title for your essay," she remarked, as if she hadn't already read it several times in the judging process. "What prompted you to decide on that topic?"

"I've always been intrigued by the idea of exploring other worlds. I've read everything I can in fiction and nonfiction about it. I knew that a lot of people think that the idea of aliens, as in many of the television shows out there, are purely fiction and not possible. I honestly think people are way too quick to pooh-pooh the idea. Just because we haven't found inhabited planets in our solar system doesn't mean there can't be aliens out there.

"Honestly, when you consider the vastness of space and the number of galaxies we know about so far, I think the odds are in favor of potential intelligent alien life. It's a little arrogant of us to think otherwise. But a lot of the people I've spoken to think I'm actually a little off of my rocker to believe it. I think they feel like I have a lot of 'growing up' to do."

Lizzie laughed. "I think your reasoning is sound. I look forward to reading your essay." (This wasn't untrue. She did look forward to reading it again.)

She leaned over and gave Jenny a slight hug, pressing one hand against her shoulder firmly. "Do you think you will be majoring in the sciences?"

"Actually, I'm considering being a scientific journalist, you know, reporting the findings and advances of technology and so forth. I think the only way we're ever going to make any progress is for more people to be informed about what's going on in the scientific world. I don't picture myself in a lab, but I think interviewing scientists from all over the scientific spectrum and writing about it would be fascinating."

Lizzie considered this. She realized her niece had some real potential to advance science from that position, more than most scientists in a lab would ever have the opportunity to do.

"Congratulations, Jenny," was all she said, however, keeping that little gem to herself. "May I see that trophy?"

Jenny happily reached onto the table slightly behind her, where her trophy sat, and handed it to her aunt.

Lizzie made a great show of examining it and turned as if to hold it to the light for closer inspection. As she turned back, she touched the indentation in the base where the entire piece screwed together. She returned it to Jenny. "I'm sure this will go with you wherever you go, as a reminder of this special day."

Jenny nodded happily as she returned the trophy to the table. "You can be sure of it. I'll be going to college in a few years, and I've already decided to take it with me when I go. It might feel a little like showing off, but it will make a nice decoration for my dresser, don't you think?"

Lizzie winked at her. "Nothing wrong with a little pride in your accomplishments. Just remember that, moving forward, you can't afford to rest on your laurels, my girl. I expect you to continue to put the same effort into your college years as you have into your honor-roll achievements so far."

"I will, Aunt Lizzie. I need to get scholarships, after all. My dad doesn't make enough money in the military to afford to support us all in our education. I know there's a lot of competition for full-ride scholarships, and a tuition-only scholarship just won't cut it. I intend to put full-time effort into my graduate studies and would like to do it without having to also have a part-time job somewhere."

"Those are good goals. Let's see if you can stick to them. I wish you well. I look forward to good reports about you from my nephew and your mom."

The reception was followed by interviews from various newspapers and a live report from the local television station. Lizzie was impressed by the intelligence of the replies by the various students, including Jenny.

One of the reporters from an obscure L.A. newspaper, a middle-aged woman with shoulder-length black hair, showed particular interest in Jenny, of course, being the author of the winning essay. She asked some pointed questions about where she lived and how much longer she had in school. Jenny replied confidently that in her senior year she would be applying to the University of Southern California for a degree in journalism with a minor in the sciences. The woman noted this with some satisfaction, and went on to the second-place winner, doing a more perfunctory round of questions.

After the little press conference, the family went to a celebratory dinner at a local restaurant. Afterward, when they asked Lizzie to stay for a while, Lizzie pleaded the necessity to get to the train station to catch her train back to L.A., since she had to work the next day.

She boarded her train feeling tired but satisfied. She could see a lot of potential not only in her niece's performance, but also in the great number of amazing minds coming up in the next generation. She knew that even after she had decided on her final candidate for her replacement as a gate guardian, she would want to continue to support future science and technology efforts by making this particular program a yearly event.

As she finally entered the train, she found a seat and continued her own train of thought. What if she could also find some worthwhile commercial science and research projects and do some anonymous funding? Her mind leapt to Bob and the workshop he had built. She made a mental note to find out more about the personal projects he was working on.

Over time, the workshop had begun to feel like it was a part of the neighborhood. Lizzie liked Bob and his family. His wife was kind and a good mom. Christopher still couldn't make up his mind whether to answer to

Chris or Cleo and was becoming a nice young man, intent on his studies. He was very involved in the ROTC program at school and was gravitating towards military service.

Although Bob was definitely making a good living working for other labs and tech firms, Lizzie speculated on what would happen if he got a grant funding his research.

"Is this seat taken?" a rich alto voice asked, just as the train was getting ready to leave the station, breaking Lizzie out of her reverie.

Lizzie looked up to see, to her surprise, the reporter who had attended the press conference, who had been so interested in Jenny.

"No," Lizzie responded. "By all means, do sit down. Where are you headed?"

"I'm off to L.A.," the young woman replied with a smile. "I'm a columnist for a local paper. My column focuses on science and technology. I thought the NASA contest story might be of interest to my readers. Marie, by the way," she said in introduction, extending a well-manicured hand.

Lizzie shook the offered hand. "Lizzie Japhet. What did you think about the festivities there? Seems like a long way to go for a story."

"Oh, I follow the scientific journals, and the contest was mentioned in the NASA updates. I thought this was worth people knowing about. It seems to me that space exploration is a lot on people's minds these days. The piece might be of enough interest to my readers that I can do a few follow-up pieces in the future. It'll be interesting to see what these young people do with all of those smarts.

"So, where are you heading?"

Lizzie didn't have to think about what to tell this curious stranger. By this time, her cover story was so ingrained in her and was so well-documented that she easily reeled off her explanation that she worked on projects for a technology firm that she couldn't talk about because of the non-disclosure agreements she signed when they had hired her.

"So, Japhet, you're related to Jenny? You were there with her family, weren't you?"

"Yes, Jenny is my niece. I think she has some serious potential. I was very impressed with her essay, and I want to encourage her to do well. I've noticed that she is a very determined young lady, focused very seriously on her studies. One thing I've learned about her is that when she sets a goal, she sticks to it."

"That's impressive, considering the general attitude of high school students regarding education. I think a lot of them seem to feel like school is just an interruption of their preferred activities of sports, watching television, and playing video games." Marie remarked with a twist to her mouth.

"I think there are definitely a lot of those out there," Lizzie agreed, reluctantly. "However, don't sell them short. We were all young once."

Marie nodded in agreement. She looked to be in her mid-thirties, still young enough that she may not have gained a lot of perspective in that direction. Times like this, Lizzie felt her years fairly poignantly. It didn't seem all that long ago when she was a young person, still trying to figure it all out.

They chatted about science, education, and the state of the world and speculated about what might lie in the immediate future. It passed the time pleasantly as the scenery sped by and as the train stopped at the various stations between San Diego and Los Angeles.

About three hours later, as they prepared to leave the train at the L.A. station, they exchanged phone numbers and agreed that they would like to continue their conversation at greater leisure in the future.

It was dark when Lizzie's cab pulled into the driveway. She knew Ynni would be at Tarafau's house until tomorrow morning, so she went into her quiet, dark house and went to sleep thinking it had been a very profitable day.

As the weeks rolled on, Lizzie had several opportunities to introduce Marie to her neighbors. She was a personable woman who always had something interesting to discuss whenever she came by for lunch, oftentimes with Lacey and Melinda out on the patio, under the awning or out with just the two of them at the small wrought iron glass table with the matching chairs that sat beside the koi pond shaded by the little yew tree.

She had shown a great interest in Lizzie's garden. "I have a little balcony garden on the patio of my apartment," she had commented. "I attend meetings at the garden club from time to time. You should come with me and bring some photos of your garden. I know they'd be fascinated to see what you've done with the space."

She had told Lizzie early on that she was a widow, with two teenagers living at home. She earned a sparse living as a reporter and occasionally wrote magazine articles under various pen names.

She, Lizzie, Melinda, and Lacey started attending the garden club meetings together. Marie called it "girl's night out," and they usually had supper at a local restaurant afterwards with several other of the garden club members who were indeed excited about what Lizzie had done with her garden space.

At one point, Marie had asked about the storage building. "Another workshop? I know Bob does a lot of hush-hush stuff in his. Do you bring work home as well?"

"Sometimes," Lizzie admitted, which was perfectly true, but not in the sense that she thought Marie meant it. "I occasionally need to finish something off that I can bring home. The front half is just storage, though. I have inherited a bit of office furniture and such from the previous occupant. I didn't want it cluttering up my garage."

"Not that you use it much," Marie commented wryly. "Are you ever going to sell that old car?"

Lizzie sighed. "I probably should. I understand it's a classic and it's in mint condition. I might be able to get a lot for it, but I really don't need the money."

Marie laughed ironically. "Well, maybe you could put it in a raffle and use the funds in the community then? I understand you and Lacey are very involved in helping out local schools and that orphanage down the way."

"True. I'll think about it. Are you working on any articles I should know about? That last one about the guy who is challenging Einstein's theory of relativity was entertaining, to say the least."

"I'm thinking about doing one on the trend towards home computers. It's amazing how that industry has bloomed over the past several years. I remember when computers would take up entire rooms, and most businesses didn't have a computer on the premises. Now, it seems like most people are beginning to think they are essential.

"Speaking of progress, how is Jenny doing? I understand she got that scholarship she applied for. Has she been accepted at the university?"

"She has indeed. Surprising at her age, but I've seldom met a more diligent student. The full-ride scholarship will allow her to concentrate on her studies. I see a great future for her..." and Lizzie's eyes went soft as they usually did when she thought about her niece. "In another four years, I think she will surprise us all."

"Obviously not you," Marie said, an odd note in her voice.

Was that a bit of sarcasm Lizzie detected from her friend?

"Well, I am her aunt. Of course, I'm following her progress. Her parents are very proud, although they worry about her living in Los Angeles, so far away from them. I assured them I would watch out for her, though."

"I'm sure you will," Marie responded in that same wry tone.

And during the following four years, true to her promise, Lizzie did follow Jenny's progress, but not quite in the way her parents had expected.

That day at the awards ceremony, Lizzie had not only planted a kind of alien bug onto the trophy, expecting that wherever Jenny went from there, the trophy wouldn't be far away, but her firm pat on Jenny's back when she had hugged her had inserted a microscopic surveillance device under the skin of her back. Lizzie knew nearly everything Jenny went through, listening in on conversations both with her friends in her room and on the phone.

In some ways she knew it was cheating, but she needed to know this young woman very well, if she was going to be able to eventually recommend her for the position of Gate Guardian. Gaston had his ways, and she had hers. She did wonder, however, what Jenny would think when she finally told her what she had done.

Chapter 22: Echoes

(Jenny held her sides, sore from laughing. Her aunt had definitely cheated. "Darned dastardly alien tech!" she chortled. She had often wondered, considering that she had only had two very brief conversations with her aunt over the years, what had even made her consider her remotely for this important post.

Now, the cat was out of the bag. She had shivered when Marie's name had been introduced, knowing with a sickening feeling the role Marie (aka Sam) would eventually play in her aunt's demise. She had wanted to cry out, "Don't listen to her! Stay away from her! She's not your friend!" when she had come to the passages talking about their friendship.

She noticed that she and her aunt had a lot more in common than she had ever realized. Both of them were intensely focused on learning and exploring, and both of them wished they could do more. Both of them had lost people they loved and liked, and both of them had found themselves caught in difficult and unexpected circumstances that had put them unexpectedly into leadership roles they had not felt entirely prepared for.

And both of them had trusted someone who eventually betrayed her, and in Lizzie's case, fatally.

Now that she was almost to the end of this final journal, she felt like the time had been well spent.

She stood and stretched and wandered, journal in hand, out to the patio. She felt it was appropriate for her to read the last words her aunt had bequeathed to her in the garden she had loved so much.

Letting out a contented sigh, she settled onto her padded chaise, facing the little yew tree, the koi pond, and the strawberries that were just beginning to bloom. She was ready.)

"The funeral is on Wednesday," Elias said to Lizzie, his craggy face wet with tears. "She just collapsed. We had gotten home from that cruise she had always wanted to take. I could tell she was tired... we're both getting on in years, after all. Heart attack. It was instant; she didn't suffer. But Lizzie, what will I do without her?" and the usually stoic man put his head in his hands and sobbed unashamedly.

Lizzie didn't try to hide her grief. Melinda had been a good friend, and she hadn't really expected anything like this, as she had always seemed healthy, even if she had slowed down a bit the last few years. With tears streaming down her face, she asked, "Elias, is there anything I can do? I know Melinda had a lot of friends, but I think she is the youngest in her family, if I remember right, and there are no family members on her side left to help out."

He shook his head, wiping his eyes on his sleeve. "Nope, it was just me and her and her friends from the library, the orphanage, and the garden club. I think we're going to do it kind of quiet like. She wouldn't have wanted us to make a fuss."

Lizzie sat down next to him on the little love seat and put her arms around him. "Elias, we will all miss her. She gave so much. She made friends everywhere she went. And she loved all the wonderful trips you two have made together since your retirement. She was happy; and most of all, she was happy to be with you."

They cried together for a while. As he calmed down, he agreed that it would be good to have a quiet meal here in the garden after the burial. Melinda had loved it so much and had contributed to it from its beginnings.

Lizzie knew that as she got older this kind of thing would happen more frequently. She didn't have to like it, however.

Over the next few months, she noticed that Elias almost never came out of his house, and she worried about him. Even though he had friends in the neighborhood, he had begun to avoid social contact.

One day, as she was out on her weekly shopping trip, she saw a teenage boy sitting out in front of the grocery store beside a large box. On the box, scrawled in black marker, were the words "FREE Puppies." Curious, she looked into the box to see three wriggling grey pups looking up at her with large dark eyes.

"Why are you giving them away?" she asked the young man. "They're adorable."

"They're great Danes, ma'am," he said, as if that made it obvious, then continued when she didn't comment. "They get really big, see? We already have two of them, and the pups are just a little too much."

"But you could sell them, couldn't you?"

"Yeah, but mom says she's tired of chewed up furniture and cleaning up after them. They're mostly housebroken, but they still sometimes, um, well... you know," he said, lowering his eyes.

"So, how big do they get?"

"Well, their dad is about four foot at the shoulder and their mom is only a little bit smaller, so... pretty big."

"Hmm..." she said, pondering, and once again she clearly recalled the haunted look she had last seen on Elias's face as he went out to pick up the morning paper from his lawn.

"Just a moment," she said to him. I need to go back inside for a few minutes. Save me one."

She went back into the store, picked up a pet bed, some dog food, puppy treats, and a leash and collar that looked about the right size.

When she got back outside, she noticed the cab she had called had arrived. She hurried to the cab, got the driver to open the trunk, deposited her groceries and the pet supplies, and rushed back to the young man.

"Which one do you want?" he asked eagerly. "Still haven't gotten rid of any of them. Mom will be happy to see at least one of them gone."

Lizzie looked into the large box at the wiggling pups. One of them looked up at her. Mentally she probed, "Hello, little guy. Would you like to go home with me?"

The pup, though Lizzie was sure he couldn't understand more than just her friendly intentions, wiggled his entire body, his tail thumping loudly on the cardboard sides of the box.

"I'll take this one," she told the boy, lifting the puppy out of the box. "I have the perfect home for him."

"A dog?" Elias said when she put the wiggling pup into his arms an hour or so later. "What am I gonna do with a dog?"

"Love him, train him, and give him a home. You'll be doing a kind thing. Otherwise, he might have ended up in the pound."

Elias looked at the puppy critically. "You're grey as ash and very silly. I'll have to teach you some manners. I will call you Cinder." The puppy responded to this gruff remark by enthusiastically licking his face wetly.

Thereafter, Elias could be seen every day, at least once a day walking the puppy and teaching him to heel. And although the generally disgruntled expression on his face didn't seem to change much, Lizzie could tell that a friendship was definitely blossoming.

She had finally convinced Bob to allow her into his inner sanctum, the workshop next to his house.

She was surprised to learn not only that Bob had a large number of projects all going at once, but that they ranged in detail from computer programming to robotics to the beginnings of artificial intelligence. She had been amused by the fact that before he would allow her into the workshop, he had handed her a document to sign: a non-disclosure, non-competition agreement.

"Just protecting myself. Some of these projects are my own, but oftentimes, I have a contract with an employer. Don't ask who they're for. I'm really not allowed to tell you. I know you understand, considering your own work."

Lizzie happily agreed to sign the document with a flourish, and thereafter they spent many happy hours discussing and arguing about theories, protocols, and the extent of current research on the various topics they explored together.

For a time, things seemed to go well, all things considered. Lizzie knew that her niece had only a couple of years before she completed her degree. Reports from her proud parents were that Jenny consistently made the honor roll and was at the top of her class by the end of each semester.

However, about two years after Melinda passed, Bob and Carol came by unexpectedly. They looked anxious, and Lizzie took them out to the patio to talk, knowing that this was a place that seemed to calm everyone who entered it.

As they sat on the patio, Carol leaned forward. Lizzie had noticed that lately her complexion had taken on a greyish tinge and had been wondering about her health. The look in Carol's eyes spoke volumes. "Lizzie, we just came back from my doctor. The test results are all back. It isn't good. My condition isn't curable. They are giving me months, maybe a year."

Bob sat next to her, grasping her hand firmly, his mouth in a tight line as if restraining himself from saying anything. Lizzie was stunned. She had known that the past year her friend had often been short of breath with the smallest exertion, and she had carried an inhaler with her as long as she had known her. She immediately found herself wondering if the amazing Alliance healers could have healed her friend, knowing at the same time that this hope was in vain.

Once again, she found herself bitterly wishing that she had access to technology that everyone in the Alliance took for granted as normal. But even as she considered it, she recognized the damage she could inflict on her world over time if she didn't allow them to progress at their own pace. She had seen too much over her years in the Alliance not to understand the reasons for their ban on introducing new tech before a culture was ready for it.

So, she simply said, "I'm so sorry to hear it. What can they do for you in the meantime? Does Chris know?"

"We're planning on telling him when he comes home on leave in a few weeks. He's very happy in his work in the military, but it does keep him away from home most of the time. We miss him so much," she answered quietly. "I know he'll be all right. I'm not looking forward to telling him about it, however."

Bob finally broke in. "I'm taking a leave of absence from work, maybe even retiring early. I want to be here, and I don't think I will be able to focus much on anything for a while. I know I do most of my work from home, but it still leaves her alone for long stretches in the house by herself."

Lizzie nodded. She was working hard at restraining herself from getting overly emotional about all of this. Ynni, who was perched in the yew tree with her reflection turned off, started to croon mentally, soothing Lizzie. Without even realizing she was doing it, Lizzie began to join Ynni's melody with a mental tune of her own, a sending of hope, love, and comfort to the couple before her.

She knew the two of them wouldn't actually hear the little mental symphony, but she was pleased to see the calming effect the music had on all of them. This was the best use she could think of for her mental gift.

Over the next few months, she tried to spend a lot of time with Bob and Carol, inviting them over often. She generally included Elias and Lacey in her invitations. Lacey gladly attended as often as she was able, but Elias generally still kept to himself.

Even when Lizzie dropped by his house with an offering of food, strawberries, or treats for Cinder, he generally didn't invite her in, simply thanking her in the low growl he had taken on since Melinda's death. It was clear to Lizzie that he might never recover. His stark loneliness haunted her. She knew what it felt like to lose the love of your life, but in her case, she had never had the opportunity for the years and years Elias had been given with Melinda. Sometimes she envied that, and at other times she realized that perhaps his grief was deeper because of it.

It was soon evident that Carol was declining rapidly. The deep cough became almost constant, and they spent almost more time with doctors than at home.

Jenny had sent Lizzie an invitation to her graduation ceremony in a few weeks. Lizzie was pleased to see that Jenny had been chosen as the valedictorian and would be speaking at the commencement event. Since Jenny was attending the same university Lizzie had, it would be a short cab ride to attend. She was glad of that, since she wanted to be on hand to help Bob and his wife, if worse came to worst.

The graduation ceremony was held outdoors, typical for southern California. Lizzie sat in the second row of the chairs laid out on the lawn, next to Jenny's parents. When Jenny stood for her valedictorian speech, Lizzie was gratified that she spoke about not only the potential of her fellow classmates, but also about the work that would be necessary for them to change their world for the better. It was well received, and Lizzie applauded enthusiastically along with the rest of the assembly.

"Well done," she told Jenny after the ceremony concluded. "I'm impressed with all of your hard work and diligence. What will you do now?"

"I've been working for the past year as a guest blogger and contributor to several blogs and websites," she said, looking almost embarrassed to admit it.

"It pays well, and I'll be able to do it from home. Mom and Dad are a little bit disappointed, I think, as they were hoping to see me working for a wage and getting the benefits of regular work. And they'll never get the bragging rights they would have gotten if my name was well known. As a ghostwriter, I almost never get attributed with any credit for my work. But I don't mind that, and the paychecks have been more than enough to support me."

"What kind of writing do you do?" Lizzie asked.

"Mostly I'm writing about technological advancements and science topics. It still interests me, and I'm always happy to do the research required to do it well. So far, I have worked with three different companies who like my writing and are continuing to ask for more."

Lizzie nodded. She could appreciate Jenny's parents' viewpoint. But she knew that with the technological advances that Jenny took for granted, many of her generation would choose similar careers, and the days of working one's way up the corporate ladder in a glass office building to financial success were fading quickly.

She handed Jenny a card with a nice little check in it. "To get you properly launched, she said," giving Jenny a quick hug. "I think you'll do well. Don't expect your parents to understand your career path, but recognize they come from a very different world than the one you live in."

Jenny nodded. "Thank you, so much, Aunt Lizzie. I hope the time will come when they understand, but in the meantime, I appreciate your viewpoint. There are so many who don't seem to 'get' freelance work; the question they usually ask is, 'When are you going to get a *real* job?'" And Jenny laughed a bit self-consciously.

Chapter 23: Odds and Ends

(*Jenny looked up from the journal. In the branches of the yew tree, Chidwi was crooning contentedly, surrounded by a number of curious finches who were cheeping in chorus. It was a cheerful sound. Jenny marveled that the little finches weren't at all put off by Chidwi's presence. It was almost as if Chidwi's happy croon attracted them.*

From now on, her crooning would remind Jenny of her aunt's amazing mental talent. She found herself wondering once again if she might have something similar to explore. Her own gift of sending her thoughts and image cross-dimensionally was considered rare and, at this point, especially useful and remarkable; but she loved what her aunt had been able to do with her own gift.

She remembered clearly that brief exchange with her aunt on her graduation day and the surprisingly large sum on the check she had received. She had used the money to put a down payment on the car she still drove.

She was beginning to feel like she had run a full marathon with her aunt at this point; but she also realized, somewhat regretfully, that she was approaching the end of the compelling narrative. What a rich life Lizzie had led. She turned the page.)

Lizzie approached the door to Bob's workshop with a bit of trepidation, hoping the gift she brought him would be well received and wouldn't be viewed as presumptuous on her part.

She shifted her burden to her left hand and knocked. For a little bit, she wasn't sure he was going to answer. But she heard him stirring around, and he opened the door a crack. "Oh, it's you," he said in a tired voice. "Come in. What've you got there?" he asked warily.

She entered the workshop, noting that there were only a few projects cluttering up the various worktables at the moment. His computer was on, exhibiting some detailed programming.

She had often been here over the months since the death of his wife. He didn't always let her in, and most days he exhibited the inevitable weariness of grief.

He had been working with her on programming for an AI she had been creating. She was planning on eventually installing it on her Alliance tablet, but for now it was all on the Earth laptop she had bought specifically for that purpose. After all, she couldn't have explained the peculiar workings of that alien tech to her friend without consequences.

She strode over to one of the worktables and set the covered basket in her hand on top of it. "I thought you could use a lab partner," she said simply, and removed the covering.

Inside, almost ugly in its early stages, was a baby hyacinth macaw covered in pinfeathers, looking like nothing so much as an ugly beaded bag. The colors were beginning to show through the nearly transparent coverings of the not-quite-blooming feathers. The little bird's head appeared to be too big for his body, and his eyes seemed to be too big for his face.

"This is a rescue project," she explained, seeing his incredulous expression. "A friend of mine has an adult macaw that had a nest full of babies, and she asked if I would adopt one. I told her I was away from home a lot, but that I had a very kind neighbor who might have the time and the presence to be able to care for one of the little ones."

She didn't want to say or even imply that this was because she knew he was lonely and still mourning the loss of his wife.

"He'll need a lot of care at first. He needs to be fed some special gruel-like stuff every few hours the first few weeks. Not to worry, I have a month's supply of it. I'll be bringing over his cage, the feeding supplies, and a few chew toys after we talk about it. I know it is assuming a lot, but I kind of felt like he might be a project you would enjoy.

"Macaws usually learn to speak and are very intelligent birds. Hyacinth macaws get pretty big, and they have long lifespans. It is estimated that they have an IQ similar to that of a human toddler, they're very good at solving problems, and they generally have congenial personalities when they are kindly raised.

"This macaw is from a long line of domesticated birds, not out of a jungle environment. My friend tells me that putting him into a jungle environment at this point would probably not be a good choice.

"He doesn't necessarily need to be caged. Generally, my friend only puts her birds in a cage at night. You can 'potty train' him so that he won't be pooping all over your equipment. I think that just about covers it. What do you think?"

Bob looked at her blankly. "Um... I dunno. Never had a bird before. We never owned pets, as Christopher was allergic to most furred animals, and a bird never occurred to us. It's true. It's awful quiet in the lab and the house these days...." He trailed off, shrugging his shoulders, his head momentarily bowed.

Lizzie knew he was in thinking mode when his eyes glazed over like that. Typically, he looked down at the floor when thinking, so she waited patiently, realizing that now was not the time to talk.

After a few minutes, he put a tentative finger out to gently touch the little bird's head. The bird nodded his head, rubbing it against Bob's finger, eyes closed, happy to be stroked gently.

"What about those pokey things; shouldn't there be feathers?" he finally asked, continuing to gently stroke the little head. The little bird had begun a kind of croon in his throat.

"They will come out of the pinion shells over the next few weeks. You can help that along by doing this..." and she demonstrated rolling one of the pinions gently and slowly between her finger and thumb. The plastic-like husk broke up, and a tiny, deep-blue feather emerged. "Notice that he enjoys it," she added, as the little bird nuzzled her hand with its beak.

"You'll show me how to feed him and take care of him? Like I said, I know nothing about birds except that they fly and like to sing."

"This guy will not only sing, but he will also squawk and talk and make a number of interesting noises. He will imitate your speech or any noises he hears. I noticed that you do tend to talk to yourself as you work, and he would be an avid and interested listener."

"Well, if you promise not to leave me hanging...."

"I promise I will help you take care of him until you're both ready to fly on your own," she agreed with a smile.

"Then I think I'll call him Ignatius, after a professor of mine who looked a lot like him, big beak and all," he replied, once again stroking the head of the little bird.

Lizzie hadn't heard from Marie for a long time, as she had moved away to be with her grandkids, and Lacey had become so popular in the lecture circuit that she was seldom at home. Bob had taken to Ignatius right from the start. These days, as she stood in front of the door when she went to visit to work on her AI, she often heard what sounded like arguments coming from within the workshop.

She continued to visit Promisia and Linaria, where she was considered to be somewhat of a legend. Every time she returned to either place, it was assumed that she and Ynni would do one of their spontaneous concerts. On Promisia, the mbira had become the traditional instrument of choice on the planet, but they had also begun producing harps, flutes, and various percussion instruments and had, by that time, organized a few sizable orchestras and bands for public entertainment.

She, Tarafau, and Ynni often also visited with Amenia and Elizabeth and the linkling tribe which had not only grown, but by now they had expanded to establish similar tribes in various parts of the planet. The Daringi, along with the other intelligent species on the main council, had decided that the linklings not only were agreeable little citizens but were also helpful in any environment in which they found themselves.

The general populace had begun to consider it a great honor to be chosen for bonding with a linkling, and it seemed to be a rare symbol of status and reliability, as linklings wouldn't choose to bond with anyone who wasn't honest and kind.

Lizzie continued to watch Jenny's progress with great anticipation of her future prospects. She found herself wondering if Jenny would accept the post as a gate guardian if offered it, however. She could see that because Jenny was talented, humble, and hard-working, and people seemed to like her, it boded well for her potential to move up the ranks in her chosen field.

She was surprised one day to see Marie pull into her driveway as she was trimming the bougainvillea. She had just hired a young landscaper to tend her garden and yards, but she still enjoyed puttering with her plants.

"Hey, there, Lizzie!" Marie greeted her enthusiastically as she got out of her car, a small shopping bag in her hand. "Long time no see. Have time for some tea and chat? I've got some mint tea bags, and we can ice it and add some of that vanilla sugar you're so fond of. I even brought cookies!"

Lizzie laughed and hugged her friend. "Good to see you, Marie. How're the grandkids?"

"A handful, as usual," she replied as they entered the house. "You know... kids these days." And she shook her head, only somewhat amused.

They went straight to the kitchen and chatted about inconsequential things as they set the kettle to boiling and got out plates, the special sugar that Lizzie made by keeping a vanilla bean in the sugar canister, cups, and a lemon cut up for the tea.

As they set everything out on the table on the patio, they continued to catch up—Marie about the antics of her grandchildren and Lizzie about the goings on in the neighborhood, as Marie had known all of Lizzie's neighbors when they had enjoyed similar chats out on Lizzie's patio beside her amazing garden.

At one point Lizzie asked, "So, are you moving back to L.A.?"

"Yep, I've had about as much as I can handle with the grands and all the drama. If they want to see me, it isn't a long trip from San Jose. I just need my own space, you know what I mean?"

Lizzie laughed. "Yes. I admit I enjoy just being at home sometimes. It's been very quiet around here the last few years, with Lacey constantly gone on the lecture circuit and my two widower neighbors not being nearly as social as they used to be...."

Marie nodded solemnly. "I get it. But we're all getting along in years, aren't we?"

Lizzie chuckled ruefully. "I've outlived all of my siblings and my parents, of course. I keep wondering who that old lady is who keeps looking out at me from the mirror these days."

Marie came back several times over the coming weeks, always bringing some kind of treat with her to share while they just hung out on the patio and talked about nothing much in particular. Lizzie enjoyed the little breaks, feeling like Marie was probably lonelier than she wanted to admit.

Over the weeks that followed Marie's return, Lizzie noticed that she felt so very tired, most of the time. Realizing that she still had work to do, she decided to begin working on what would be needed to transfer the guardianship to Jenny. Maybe she would retire soon and, like Gaston, take up residence in Sanglarka.

The guardians there weren't the same as when she had first become an agent, but she had become good friends with them. Arvid was still there, of course. He had taken over the cooking and did much of the physical training under Lova's administration, and it was always fun to watch him and Tarafau banter on their visits.

It had already been decided that Tarafau would take over as Jenny's guide, assuming she accepted the post, so she put Tidbit in her will, making the keeping and caring for the cat a prerequisite to inheriting the rest.

She made arrangements for all of her financial resources to transfer automatically to Jenny and, having finished the programming of her AI, she transferred it into her tablet adding a protocol that would immediately transfer the login to Jenny as soon as she signed into it upon assuming her responsibilities as a gate guardian.

She looked forward to hearing about Jenny's adventures as an Alliance agent trainee, and she found herself anticipating retirement with a certain amount of contentment.

Her last entry as she continued to feel weaker and more tired, was directed specifically to Jenny: "I hope you find as much joy, excitement, fulfillment, and adventure as I did on my own journey, Jenny. It is my hope that much of what I have written here will be helpful to you moving forward. I know you can do this, and I am so hopeful you will accept this undertaking with a willing and happy heart. Love, Lizzie"

Epilogue:

As Jenny sat on the hospital bed, Chidwi perched beside her. She had completed her time on the treadmill, and now the healer listened to her heart and then looked into her eyes and ears, finally running her hand down Jenny's spine, which made Jenny shiver from the resulting tingle. She ran an instrument from the top of her head to her toes and looked at it, her face unreadable.

"All is well, with you, Jenny," the healer finally sent with a satisfied smile. *"I will release you for full duty. That being said, I will want you back in for a follow-up in about six weeks, just to be sure we didn't miss anything. If you find yourself feeling at all light-headed or start having unusual headaches, please see me as soon as you can. We still don't know the long-term effects of 'the shout,' and we don't want to take any chances with you."*

Jenny nodded, grinning. Burt sent to them both, *"I'll keep an eye on her, ma'am. I expect we'll be spending a lot more time together over the next few hundred years."*

"We have just one more thing to do before I go back into the fray, however," Jenny reminded him.

"Of course. Get your street clothes on and let's take care of that detail together, shall we?"

They walked hand in hand, Chidwi perched happily on Jenny's shoulder, to the elevator that took them to the gate office. They let them know their destination and traveled through the gate to the top of a hill overlooking a small city surrounded by two rivers and farmlands that stretched far to the edge of the valley.

On either side of the path that led down the hill to the city were brightly colored stones that sparkled in the sunlight. Over time, the Promisians had also planted flowers beside the stones, as well as flowering trees, so that the walk was like a pleasant stroll downhill through a city park.

At the foot of the hill, they were met by a delegation from the town council. The Promisians, in their delicate flowing finery in soft pastels, waited there to greet them effusively, each one of them introducing themselves to Jenny and Burt, gently touching them on the cheek and including Chidwi, who returned the gesture with her own tiny hand.

"We greet the niece of Lizzie, the hero of Promisia, and Burt, her husband, and their little companion. We greet the Gatekeeper and the Agent of the Alliance. We are so glad to have you here and have organized a special celebration in your honor. Please follow us to the inner park."

"Thank you," Jenny replied, feeling the intents of joy and welcome in the sending. She took Burt's offered arm and they began to walk into the city. Along both sides of the roadway were people, waving, cheering, and laughing joyfully. The waves of mental greetings were almost overwhelmingly strong.

As they neared the large building that Jenny recognized from Lizzie's description as the community building, music swelled around them. Promisians of many different ages carried instruments of many types, and most of them were singing. The mbira outnumbered all the rest of the instruments by far. The sweet reverberating tones of the thumb pianos gave the overall effect of something both ethereal and ecstatic.

Chidwi joyfully joined in, crooning an exultant descant as they walked.

At the top of the circular city park was a low dais. The procession proceeded up the steps to the top, and their leader gestured for them to be seated in the chairs that lined the platform.

The chief councilor moved forward to stand facing the crowd that had followed their procession to this place. She raised her hands for silence, and the crowd went still, all eyes riveted on her.

"My dear friends, what a glorious day! Here in our beautiful valley home, we have the honor to receive the niece of Lizzie, the hero of our unfortunate exodus and a principal co-founder of our new beginnings. I wish Lizzie could see what she has wrought for us and all future generations, but we can take this time now to honor her and to look forward to the continuation of her legacy. I give you Jenny Japhet Scout, the Gatekeeper of the Dimensional Alliance and Lizzie's heir."

She gestured for Jenny to come forward. As Jenny rose, a great cheer went up from the crowd. It was nearly deafening and filled with such joy and welcome that Jenny found her face wet with the overwhelming emotion pouring from this group.

She looked down at their faces and scanned the assembled Promisians. They were, like all beings, each unique. Some were obviously aged, but there were so many of the young and small children that it was obvious this once-forlorn group was prospering and happy.

At first, she was at a loss for words, the strong emotion that enveloped her like a warm blanket on a cold day making her hesitate. But then it came to her what Lizzie might want to say to these dear people.

"Lizzie and Reloi are smiling right now," she sent, bringing herself under control so she could say what was in her heart. *"Both of them sacrificed much over the course of their lives for the people they loved. My aunt never forgot the Promisian people, their resilience despite their disastrous past, their diligence and persistence in the trial of their faith, and their incredible focus on the positive aspects of life.*

"Your joyful music ascends to wherever she is, and I can hear the song of her heart as she receives the message that the sacrifices she and Reloi made were not in vain. Each of you, and those who come after you, are a monument to them both. I rejoice with you. I only hope that I will live up to the inheritance she left to me. Let us rejoice together. I wish to meet you and hear your stories and also receive the inspiration I will need moving forward.

"There are others suffering in the multiverse, dreadful and dark things. It is the desire of the Dimensional Alliance to relieve that distress and hopefully to bring about the kind of healing that all Promisians now feel as a people. I will carry your enthusiasm, optimism, and courage with me as we push onward in our quest for justice and freedom for all of those who have suffered from the incursions of the dreaded Insenium."

The cheer that followed nearly blew them off the dais. Burt stood and moved next to her, putting his arm around her and pulling her close to him. "Well done, Gatekeeper," he said into her ear. "We can't fail, as long as we do this together."

The End?

Follow the further adventures of Jenny, Burt, Chidwi, Tarafau, and all the rest in the next book, coming November 2023, *Threads of Infinity*, seventh book in The Dimensional Alliance series.

And, if you have loved these books, please take a moment to post a review on the official website:

https://dimensionalallianceheadquarters.com/reviews

About the Author:

To write or not to write has never been the question...

I wrote my first 26 line poem at age 8, entitled "My Christmas ABCs". I then memorized it and performed it for the church Christmas party. This wasn't terribly surprising to the people who knew me. i started reading before Kindergarten and Dr. Seuss was one of my favorite authors, so rhyme came very naturally to me.

I have been writing all of my life, as long as she can remember. A lot of poetry, short stories and, of course, the usual school reports. I always got high grades on my writing assignments, even when I didn't in other classes.

Then, adulthood set in. Always a voracious reader, I dreamt of writing a novel, but after enlisting in the U.S. army, i got gloriously side-tracked with a wonderful husband and six amazing children. During that time, I still wrote: Musical plays for my kids at church and school, songs, poetry and even an occasional newspaper article streamed from my pen.

I got involved in jobs that required clear concise writing and a lot of marketing copy. I put up her first website in 1996 and made my living on the internet for over 20 years, writing everything from blog posts to sales copy to scripts for online videos, not to mention copy for the websites I built for my clients.

At age 64, at a time when I thought my adventures were over, I finally published the first novel in a nine book series. "The House on Infinity Loop" is the first book in the first of three trilogies of the Dimensional Alliance series.

To my readers: Never give up on your dream. It is never too late. There are many more adventures to come.

Also by Bonnie K.T. Dillabough

The Dimensional Alliance
Links to Infinity

The Dimensional Alliance 2nd edition
The House on Infinity Loop
Infinity on Fire
Mirrors of Infinity
Ripples of Infinity
Chords of Infinity

Watch for more at https://dimensionalallianceheadquarters.com.

www.ingramcontent.com/pod-product-compliance
Lightning Source LLC
Chambersburg PA
CBHW010346220726
48290CB00016B/2655